# Flying Fish, Giants And Black Coffee

## A Tale

Jill Bates

10·17·11

This book is a work of fiction. The names, characters, places, incidents, and dialogue are products of the author's imagination or are used fictitiously and are not to be construed as real. Any resemblance to actual events, locales, organizations, or persons, living or dead, is entirely coincidental.



FIRST EDITION


ISBN-10:1463791437
ISBN-13:978-1463791438

To Max my forever friend

To Sabryna for that amazing turkey sandwich, even though I am a vegetarian, I will never forget

My thanks to Kathy
And Lynn
For putting my book on top of the mountain

# THE BEGINNING

Strange things happen. Some much stranger than when the child in the yellow mackintosh dipped his hand into the small puddle outside the gates of the Tower of London - all because he saw a giant pike waving his fins and smiling. The pike grabbed a hold of the thumb with his grinning mouth. Red wellington boots were the last to disappear as the pike swam down through the solid pavement, dragging the child with him. Strange things do happen, and they did, on the day that the Giant was born. A rickety old house appeared on the corner of Main Street full of witches and children's souls trapped in a framed painting that hung crookedly on its wall. Kelly Keen died, but she left the morgue walking on her own two feet. And a snow-white cat with purple eyes came to help, dropping with a plop through the ceiling into Carly Jones's kitchen.

# CHAPTER ONE
# FELICE

In town, close to Chetsy Chocolates, Felice was working hard at the cafe. She stood tall over the counter, her square jaw and prominent cheeks depicting her toughness. She had cut her jet-black hair just this morning, cropping it almost to the skull, allowing her face to do all the talking. She was stunning to look at. *Better hurry,* she thought, *nearly time to open.* She walked over to the sign in the window - the one that said *Lance's Coffee House Open*. She flipped it over.

The line outside was long. It was almost unbearable for those waiting, with the dark intoxicating aromas drifting out – enticing - like the dream of living in some foreign land. Felice opened the door to one long row of feet - from boots, to tennis shoes, to sandals, to high pointed heels… bright pink ones, with open toes and a bow. Her attention was caught by the ridiculous heels half way down the line - *now why on earth would someone wear shoes like that?*

"Come on in. Hey, Steve. Ah…" *should have guessed,* as she watched the atrocious things tottering toward her - it was Sheila. "Now don't trip!" she announced to the pinkies as they moved toward the den of iniquity. The bouncy legs and mini skirt above the six inchers, curtsied, and the bobbing head did a sarcastic toothy smile. Sheila had caught the tone. One of the heels poked at Felice, sharp and quick, like a giant yellow jacket jousting with its stinger.

"Don't worry, I wont!" said Sheila, retrieving her footy dagger from Felice's well-worn boot.

Felice grinned as she moved outside to raise the sunbrellas. *What a bitch...* she thought, before dragging the wrought iron tables into place.

Business was brisk, but Felice took her usual mid morning break, leaving her sister to cover. She left Lance's, a small leather bag slung over her shoulder. The straps of the bag were long, so that it hung down to her hips - inside, snugged away, was a magic book. One hand rested peacefully over the satchel, posturing in a protective yet loving way. Her hiking boots clip clopped along as she made her way to the library, the swish of her skirt announcing her arrival.

"Morning." She nodded to the librarian. *Just a quick look today* - she was never able to pass the library or a bookstore, used or new, without at least a glance, just in case a book of magic had shown up. She scanned the aisles quickly knowing what to look for, but came out empty handed. "Always tomorrow, one never knows," she announced to herself as she marched up the lane for her daily walk. Knowing her route about town like a spider knows it cobweb, she noted everything - that is why she pulled up short when she reached the corner of Main Street. There was an old, creaky house on the corner.

It had not been there yesterday!

Outside the house, close to the street, hung a sign

that swung like a corpse. The lettering was red, hand painted onto a black background - it said.

Used Furniture          Trade and Sell

Felice pondered for only a moment before she followed the curvy path that meandered across the lawn. It was as cranky as the building itself, escorting her to the three, rough stone steps that led to the dark entrance. Before her hand could touch the sticky green moss atop the moldy wood, the door squeaked open. Stepping in, she was greeted by a tall, thin woman who tried to place an arm around her shoulder - like long lost friends. Felice stepped away, ducking out from under the human scythe. A frown creased the stern face of the rake before her.

"Come in. Come in. Take your time. Take a look. Let me know if I can help. Have a cookie... please."

Felice declined, simply shaking her head. That is when she had her first chance to glance around. There was furniture everywhere. Tables, chairs, desks, lamps, footstools; queer looking things with no names; old milk churns, chinese hutches, armoires, glasses, plates, sofas, plant pots, stuffed dolls and more. She looked in amazement at the amount of things that were crammed into the small space. As her stare fell into a shady painting on the back wall, a faint, musty smell entered her nostrils. It was a smell she knew. But not one she liked. Her nose twitched like an armadillo's. Just then, the door creaked opened again. It was Sheila and her friend, finished with their coffee.

"Hi Felice! How's your foot?" Before Felice could

answer, Sheila turned away, not caring for an answer. She was more interested in the beady-eyed woman holding the cookie platter. "Hey! Hello! I never noticed this place before. How long have you been here?"

Better B. Better was quick to respond, but not before she offered a cookie, holding the china plate out toward them. Both Sheila and her friend took one. Felice almost said something but knew that it would be safer to keep quiet. She was here on her own. She should wait.

"Well, I just opened today," said Better B.

"No. No, I mean the house. It wasn't here before... was it?"

As the question fell off Sheila's lips and as the cookie was finally finished, she found she could no longer remember. She looked quizzically at her friend who just shrugged her shoulders.

"Oh well. Anyway. It doesn't matter." Her eyes scanned the room. "Ooooh. Look at all this stuff. Is it for sale?" she asked as she waggled her buttocks over to a brass moneybox in the shape of a bear.

Felice grabbed her chance to leave as Better B. took the two ladies in hand.

"Bye!" she called as she exited. Her breathing was rapid as her pace quickened. She had found the place. She knew she had. Her thoughts bounced as she moved along - *it's going to be a long two years waiting for that damn Giant to grow - hurry back Bunting, and why won't that idiot, Carly, wake up!*

Back at Lance's Coffee House the day was a long, slow one for Felice, she could not wait to get home.

She decided to leave early. Her home was just on the outskirts of town, so she walked. It was only ten minutes later that she was placing the giant brass key - the one that she kept on a chain around her waist - into the rusty keyhole of the thick, heavy oak door. This was not the front door, this door led to her special place, her private place away from her adopted sister. Slipping easily through the doorway, she turned mid stride, key in hand, clicking the heavy lock shut again. She sighed relief before entering the room, her eyes softening. Books lay everywhere, worn and weathered. They were on the floor, on the table, the chairs, even under the stairs. There were brown ones, red ones, blue and white stripped ones. Some were jet black, a few were delicate pink with tattered corners, and finally there was the one giant orange book, so thick it could never be finished.

Felice moved slowly, placing her palm on the orange binding. She lifted its huge cover, turning to page eight hundred thousand and one. The parchment was full of swirling letters and crazy marks. The fire wand that was fizzling in its stand lit up, so that she could see better. Reading down the page, her finger moving from line to line with her eyes. "Hmm. Just as I thought - this is not good news." The smell she had detected in that place was exactly as she feared. "I need to think about this..." ... as she backed toward a majestic seat tucked in the corner.

Her Thinking Chair was made of mahogany with a pair of eagles carved into the backrest. Each eagle head peered over her shoulder, sensing her worry as they wrapped their wings gently around. She was still. The only movement was made by her skirt as it cascaded over the edge of the seat in waves of purple mist - it's cloth full of history and secrets that whispered in the room. There she stayed, enveloped in feathers as thoughts skittered across her face.

# Chapter Two
# KELLY KEEN

Kelly Keen's eye clicked open as she lay in a drawer at the morgue - dead for three days, ready to travel from there to her grave. *Drat! Thought I'd finally left this earth!* Scowling under her breath, she reached to touch the smoothness, her fingertips grazing the cold surface. *Hmm? Freezing. Metal. Drawer.* She remembered working in Chetsy Chocolates. Bored to death. "Guess I really was!" Her palm covered her mouth at the sudden loudness - then she laughed, her own humor getting the better. She had been so fed up, that the chocolates and coffee machine had the temptation of a million dollar stash found on the beach. She couldn't help herself. Reaching into the display case, she grabbed her favorites first. Thirty-one chocolates, in quick succession, then heady strong triple shots - with six wrist curls, one after the other, the lethal brew went down.

"Whoa! Holy bejeezus! Whoa!" Her head swam as her heart pounded! Before she could think any more, death came a knocking

Now here she was lying in this cold drawer - shivering.

"Thin, shitty sheet," she grouched, pulling the cover around her neck. She grumped some more, thinking about having to drop the only warmth - *guess no time like the present, better get moving.* Silently, the drawer slid open. She climbed out. A naked, nimble cryptess, her long bare legs straddling the sides, reaching stealthily down. Her bare bottom and flagging hips hindering her not. *Hah, not bad, not bad at all for a seventy-one year old dead person.*

She snickered. *I could get to like this... this being dead, then not.* She felt good. Old bones did not ache.

Her flat feet touched the icy slab of a floor. Her eye twisting here and there, making sure no one was around before she tiptoed out the swinging door. *Now, where would they be?* She pulled open several drawers before seeing the one with her name. Her clothes were inside. She pulled on pants before pushing her graying head and wrinkling arms into the cashmere sweater. Her sagging body covered, her breasts flopping back into place. There was no money that she could see, but when she pulled open the next slider, there was a wad thicker than a drinking man's belly. Kelly's hand wrapped around the pile of notes. She looked around once more, about to leave, her lonely eye taking in everything.

Her feet padded toward the exit sign before her memory remembered. *Tst tst. Silly me.* She stepped back to the drawer, pulling it open once more. An emerald green glass eye blinked. Looking for her. *Hello there.* It blinked again. Gently, her fingers holding the globe, she raised it toward her face - pushing, feeling - popping her sight easily into the black socket. "Hah." She squinted. Both eyes. "Now, we can go home!" She said this to her new friend - the one that had inhabited her body.

The next day, the shop door of Chetsy Chocolates

opened - the bell tinkling overhead. Two shadows stepped over the threshold along with an old, yet spry woman. Kent was working, not having hired anyone yet. He looked up.

"Kelly?"

"I'm back!" Her mouth chortled.

And she was. But not on her own.

## CHAPTER THREE
# CARLY JONES

At a small log house on the outskirts of town, the door opened. David stepped out, striding across the lawn toward a balding man sitting in the corner.

"Do you want me to feed Able?" he asked. Even though he could not see the bird himself, he liked to humor his partner. He didn't care if Carly was a bit crazy - he loved him anyway.

"Hmmph..." Carly nodded, he was engrossed in his painting - a dainty cup in one hand, a brush in the other. "Feed the cat too..."

David stopped short. He watched as Carly placed his brush on the table, reaching down to pet something that wasn't there. *First the parrot, now a cat,* he thought. Then he shrugged his shoulders and walked back into the cabin. When he came out later with tea, peanuts and a bowl of tuna, he placed everything on the small table, stepping back to watch with folded arms. His eyebrow cocked as the peanuts and tuna disappeared. He hadn't quite figured that one out yet.

"Don't think I'll worry about it," he muttered, walking back inside. "At least he's happy."

Carly continued to pet the cat that was now on the table. He stroked behind its ears, along its back, tickling its belly as the creature fell on its side. The purring was so loud it started to buzz. The purple eyes did not bother Carly. He liked them.

"How lovely," he murmured as he rubbed harder

on the humming cat's ears.

Carly Jones had been in the living room of his tiny cabin when the Giant was born. He didn't see the white curly haired cat appear in his kitchen. It was just there when he went to make a cup of tea. Now it was rubbing its head into his hand again. Just like it had the first time.

"Hmmm? What's your name?"

"M e e o w n d y..."

"Oh...? Mandy... How nice to meet you." The cat just purred louder.

Carly was sitting at the edge of his garden, under a trellis laden with wisteria and sweetly scented roses. He turned back to his passion, closing his eyes, feeling some creature emanate from his being as he painted onto the pottery. The creature itself crawled from his fingertips, crying in pleasure at the moment of its birth. Carly opened his eyes. The painting on the cup was wondrous. *Best yet my lad...* a female voice whispered... a familiar voice - one that he heard all the time in his head - his mother. Just then, white, purple and yellow snow fluttered down, warming his baldness - *Huh? H*e looked up, his trance breaking. It was Able. Restless. Plucking amongst the flowers.

"Able. Stop that. Mind the paint..." The parrot looked down with ink black eyes before stretching his wings to fly over to the rough wooden sign that was nailed to the gate.

As he landed, not so lightly, the sign said in a very stern voice, "SHUT!"

"Shut up yourself!" squawked Able.

Carly laughed. "Its alright Sign. Its just Able."

The poor sign just groaned in a creaky way. That's

all it could do besides say OPEN or SHUT.

Carly leaned back in his chair, hands hooked behind his head, looking around. It was a grand day. He was content to sit glancing about this beautiful place. The shining sun glinting off his outdoor art gallery. A kaleidoscope of colors, of plates, vases and birdbaths, of bizarre clay creatures hiding beneath leaves or in the bamboo forest, all littering his wonderland of a garden into which he welcomed everyone. Although there were times when he wanted his privacy. That is why he had put up the sign. Now was one of those times. He had a strange feeling inside that he couldn't quite place. It was gnawing away inside.

## Chapter Four
# THE BIRTH

The days of Hayban were past, but his house still stood on the outskirts of Chetsy. It was a wild house that stretched into the sky with high ceilings and big wide doors. Three gigantic, silver grey stone chimneys stood sentry over the busy gardens, with scents of frangipani, jasmine and crimson lilies filling the air. Powdery fungi, croaking toads and bulbous nosed frogs lived in a corner of the wildness, the crimson red pond rippling as they dove for fun. In one of the drooping gutters, a small stray moon had come to rest, tilting that side of the towering structure to the west, its stone walls cracking as the building bowed gallantly toward the enormous willow that wept graciously into yet another pool - this one gold in color - a palace to seven black swans swimming to some melodic waltz.

This was a house built by a giant, for a giant, but, alas, at this time no giant lived here - only Hayban's granddaughter. Five foot six. Although this absence was soon to change for Theadora was giving birth. It would be her first and only child. She was thankful about this as her delicate hands held onto the back of a stout wooden chair. She was in pain, her grinding teeth making fudges of tiny flames. Her lips burned. The smoldering in her abdomen had begun as soon as she had started to drag the birthing ingredients up from the cellar. The white sear that ate her insides was becoming harder to bear as she blended the secrets together, binding forms that would bring to life her son. But still she carried on, fighting the stabs in her gut, tossing the Dittermore's tongue into the smoldering mash, leaving the fairy wings to flutter lightly on the dark oak table, waiting their turn, waiting to be gently folded into the brew that was now bubbling inside the giant skull.

"Taiama wuds lickety tay..." she muttered, finally lifting the silken beauties from the tabletop. Their gentle beating made her fingers tingle. She hesitated, afraid to let such treasures fall. Still, her son was paramount, his birth the most important of all. Her tender hold loosened, the wings dropped, their fluttering not able to stop the decent into the heavy oily liquid. The mash started to rise. Iridescent bubbles with shimmering simmers of rainbow colors plopped to the surface. Her whispering chant continued, until at last, she reached for the final ingredient - it was Jebber's finger, her father. Eyes clenched, she let it fall into the heavy, thick boned dragons skull. As the gnarly knuckle hit the surface, a cramp grabbed her, taking her down - *oomph, belly really hurts.*

She lay on the floor, exhausted, clutching herself, hearing the bubbling above, the cries of the spirit, writhing, waiting for release. Finally, she reached with her arms - her white knuckles a guiding light. Grabbing onto the edge of the weathered table she pulled herself up. Standing once again, although stooped, she carried on, not letting the pain stop her.

"Tay zemussy pin nontay!"

She grunted as she hauled the boiling and bubbling skull across the cold slate floor, sweating profusely as her arms flexed to finally toss it into the roaring flames. The giant hearth howled in glory.

"Mienet tu salasti de manontay!"

As the last words dripped from her lips, the fire roared its rapture, spitting molten swords at her face.

*Uuuugh I'm burning...*

Her knees hit the brick hearth as she fell again, her abdomen cramping tighter than a hangman's noose. A trickle of blood dripped down her sweaty shin.

Laying there, her face tilted toward the flames, she saw him - her son - for the first time. He simply appeared. Standing three feet tall in the fire. Looking right back out at her.

*Oh, you are so beautiful!* She struggled to her feet as his need for life seeped its energy into her efforts. Her body bent toward the flames.

"Come... step out to me..." She beckoned, holding her arms toward him. "Come on.... you can do it, just come toward me."

She held her breath. He looked so puzzled. Frowns creased his good looks. Lips pursing.

How?

"Think not of the flames, only of me. Come on. Step forward."

*Stay calm. Be with him. Do not lose your son to the fire....*

Don't think I can.

"You can! You can! Come forward. I love you."

She pulled her tallness taller. Her strength stronger. Her jaw more set. Their eyes held, cobra in their intensity. His blue. Hers green. Locked in love. His frowns smoothed, an ocean with no wind, not even a breeze. Then, at last, he moved.

Her smoldering inside hissed and sputtered. Sweat from her brow trickled, blurring vision. She blinked - hard. Tossing her head in an effort to shake free of the pain, her beautiful ebony mane tumbling around her face, her clothes clinging in desperation to her shapely form.

*Keep moving... keep on... come...*

"Come on, my son. Come out to me!"

He tried, he really did. To no avail. The flames rose, wrapping his body like a shroud. Only his head could she see.

Her stare bore into his. *NO!* She would not let him be taken!

"Come! My son. Come!"

*Don't let him fall into the flames. Move. My son... Move!*

The yellow tips licked at his chin. Wanting to taste his eyes, his hair.

Theadora gave one huge determined effort, clutching at her will as the licking devil started to wrap its arms tighter, reaching up over her son's head. Her suffering was nothing. Her son was everything!

"Push them back, Willman. Push them back! Like this!" Her mind a catalogue, pictures flipping fast, she sent it to him. *Like this...* *see...*

She clenched her teeth so hard they sent out sparks. She forced herself to relax, releasing the incredible tightness in her belly. Calmly. *Feel my mind son... feel me...*

"Oh! My!"

That is when she felt him for the first time, tugging and pulling at her insides. Until her strength became his. Then, finally, he could look beyond, into his depths, reaching for something, searching, deeper. He moved. His arm first, followed by a hip, then a long spindly leg. Until at last, the flicking tongues dropped, leaving him naked. Exposed in his glory! The orange lashes licked at his feet, squirming, smarting. Begging for court again.

NO! Stay back!

He freed himself, strong now, kicking them aside. They yelped, tongues hacking back and forth. He stepped forward, moving out of the cowering flames into his mother's arms. Kissing him on the head, her hand cradling his skull, she looked into the hearth, relief flooding her inner depths as the fire receded. She laughed.

"At last. My Giant is born! Love to you," she whispered, her tears washing his singed hair. She knelt down, their eyes on a level, her hands cupping his cheeks. "My Son." He leaned forward to kiss one of her tears before putting his arms around her neck. Then he snuggled his face under her chin. Time stopped, although the clock still ticked.

TICK TOCK
  TICK TOCK

TICK TOCK
  TICK TOCK

The fire went out.

TICK TOCK
  TICK TOCK

Neither one moved, until she heard the red door open. She stood.

"Come my son, we must move fast. Your youth is gullible, easy to find. We must leave." Moving him gently away from her sweaty form, she reached down to take his hand. His fingers were hot, making her flinch, but she did not let go. She felt so tired, but not too tired to look after her boy. Hand in hand they quickly left the warmth of the kitchen, their feet tapping a morse code as they headed for the Room of Secrets, passing down the corridor toward the shiny mahogany door that opened its mouth before them.

They both stepped forward, across the threshold, each using an arm to knock the spidery webs aside that fell as veils over their heads. They breathed in the misty air, the cold stone floor echoing every movement. The door clicked shut behind, their guardian, gently locking into place. It knew they would not return to this house, or to Chetsy, for well on two years.

Thea glanced around, blinking at the darkness. *We must move quickly son. No time to waste.* His mind easily read her words. They waited, two ghostly figures, until the gas sconces lit themselves, framing their bodies in a soft moonlight glow.

"Where are we going?" asked Willman, his head cocked up toward his graceful mother, glad that he could now see through the gloom.

"Through there!" she said, pointing forward toward the towering mirror that hung majestically before them. As exhausted as she was, Theadora knew she could not stay here. Her son's life, and hers, were at stake. Her bare feet moved forward, disturbing the fine carpet of dust, her eyes boring into the tantalizing shimmer before her. She took her son across the room, until her step melted into the glass. The Willman followed, never questioning, for he already knew. As they entered, the mirror bowed, the glass bulged, until their bodies simply dissolved out of this world.

As they exited the mirror on the other side, Tizzie the Pixie greeted them.

"Theadora! Theadora! Oh, you came home! How beautiful, your son. I remember all those years ago you picking his name. The Willman, T.W. Is it so?"

Tizzie ran up to Theadora, gazelle like in his movement. She bent down to kiss him on the cheek, her exhaustion lifting.

"Tizzie," she whispered, "how wonderful. I've missed you, you little beast. It's been too long. And yes, that's his name, since before he was born."

"You know, I thought you would never ever come back, Thea. I sit here every day waiting. Worrying."

Tizzie pouted then. A well rehearsed Pixie Pout.

She bent down again, her fingers grazing his silken cheek. She smiled to herself. Tizzie would never change - he had been her family forever. This kind witch then stood tall, looking around as she did. Her land had not changed, even though she had remained on the other side for so many years. Torn between her two homes. Her lungs filled with the freshness of the air, the swelling scents of honey suckle and orange blossom overflowed her mind. The croaking of the frogs, the snippetting of the crickets and the low cackling of the Delfars were more blissful than she remembered. She looked up at the multicolored frogs littering the small trees. Some wore polka dots. Others were striped - like zebras. The ones that clung highest in the branches looked more like abstract paintings. It was quite the sight. The Willman pointed, his mouth an O. She grinned as her son switched his stare to the giant crickets. They were the size of baby pigs, with big fat legs and cheeky faces. Their tubby green bellies rubbed on the ground when they moved. Being sedentary creatures, they had nothing more on their mind than to make bizarre clicking and crickety type sounds. They did not like to leap around. They preferred to click.

The Delfars, however, were something else. Swinging from branches. Tiny monkeys only six inches tall. Inquisitive. Full of mischief. Naughty. Their pinched pink faces always grinning, even as they groomed each other - their long silver hair laying like silk on their heads. They had a slight odor. But not bad at all. It was a smell of the earth, freshly dug. It was then that Tredor, the King of the Delfars, landed on T.W.'s shoulder. Tredor's long fine mane was pulled back into a ponytail that bobbed up and down as he moved, even as he reached up to poke a finger into the little boy's ear, twiddling it, which made T.W. gurgle in laughter. Tredor screwed up his own face, snickering to himself. The naughty monkey gave one more twiddle before pulling his finger out, then he grabbed a hold of the boy's rapidly growing hair - using it like a vine, he swung around to plant a kiss squarely on the laughing lips, then scattered before Thea could reprimand him. Tredor now sat in the twenty-foot tall orange tree, with oranges bigger than watermelons, cackling quietly to himself. His mate joined him. He kissed her on the lips too! Theadora waved a finger at him.

"Tredor! You need to behave. Teach you and my son some manners!" Behind her finger wagging she fought back yet another smile. She was so glad to be back. T.W. disentangled his fingers from his mum's so that he could use both arms as he jumped up and down waving.

"Tredjor! Tredjor!" he yelled, a huge grin playing on his face.

He had found his first friend.

Theadora took her child's hand, striding purposefully through the grove of orange trees, careful not to knock her head on the giant fruits. Tizzie leaped along beside. Tredor, his bride and their entourage, swung from tree to tree, dancing to the song of the giant crickets. In this way, Thea moved through the woods to her home, her home on this side of the mirror. The trees cleared away, becoming only sparsely scattered in amongst the small dwellings that she first encountered, the dwellings of her friends. Not one of the homes was the same. Some were round, some square, some domed, some triangular, some set in the crooks of gnarly trees, some oblong. None were big. But each one was a different color. The only thing they had in common was a large number of exquisite looking flowers that climbed, crawled and creeped into every nook and cranny of each house. Some of the flowers that looked like roses or clematis could have been, except they were at least three feet in diameter. Everything gave out a scent but none of it overpowered the freshness of the air around - just a mingling of citrus, of vanilla, of strawberries, of custard, rosemary and mint. All so mild it was difficult to identify. But there.

The path through the village was meandering. Her friends greeted her, hugged her child. Kissed her cheek. Until finally she reached her own home. Her father waited for her there. He was sitting on the low stone wall in front of the house when she came. He couldn't wait. He stood to move forward, just as she ran to him. "Oh dad, how I've missed you..." "Sweetheart..." he responded as they enveloped each other, arms reaching up, arms reaching down, folding around. Close behind his momma, T.W. ran.

"Granda!" He cried. "Granda!"

He knew. He was smart. The small boy looked way up into the air at his granda's towering form.

"GIANT!" Willman was beside himself with glee.

"Hmm, he has quite the vocabulary already, Thea."

Granda, as big as he was, stroked his grandson's head. His large hand with a missing finger was gentle. The Jebber was so happy, a huge tear dropped off his face plopping to the ground making a mud puddle. Willman slopped his feet around in the mush, then looked up at his Granda and laughed. His Granda laughed back.

It had been a really hard day for Theadora, as she watched, her lids flickered, her stately form drooping. Her father caught her before she fell. He knew it was time to rest. Beds were sought and sleep came. But not for Tizzie. He rocked gently in the small chair on the porch, eyes wide. Alert. Tredor, as always, crouched close by.

## CHAPTER FIVE
# THE USED FURNITURE STORE

The inside of the used furniture store was on high boil, waiting for the lobsters to scream. It was immediately busy. Hopping. Alive with activity. Interesting pieces started to appear; old chopping blocks from England; ancient sideboards from the orient; tables lovingly worn with a hundred years of use; plush velvet chairs, green, gold, red and pink. Strange masks, gargoyles and monsters. Etchings, paintings, carvings. Shiny chandeliers with shimmering crystals. The furniture moved in and out. Men, women and teenagers started to buy things they didn't want, arguing with their friends about who should get the candlestick or the chair or the carved wooden pig.

Better B. Better rubbed her hands in glee. She was more than enjoying herself. She could not believe how quickly this place was becoming her dominion. Her plan was going to work. She was going to suck every ounce of energy out of this small town and the people in it until she was ready to explode with power. She would be a bomb that needed no detonator, and to top everything, she would be rid of that stupid village full of witches.

She hustled. The busier she was, the sooner she would rule! It came as no surprise to the townsfolk when one day, there was another lady working in the shop. A woman from an old friendship of many moons ago. The new lady was plump, short and loud. Much too loud! There was a constant babbling of voices inside the building.

"What on earth is that in the corner?"

"Oh, its beautiful Seteeva. I don't really need it. No, don't have room. Yes, it is a good price. But. Oh. Well, alright. Yes, please. I'll take it."

Furniture, books, dolls and odd pieces moved in and out of the little shop. The desire for things not needed started to grow. The competition to obtain became more and more unhealthy.

"Seteeva. Could you help? What do you think? Should I get it? Think I will. Doreen told me about it, said she was coming back to look at it again later. I'd better take it now, don't you think?"

"Of course. Absolutely. Don't wait. Buy it now before Doreen gets her greedy mitts onto it. Best that way."

Seteeva Haar was highly amused. Amused, but bored. She stepped back into the shadows, a strange twist to her lips as she watched people pile in through the door. Her hand dug in her pocket to finger her pipe that was stuffed with a root that she grew in her garden. She thought about that root now - *should harvest tonight* - her twisted face turned into a smirk. As the skirmish continued before her she daydreamed about pulling the black root from the ground, after which she would pulp it into a mash before smoking it in the smoker. Then finally, she could stuff it into her pipe to smoke herself. Her smirk became a huge grin. She could taste the fresh pipe already, so she wasn't happy when somebody grabbed her arm.

"Seteeva! Tell Beatrice that I already bought the yellow chair! Tell her! She's taking it!"

She was jerked back to the present to see a fat lady in pink sweats hauling a plumply stuffed yellow chair toward the door - the arms carved most majestically with lion heads, the feet giant paws with claws. It was a superb piece.

"Seteeva! I already paid you!" the voice exclaimed in her face.

"You did?" Her fingers cradled the pile of twenties in the pocket without the pipe. "Hmm. Are you sure?"

Beatrice was almost to the door, beads of sweat on her pudgy brow. She glanced back toward Seteeva, smiled, baring her teeth at Sonya who was now glaring back, fume and doom seeping from her eyes.

"Seteeva! That is MY chair!" The small woman was eye to eye. Seteeva decided to move.

"Yeh. Yeh. Alright Beatrice. Stop. That's Sonya's chair. Give it up."

Beatrice was aghast. "Bu, but, but... yu you said I could have it yesterday..."

"Yeh. Well, didn't pay did ya. It's Sonya's."

"You promised, Seteeva," Beatrice growled. "You said you'd hold it for me."

"Sorry dolly, chair's not yours. Now, if you want to give me more than she did, well... then... hmm, maybe..."

Sonya glared at Seteeva before grabbing the chair out of Beatrice's sticky grasp, hauling it the final two feet out the door. A hiss followed her, Beatrice's flopping rolls of lard greasing the way for hatred to follow. Just that morning - as they had done for the past ten years - the two of them had played golf together, with Beatrice sharing her excitement of the chair that she had to pick up at noon. Beatrice had wondered why the game had ended early. Now she pictured Sonya's head on the tee as she swung mightily with a number 5 Wood. Interestingly, the thought gave her pleasure. Strange, since she had never thought ill of anyone in her life.

## CHAPTER SIX

# JIMMY

A few days after the shop on the corner of Main Street opened, Jimmy found himself wandering down the middle of the road in his pajamas. Last he remembered, he had been tucked in by his brother and off to sleep he went. The dreams had been weird, being sucked out of his bed, down the stairs, under the front door toward a big gaping black hole in the middle of the street. From deep in the hole came a voice, a mix between a man and a woman's. Not nice voices. Not nice words. Then he was back in the house where gingerbread men with extra long legs chased him around the kitchen while brandishing glinting butcher knives. They chased and chased until he was sucked under the door again. Then he woke to a giant stuffed doll laying next to him in his bed, but not really waking because it was a dream. Right? It was when the doll sat up to look at him, pulling back its lips, exposing jagged pointed teeth that he screamed for the first time. Trying to hang on to his headboard because that sucking and swooshing sound was getting louder. Pillow over his head.

"Go away. Go away." He gasped in absolute terror.

Even though he tried to stop himself, a sudden force whooshed him out from under his duvet, down the stairs and under the door. He barreled through the air toward the hole, the demonic voice talking to him, beckoning him, his body flying toward the blackness, the voices sounding more and more evil, the horrors of what were in that hole becoming all too obvious. He didn't want to see those horrors! He didn't! He screamed again.

"No! No! Nooooo!"

And now, all of a sudden, the hole was gone and here he was tottering down the street. This was real. He really was walking alone, in Chetsy, in the middle of the night. This was not a dream. Except now the voices were coming from inside the sinister old house instead of out of the hole.

The house that said.

Used Furniture        Trade and Sell

Jimmy was terrified.

He became even more terrified as he watched the door creak open, then the lady he had thought was nice yesterday was standing there. She looked at him, dead on with a piercing stare. Jimmy wanted to look away, but he could not make his head move at all. In that moment of silence, he stood stock still, bitten by poisonous fangs, feeling paralyzed - the only struggle left was in his mind. He had heard those nasty voices coming out of the house and now there was the lady he had thought was nice. He was very confused.

"H e l l o," he ventured.

Better B. answered back, her fierce stare softening.

"Hey, little boy, don't I know you? What on earth are you doing wandering the streets at this time of night? Come on in. I remember you now. I'll call your Dad. Come on over here. Do you want a cookie while you wait?"

Jimmy hesitated, but not for long. He didn't like standing in the street in his bare feet. He was cold and besides she said she would call his dad. *Couldn't hurt...* he clenched his little toes while he thought. He took a step forward, then another, his bare soles not feeling the stones beneath. He walked the curvy path, up the steps, through the door that closed behind him.

He was only seven.

## Chapter Seven

# JIMMY, BIG BROTHER AND TOM

Meanwhile, Jimmy's elder brother was starting to feel upset with his little sibling, it was ten o'clock and he was hiding. He had gone to check on his young brother in bed and guess what, not there. Again! How many times had he told Jimmy not to play this silly game – he just didn't know what to do with him. Maybe the next time he had to baby-sit for the little twerp he should just lock the bedroom door and leave him for the night. But for now, he was stuck wandering their big odd house, looking under beds, in closets, behind sofas, until finally he tried the smell of popping corn to lure the little punk out of his hidey hole. It didn't work like it normally did, which left big brother with a gradually sinking pit in his stomach. Dad would be home soon then there would be trouble.

Tom arrived home at about a quarter past eleven, pumped up about the new play he was in. Rehearsals had run late. He searched the house along with his firstborn, frustrated with Jimmy for once again playing his hidey trick. It was giving him a headache. Sitting down, he put his head in his palms, his thoughts jittering about - *this was an old rambling farmhouse, but this was not possible.*

"Jimmy!" he called out again, but halfheartedly this time.

After over an hour of searching, he called the police - small town police where everyone knew everyone. They told him not to worry, Jimmy had done this before, hadn't he?

"But not for this long," sighed his father.

"He's probably fallen asleep in his hidey hole, he'll wake up soon and come out," the voice echoed down the phone. The receiver now back in its cradle, *just where Jimmy should be,* thought Tom. By four in the morning his head was a smoldering mash. As he went to pick up the phone again, he heard a faint sound upstairs.

*What was that?*

His legs took the rise two at a time, feet pounding, but not as hard as his heart.

When Jimmy woke, he was curled up in bed, his Spiderman pajamas wrinkled around his sweaty body. His eyes felt heavy. His hand lay clenched in front of his face, whiter than the sheets. His fist uncurled as he reached down to eat the last crumbs of the cookie that lay concealed in the folds of Spiderman's web. *So hot! Just too hot!* He threw back the covers, knocking his giraffe that he had made in pottery class to the floor. It landed on its head, its neck breaking before the body exploded like a pomegranate hurled at a wall. A minute later he saw his dad, moving across the room toward him.

"Jimmy?" Tom hugged him tight, not noticing the pale skin and dark eyes of his son. Relief made him blind. "Don't worry me again like that. Where the heck were you hiding?" Jimmy made something up, saying he was scared to come out after a while. The lie came easily as the buttery flavor of the last crumbs filled his mouth. They lay down together - father and son - Jimmy cradled in his dad's arms. Sleep came quickly to the little boy.

# THE TALE

## BACK ON THE OTHER SIDE OF THE MIRROR

## CHAPTER EIGHT
## THE WILLMAN

When morning came, Theadora's eyes sprang open. Her son was not by her side. Covers slung, feet pounding the floor, she raced to the wide open doors leading to the courtyard of the house. She heard her son then, his gentle voice singing a tune. One she did not know, but it seemed like Tizzie did - the two of them enjoying the ballad together.

"That was fun Tizzie Dizzie!" laughed T.W. "Another one!"

Thea stood back, watching. Tizzie started another, but this time it was more of a rhyme. This one she knew. Tizzie repeated it only twice before her boy picked it up. When Tizzie said it - it was one thing. When T.W. said it - it was another. As the boy uttered the last word, the little pixie's ears grew to four times their size.

At first, The Willman was shocked, but only for an instant, no boy could resist. So he repeated the rhyme again and again and again. By this time, Tizzie's pointed ears were so big he couldn't stand up. He kept trying to struggle to his feet, but each time he did so he tipped to the side, his giant ears like dumbbells weighing him down. They both started laughing in that uncontrollable giggling way, so that the pixie's requests for the boy to stop were lost. In fact, the pixie was laughing so hard by now, that his belly hurt.

Thea looked down at her giggling son and the ridiculous pixie.

"Listen to me. Change the word at the end of the rhyme to 'tautetoma'... it will shrink his ears."

Her boy did, finishing with a flourish... "Tautetoma!" He repeated it several times, causing Tizzie's ears to shrink in size, again and again, until only a tiny black hole was present on each side of the little man's face - with no ears to hold it up, his hat fell down over his eyes. They both started to giggle again.

"OK! That's enough!" Thea stared sternly at her son. "If you can't stop at the correct point, then you need to change the last line of the rhyme to 'clawaskia tia klo malinand,' so that Tizzie can return to the way he was."

Willman was more than happy to comply. The points of Tizzie's ears came out of the black holes first, rapidly growing until the rest of them appeared on the sides of his head. The pixie could see again as his hat was pushed upwards. They both clasped each other, two little people, three feet tall - arms around the other, rolling on the ground laughing.

Thea let another smile play on her lips. Her son was going to learn fast. He would surely be the wizard she had hoped for.

## CHAPTER NINE
# THE POWAMANDER

It was a few weeks after the 'ear game' when Thea woke up to her son being gone yet again. It seemed to be a pattern. She knew she must remain wary, to protect him, be on guard while he grew. The Jebber was here, so was Tizzie and Tredor, along with all of her friends. Still, she knew enough of evil to not let her ears or eyes close. So again, she leapt out of bed to venture outdoors in search of her son.

This time he was not in the courtyard. Neither was Tizzie or Tredor. Jebber was traipsing around at the side of the house. She went that way. He simply nodded, pointing off into the trees that led away from the many small homes. She followed his finger - passing through the arched gateway that connected each end of the low stone wall - marching off, once again careful not to knock her head on the giant citrus fruits.

Several of the crickets lay around escorting her with their clicks. The frogs were also vocal. They had a duck like voice.

Qualackity. Qualackity. Qualackity. Qwik.

It was a soothing escort until the cacophony of another noise came to her. The Delfars were cackling so loudly, it was deafening. *What on earth was going on?* Her step quickened. She rounded a few more trees before she saw Tizzie jumping up and down on the spot. Squealing in delight. Looking up.

Thea didn't think it was a good idea, but she

looked up anyway.

Her heart stopped.

Almost at the top of one of the tallest trees was one of the watermelon size oranges – it was bigger than all the rest. This one had been hollowed out by the Delfars – like a snail shell without the snail. Small oval windows had been chewed into the skin, after which the orange hide had been coated with the sap of the dingler weed to preserve it. There were two entrances, one on either end. This was where the Delfars slept, inside these hanging citrus skins. There were many of them throughout the grove.

As Thea looked up. Willman looked down. He was smaller than she remembered and was beaming from ear to ear, waving to her from one of the windows.

"Hey, mum!"

Tredor hung out of the other window, hanging on with his tail, jabbering and cackling away. It seemed that every other Delfar was here, all applauding her son's newest feat.

The cackling grew in pitch. Tizzie jumped higher. It was a celebration. That is when it happened. The Willman was leaning too far out of the window. He fell! At least Thea's hitched breath made her think that.

"Willman!" she yelled, moving forward to catch him.

Then to her surprise, he didn't just plummet to earth in a splattering way. He simply floated down. That is when she noticed his arms above his head, his hands holding onto a downy feather ten times his size - the feather was a brilliant peach flame, fluorescent. He landed close by. She heard him utter a few words and watched him grow from his tiny eight-inch height back to his normal size. Tizzie ran to him, again they became entangled in their laughter. Theadora was amazed. *Already,* she thought, *he had befriended the Powamander. The bird of fire!* She knew that The Powamander lived quietly in the woods, a hermit of sorts. He gave his feathers to few - they never fell out - only plucked by the creature himself to be used as gifts. As she pondered, Tredor scrambled down the tree to sit on top of Tizzie's hat, arms in the air, clapping loudly. His pink face was stretched wide in laughter, even pinker than ever.

After the commotion died down, they headed back home, followed by their entourage. Thea didn't even want to know how her son had gone up to the house in the sky, so she didn't ask, although the shimmer of a smile still played on her lips.

CHAPTER TEN

# BUNTING ARRIVES

Jebber heard his family coming and greeted them at the gate. He knew what mischief his grandson had been up to. He smirked proudly. Knowing he would have little time with this boy, he turned to his daughter.

"Can I take T.W. out to visit? Remember, he is growing fast and our friends want to see him as a lad."

He was right. Willman was growing fast - sometimes an inch a day. He would stop growing at six months having reached the massive size of his grandfather, along with developing the looks of an adult man. But he would need more time beyond the six months to reach his maturity inside.

Jebber pushed his point, seeing that Thea was reluctant.

"And Bunting is back. I saw her lights on and her rooster is back on the roof - a sure sign of her return. Anyway, Tonya (Bunting's sister) told me that Bunting is insisting on seeing your son before she has to go back to Chetsy. Besides, I hear she's cooking."

This last comment made Theadora's eyes light up.

"Oh, really... Well, off you go then. Find out when we are invited."

The thought of a meal prepared by Bunting made Thea's mouth salivate. No one. Absolutely, no one - could cook like that woman.

Her dad knew that would get her. Laughter flowed

from his lips as he walked down the garden path. He lifted his grandson with one swoop of his arm onto his shoulder. He did the same with Tizzie, placing him on the other. The two small ones hung on best they could, but Jebber would let no harm come. He placed his large hands lovingly over their legs, holding them in place. They needn't have worried. In this way he marched - his long strides covering the ground, passing by a triangular house first, then a yellow home built in a tree. All of the houses were small, much smaller than theirs, because they were the only family in the area to carry the giant wizard gene. Their own house sat on the outskirts of the village because it was so big, but it was obvious that the village had been built around a giant's presence. This became even more obvious, as they rounded Mr. and Mrs. Walklate's pink house with a steeple roof. Willman yelled out in excitement, his hand pointing.

"Look at that, granda! Look!"

Before them was a large structure, like a great big bandstand, only bigger. Giant size! Around it grew the assortment of flowers that were in all the gardens. They climbed the towering poles that held up the roof. Creeping along the bannisters that bordered the perimeter. At one end of the covered area was a big round fireplace made of turquoise stone, which sent heat into the gathering place and heat onto the lawn that surrounded it. That way, if it was not damp with rain, but cool, everyone could sit on the grass to gather, but still enjoy the warmth. The floor was of a purple marble that was not hard - it had a squishy feel like a carpet of moss. When the lanterns were alight, the purple glittered, sending up a low rise of sparkles - a ground mist that reached the ankles. Feet were lost, but the rest of the body floated above the crystal haze.

This was, The Meeting Place.

Jebber rounded the last bend with the two still on his shoulders. Everyone had known he was coming - they stood waiting, out on the lawn, some in the shelter.

"HELLO!" Boomed grandad to everyone. T.W. and Tizzie both stepped onto the palms of his hands when he presented them - in this way, he lowered them to the ground.

"Come!" yelled Tizzie in excitement. "Meet your people!"

The group welcomed with open arms. Exclamations ready.

"Oh! How you've grown...."

"Aren't you beautiful...."

"I hear you are quite the wizard already..."

And so it went on.

The Willman enjoyed himself - all these people, their friendliness, their warmth and honesty. He noticed that there were a few babies around, much smaller than he... and they actually looked like real babies. They couldn't talk - they only made little ucky sounds. They had no teeth, poohed in their pants and vomited their food. They couldn't sing, walk or run.

*Hmmm?* He thought. *How could this be?* He knew he had been born only three weeks ago. And yet some of these funny pink piggy looking things were six months old already.

He decided to ask his granda.

"Granda? How come I don't look like the other babies?"

"Because you were born different, son. You are of a different kind than they."

WELL! That just wasn't good enough...

"Granda! WHY?"

Jebber all of a sudden felt overwhelmed. He didn't know how to answer that question. A frown grew on his forehead as he contemplated. Luckily, at this point, Bunting stepped in.

"Jebber! Goodness. I miss you on the other side. But now I see why you had to do it. Looks like we may be in for a hard time in our human land. I know that Theadora saw the need for her son at this time in order to save Chetsy. I think she was right. The evil is stirring. I cannot stay here long. I should get back to keep an eye on things - although Felice and Carly are there - if he ever wakes up. So, first, time for a party! I'll cook! What do you think?"

Glad of the respite from the staring Willman, grandad leaned down to hug Bunting.

"Absolutely. Yes! Theadora can't stand to be away from your cooking you know. I only had to mention your name and I saw the drool dripping from her chin."

They both laughed together.

This respite was short lived. T.W. had been patient long enough.

"GRANDA?"

The frown came back in an instant. A look of resignation started to take over. Lost for words, Jebber started to stumble...

"Well... hum... I think... hum... that, umm..."

He just wasn't good at this sort of thing. Not being quite sure how much to tell this young boy, or even how to do it.

Bunting laughed. Her hearty, merry laugh.

"Oh Jebber. Stop! Let me."

She reached her hand down to the questioning body. He looked up at her, his face beaming. He knew he was going to get the information he wanted. As they walked away, he looked back at his granda, his tongue stuck straight out - a big fat pink slug - and his eyes saying... SO THERE!

## CHAPTER ELEVEN

# FINDING OUT

Funny as it was, the two were like long lost friends. Bunting towered above - yet in only a few months from now, the small boy would tower over her. She did her best to explain, telling him that most of the witches gave birth in the normal way.

"What is normal, Bunting?" asked T.W., this being one of the questions his grandad had worried about.

She told him what normal was before saying.

"It is only the giant wizards that cannot be born in the normal manner. But all births, no matter which kind, have to happen in Chetsy. It is our chosen birthing place. It can not happen on this side of the mirror."

The Willman learned that he would not have had the special wizard strength, only the size, if his granda had not of sacrificed himself. He had cut off his own finger to be used in the birthing process, for it was the finger that passed on the wizard strength. She told him that only one wizard giant could inhabit Chetsy at any one time, so by stepping through the black pond instead of the mirror, his granda could never return, even though he loved his life in the town. It was the only way to pass everything on.

She continued.

"The town of Chetsy is in danger. If the people of Chetsy are destroyed, then the town goes too. If that happens, then our race will die out." She told him that he was here to stop that from happening.

That he was the chosen one, according to The Scripture of Muburn. They had all read of this for many years, but no one had known when the time would be. Only Theadora was able to know that. Hopefully, she had chosen the time wisely. Everyone trusted her.

After their walk, they returned to The Meeting Place. The Jebber was sitting with his head in his hands, rubbing his frowns. He knew it was terribly important to tell Willman their history, he just hoped it was not too soon. Tredor was crouched on his massive shoulders, massaging frantically, trying to remove his worry. Tizzie lay at Jebber's feet, pouting that he had not been allowed to go with his friend.

As Bunting and T.W. came into sight, Jebber jumped up. Tredor fell, plummeting to the earth, but grandad was better than that - he caught his mistake, catching the monkey tenderly in his huge palm.

In silence, they waited. They all knew that T.W. was beyond what anyone had expected.

Had Bunting managed to quell his rapidly growing mind?

The answer was immediate!

The young giant dropped Buntings hand so that he could run toward the threesome. As his strides covered the ground between them, he yelled out a rhyme.

"Sitzlle tramble ketterlor!
Caldon zi plimetey!
Yolendo vettle talando!"

The results were instant! Tredor's head grew to the

size of a giant pumpkin, Tizzie shrank into nothingness, and Jebber felt a shimmering of his body that made him almost translucent.

*All this at the age of three... weeks....* thought Jebber.

"MY GRANDSON!" He boomed, beaming from ear to ear.

As T.W. reached the feet of his granda, Tizzie reappeared, Tredor became kissing material again, and everyone fell into fits of laughter. The Willman, it seemed, was going to be more than capable of his task at hand. That is, if the wicked witches did not turn out to be stronger than he.

CHAPTER TWELVE

# CARLY JONES'S HOUSE

On the way home - only four days before the grand party - they passed a shuttered house with a sagging chimney and caved in roof. There were magnificent vines climbing everywhere - up the walls and over the stout wooden trellis that marked the entrance to what was obviously once a garden full of pride. But the enormous blooms that should have been glorious were wilted, shyly hiding their beautiful faces - not one flower faced the sun, in fact, they seemed to be weeping. The spirit that usually inhabited the front door was gone, leaving it lilting and alone, so that it no longer opened of its own accord as did all the others in the neighborhood. It did not speak to the witches and wizards that wanted to enter. It had left, along with its master. The door simply did not open, so no one tried anymore. It had been so for many years. No one ever got to see in the house, but oddly enough, the rooms inside were still bright. Some cobwebs. But still bright.

In the living room, the parrot perch that sat in the corner had not rotted and the cat bowls stayed full of fresh food and water. The fish tank did not grow algae. The only visitors were the rabbits and voles that went in and out, through a small square hole in the floorboards. A mouse seemed to hold permanent residence, along with other unusual creatures; a badger, a hedgehog and an elf. Although as of late, even they seemed to have left - except their wardrobes were still there and the mousey had left his favorite martini glass behind, the one with the letters *'M M'* etched on the side. So maybe they had just gone on holiday.

As The Jebber passed this unusual place with his grandson and Tizzie on his shoulders, he heard a cry. It was really close to his ear.

"STOP! GRANDA! STOP!"

He did as requested, lowering the two to the ground in his usual manner.

"What, grandson? What is wrong?"

"This place is so sad, granda, what happened? I feel lost when I look at it."

This time he had no problems explaining.

"This is Carly Jones's house, my son. Carly Jones. His mother left us to give birth, but she never made it back. Her husband was from another village, not good, a temper on him. He smashed the mirror first, before he smashed her. We are not allowed to interfere on that side, he was raised in an orphanage, not knowing his heritage. We are still waiting for him to awaken. Once he does, we hope he will be able to find his own mirror so that he can return.

This short story filled T.W. with loneliness. He felt the creatures of the house. He felt their loss. Their commitment would probably never end. He asked his granda not to lift him back up. For the first time he felt real sadness. His steps trudged along behind his grandfather. His sadness did not just overwhelm himself, but it seeped into the bodies around him. Tizzie slogged on behind, as did Tredor, swinging limply in the trees, followed as always by his clan. Everyone felt heavy at the memory of Carly Jones.

## CHAPTER THIRTEEN

# PARTY PREPARATIONS

Two days later, things were better. The Willman knew that Carly would someday find his way home. For now, he needed to keep on growing. Their lives depended on it.

Besides, they were only mornings away from the grand party.

Theadora was at Buntings house, helping as much as possible. There had been pots and pans sizzling day and night. Batches of dough were mixed, kneaded, rolled. Yeast fermenting. Batter bubbling. Fruit squeezed into crystal bowls that sat next to cold vats full of brewing beer. Bunting was cooking up a storm. She was chatting to her friend while she popped more bread into the oven.

"Well, Thea? Thought any more on calling in help for the festivities?"

Thea had, long and hard. Just the day before, she had decided it was necessary. She needed to call upon the family of Benglings to help. After all, this was a very special event... the coming of her son, the gathering of The Witches - the time of recognition to save Chetsy and themselves. Besides, it would help her son grow into the wizard he needed to be. It would be good for him to see what others could do. She had seen their work many years before and it was outstanding. Most had forgotten, but she never would.

It was an iffy choice she knew, to call on The Benglings - a family who lived on the outskirts of the village - whose presence was not appreciated by all. In fact, by some of the townsfolk, they were banned due to some previous party mishaps.  Still, she decided to take that chance. She invited them in.

CHAPTER FOURTEEN

# THE BENGLINGS, WOODSORS, SITZERS, ZOOMALONGS AND HIFFIZARS

The Benglings came, but not alone. With them they brought their neighbors - the Woodsors, the Sitzers, the Zoomalongs, and the Hiffizars. It was way more than Theadora had imagined, or had any idea of, or even thought possible. She was starting to regret her decision when Mr. Hiffizar approached.

"You do know that I am an expert pilot, don't you?" He asked of Thea.

Actually, she had heard of his escapades and didn't think of it as expert, but decided to stay on the positive side. She nodded her head.

"Good oh, then," he smirked... "May I be allowed?"

Thea simply nodded again, not understanding why her head moved that way.

Next came, not just one Woodsor, but the whole family, including the bizarre five-legged creature that they claimed to have birthed. Theadora just couldn't understand this. She had studied the genetics of all under her wing. How this had happened she did not know. She was thinking it wasn't normal. Still, she went along with it, it might be fun after all.

"Yes, Mrs. Woodsor, I know your family has a knack for decorating. Absolutely. Go ahead." At the same time that she said it, she wondered if she would regret it.

Finally, well not quite, the Benglings would do that, but before them came the Sitzers and the Zoomalongs. Thea was at a loss. She knew she should tell them to go home, but she just couldn't quite muster the courage to hurt their feelings, especially since they had crept out of their holes to help.

The Sitzers were unusual to say the least, and the Zoomalongs were close behind because they were relatives. They were different in the sense that they didn't have a brain. At least not the kind of brain that is thought of. They had senses in their fingertips, in their toe tips and in their kneecaps. Besides this, they did have a bit of thought that came out of their ears and through their mouths. But nothing existed in their brain. Because of this, it made it difficult for Theadora to communicate with them. She tried mouthing words, humming songs, gesticulating with her arms, even drawing pictures. None of it seemed understood. In the end, she gave up. All she hoped for was a pleasant party. They seemed to know what they wanted to do, even if no one else did.

Then at last, came the Benglings, the only ones she had wanted in the first place. But now she was wondering about that too. The couple, childless, had turned up with five strings floating into the air, supposedly attached to balloons, but there were none. They claimed they were going to promote the celebration but had no idea how, at least not at this time. And - they were still thinking about what to do at the actual party itself.

Thea was done for. As far as she cared at this

point, the food would be great. That was all that counted. So she crept home and crawled into bed, knowing that her son was safe in the arms of her dad. Tomorrow would be a new day.

## CHAPTER FIFTEEN

# BALLABY BOO

It was the day before the party when Theadora finally saw something of her plans with the Benglings. She arose as usual, sauntering through the opening from her bedroom into the courtyard. She no longer worried that her son was up before she - he was either with her dad, out with the Delfars, in the village, or sometimes, just sitting on his own. Although, now she thought about it, he was never really alone, Tizzie and Tredor always kept him in sight, but they did know how to be silent when he needed it. *A miracle,* she thought, that the two could actually sit quietly without pestering him.

This bright morning she looked down the lane to see a wallaby hopping toward her. Theadora giggled. *Where on earth had this creature come from?* The wallaby - kangaroo like, but smaller - hopped along, its giant back feet flopping on the ground. This wallaby was not brown, it was a canary yellow and its pouch was bulging like a pregnant woman.

*With what?* Thought Theadora as she stepped into the garden to meet it, because it was coming her way.

"Hello there." Theadora spoke, expecting no response.

"Good morning to you," said the wallaby, its wallaby lips moving in a strange fashion. "My name is Ballabby. Ballabby Boo! I'm here to deliver this week's Scripture. A very special edition as you must know."

With this, the unusual creature reached into its pouch, then tossed the rolled up paper toward Thea. She caught it, realizing that it was the weekly Scripture of Muburn and that old Mr. Presley must have been given the day off. Before Ballabby Boo turned toward the next house, he thumped one foot hard onto the ground making it shake with distant rumblings.

"IT'S GOING TO BE A GRAND PARTY! Read all about it!" Sounding just like a newspaper lad yelling out the headlines on the corner of a London street. Then he moved on to the next house some ways away. She could hear him doing the same routine, and again further on. There would be no missing the news about this party. That was for sure.

Thea felt pleasant about the Benglings's opening performance. Holding the rolled up Scripture, she moved toward a bench encased in the giant flowers. She pushed some of the huge blooms aside, making room for herself, then dusted the golden pollen off her hands onto her skirt. She sat peacefully for a while before unrolling the Scripture. It was at the precise moment of unrolling, not even a second longer, that a hand shot out from the newspaper itself and grabbed her by the neck! It was startlingly fast! Following the hand, came a head - a yellow duck head with a wide smiling orange bill. It tilted backwards to look up at Thea before saying.

"Party tomorrow.
Three o'clock.
The Meeting Place.
Quack".

Then the hand and head disappeared back into the paper.

Thea was still sitting in the same position - it had happened so fast she had no time to move. Her face was still for a moment. But only a moment. She started to laugh. *Oh my,* she thought, *almost had me, that was a good one!* She had a feeling the party was going to be fun. Her son needed to learn the good ways of life. He needed to experience fun and happiness and goodness and laughter in order to want to preserve it. Her thoughts wandered a while before coming back to The Scripture in her hands. Her readings took some time, most of it much more serious news than the opening page. It was always possible if you read close enough, to find some future in the past. Thea went slowly, reading each line and each line in between.

Finally she folded the newspaper, leaving it for Jebber to open. *Hope he gets the same invite!* Then she sighed, there had been nothing in The Scripture to bring her peace.

CHAPTER SIXTEEN

# THE PARTY

It was the day of the party! Willman was more than excited. As was everyone. The smell of baking filled the village. Fresh breads, some crusty, some not; roasted chestnuts; searing and sizzling delights; tarts with whipping cream; mouth watering scents of delicious fruits freshly peeled. Tiny appetizers, a zillion to a plate. All started to appear on the great tables positioned around the perimeter of The Meeting Place. Plates full of color; yellow cloth napkins folded like clown hats; glasses colored opal white; cold pitchers filled with thirst quenching liquids. The heavy wooden tables sighed with the weight. People ran back and forth from Bunting's home - it was a mystery as to how everything had fit, there was so much. Finally a towering cake appeared, ten layers tall, dripping with frosting. It was assembled in place, on a small round table that sat on its own.

The Woodsors had done a tremendous job decorating. There were balloons everywhere, floating freely. Every few minutes another balloon would suddenly appear to replace one that had just been popped. Miniature hedgehogs were doing the popping. They floated around, curled up in their favorite way - it was their job to keep the balloons under control. Every now and then, their spines would make contact, the floating globe releasing a happy hissing sound along with the smell of whatever was favorite of the nearest person. After each successful pop, the mini hedgehog would uncurl, laughing as it did, its tiny pointed, twitching black nose and dark round eyes fixing on another balloon, before curling up again to float toward it.

Sitting on the massive beams that ran under the roof were more than a hundred peacocks with their fan tails open, their magnificent display for all to see. They were content to sit and watch the festivities, happy to see children's faces beaming at their wonder. The floor of this great place was still sparkling purple, the posts and bannisters still covered with the glorious giant blooming flowers. Chairs were scattered around, not just hard wooden chairs, but soft, comfy, with arms and high backs. Thick down filled blankets littered the surrounding lawn. Only one large covered area was left empty. This was the place to dance!

Running around the village, as people arrived, were chickens laying eggs that were already hard boiled, ready to eat for anyone feeling a bit hungry. The eggs were a cobalt blue. So easy to find. Some of the passing witches stooped to pluck them off the ground, but mostly the children wanted them. Mr. Presley, the deliverer of the Scripture, was enraptured. He probably ate the most. Well, not quite. Paylo had more than anyone. She shuffled around the entire evening, snuffling under rocks, down small holes, under flowers, in the grass, looking in places that no one would have ever thought to look. Her four feet plodding along, her belly almost to the ground, her broad head and flat nose hardly able to get into each place. But she always managed, gobbling down the egg along with the shell each time. No one tried to stop her. It would have been impossible anyway. Paylo always did what she wanted. The only thing she couldn't get that she wanted - was for her master to come home. Paylo had been born on the same day as Carly Jones. This made her Carly's dog. Living in the village. Loyally waiting.

The five-legged creature born of the Woodsors greeted everyone, carried everything, and was in all places to help. Theadora, who of course had turned up early, was amazed. He was everywhere, Siandra by name and extremely polite. He pointed out the creatures that they had brought to the party. Actually, he didn't point, he called them all by name, introducing each one in turn. It was then, as he chatted to Theadora that one of the floating hedgehogs came by. Siandra stroked the prickles, which were smooth and sculptured. Siandra sighed blissfully, as did the hedgehog before floating on.

People started to arrive. Aunts, uncles, sisters, brothers, nephews, nieces, friends, distant friends, and villagers alike.

Everyone came.

The place was abuzz. There had not been a party like this for many years. It was unusual for a great wizard giant to be born, and it was well known the reason why he was here. The Jebber had made a huge sacrifice, as had Theadora, giving birth to a son that may be killed. They all knew that their futures were threatened, but still, this village was a place of happiness, they strived for it, and tonight they were going to celebrate. Tonight they were going to live for now. Tomorrow they would live for then.

T.W. arrived with his grandfather. It was no different than his first time into The Meeting Place with everyone around. He was happy to be with his people. He knew the party was special, but he didn't want to be the special part of it, he just wanted to enjoy. His family knew this, as did all of the others, so, the celebration became simply a celebration. That turned out to be the absolute best. A party just because a party was needed. The fun began!

Mr. Hiffizar came first.

All of the villagers were moving around, nibbling on this, chattering about that, gazing in awe at the peacocks, inhaling the intoxicating scent of a popped balloon, until finally they all looked up. A loud flapping sound had caught their attention.

PHLAWP. PHLAWP. PHLAWP.

Everyone ran to the lawn - their necks careening backwards like mice looking at the hawk in the sky - to see Mr. Hiffizar astride Dreador, the recently born Carmedgeon. Mr. Hiffizar was good at flying, except that he had picked a newborn. He thought it would be a good representation for the party. The newborn Carmedgeon, a giant version of a pigeon, did not think it was the right choice. *He did not think he was ready for this yet*!

Echoing groans from those on the ground filled the air.

This was just not good news!

Dreador was still so young.

Just what was Mr. Hiffizar doing?

Dreador and Mr. Hiffizar zoomed across the sky making loop-d-loops, followed by figure eights. Then they passed high over the lawn using an advanced talent, one of flying in slow motion. The talented Mr. Hiffizar was flying an even more talented Carmedgeon who could move his wings and tail in ways that cast shadows of mythical creatures.

Despite the worry down below, this special show caused many "oohs" and "aahs".

Then Mr. Hiffizar forced the great bird to barrel straight up into the sky, to gain the altitude needed for the drop to earth that would produce the grand finale he had planned. The young Carmedgeon had not yet been trained in this area. It was a most difficult maneuver. As Dreador made the turn from way up high to make the plunge toward earth, he moved his wings into place, at least the place he thought they should be. *I'm not sure....* he thought desperately. There was that moment of stillness, when everything seemed to stop, then the dive began. It was only seconds before the out of control spin started. The drop to earth was coming alright, with no halt in sight. At least not until the two of them hit hard ground!

Every witch, wizard, pixie, elf, monkey, cricket, peacock, wallaby, hedgehog, chicken... watched in horror.

Dreador was going to die!

Mr. Hiffizar was going to die!

The screaming sound of a jet engine gone wrong echoed through the air. No one knew if the sound came from Mr. Hiffizar or Dreador - even though his beak was clamped tighter than a clamshell and Mr. Hiffizar's face was pulled back in a grimace, the whites of his teeth a startling contrast to the red of his lips.

No one moved.
Transfixed.
Horror!
Only two could react quick enough to do anything. The Jebber stepped forward casting his hands into the sky as his daughter stepped beneath him doing the same. Between them, they sent out a net that was fine as a spiders web - covering the ground beneath the falling stars - suspended by invisible wires. Dreador and Mr. Hiffizar landed. They bounced as if on a trampoline. With a sigh from everyone, including the two, the net slowly sank to the grass.
Several people ran forward. Thea being one. She loved the Carmedgeons.
"Dreador? Are you alright?"
He was crying, like a Carmedgeon would cry.
"I ruined the party..."
This is when T.W. ran up. He hugged Dreador around one of his scaly legs as he looked way up into the lovely Carmedgeon face.
" I wish I could fly like you. Will you be my friend Dreador?" he said.
That just made Dreador cry more, but he did manage to put his wing down to touch the top of Willman's head.
Mr. Hiffizar was stammering apologetically, in between his own tears.
"I'll never...ffo fo forgive...my my myself if I've ruined your...flying...c career Dreador. I am such a a f f fool."
As Mr. Hiffizar stuttered away, he felt a soft feather of a wing brush against his cheek. He knew he had

been forgiven. Still he cried all night off and on, and was the first to leave for home.

It was at this point that the Benglings decided to intervene. They told the band to start playing. The music was terrific, even Dreador started to shuffle his feet, like an ostrich would if dancing with a chihuahua - until soon the party was back in full swing. The food was fantastic. Full of magic. As the evening wore on there were more spicy comments than spicy food, and many more peppery indulgences. Hearts danced. Love flirted. It was a brilliant party. The celebrations stretched into the evening, until exhausted, everyone made their way home.

The Sitzers and Zoomalongs quietly cleaned up while the village slept. Before they too left, they rearranged any giant blooms that had been pushed aside, gentleness washing their faces as they moved. The Meeting House was left in purple glory. A cave full of amethyst crystals. Then they crept back to their earthen holes were they liked to live. Tired, worn out, but happy.

# SIX MONTHS LATER

## CHAPTER SEVENTEEN
## THE JOURNEY

It was now six months since the party and T.W. had reached his full height along with the fine looks of a mature man. He was a fifteen-foot giant, towering over his mother. He did not always have to maintain his natural form, knowing how to easily make himself smaller, or bigger, if he wanted. Today he was six feet four, broad. He sat in the garden with Theadora, holding her hand.

"It is time, Thea. I must go, so that I can become the wizard I was born to be. I have learned much here, but there is more. Our race and the people of Chetsy depend on it."

She knew that this must happen, but to let her son walk off into the unknown world was heart wrenching.

He continued, gently.

"Besides, I won't be alone, Tizzie, Tredor and Dreador will be with me."

She sighed before saying.

"I know son. Go now. Come home safe, wise and strong." Then she shed only one tear that trickled down her bronzed face. No more than when her dad had sacrificed his little finger for the birthing, having to step into the black pond to leave Chetsy forever.

Willman rose, kissing his mother on both cheeks,

then he turned without looking back. Tizzie trotted along beside him. Tredor had already said farewell to his wife and now sat on the brim of T.W.'s hat, his pink face shining bright. The shadow of Dreador followed. When they passed through the village, Paylo, the broad muscular mass of a dog was lying on Carly's front porch. She ran to greet them. Willman bent down to pet her massive head. The drooly tongue petted him back.

"Hang in there, Paylo. He'll be back one day."

She licked him again, her stump of a tail wiggling like a worm on a hook.

No one else distracted them, they simply nodded or waved knowing that time was precious. It wasn't long before the village was behind... the thick grove of orange trees came and went. There were acres of green fields that merged into miles of sand dunes and then came the canyon with the cave at the end. This is the place they were headed. The black hole loomed before them, the only place to go, either that or turn back. It had taken five days and nights to get there. Now they needed to rest. Dreador landed, scratching a hole into the earth - earthworms and salamanders scurried to escape his scaly feet. It was a huge hole, big enough for a fire around which they could all eat and sleep, protected from the wind. Tizzie was the first to sit down, his short legs had worked hard, although he had ridden on Willman's shoulders a lot. Tredor was still fresh. He skipped around picking up wood bigger than himself, his strength far greater than his size, his silken ponytail dancing with each step. While the little monkey gathered scraps, Dreador pulled bigger logs into their camp, using his beak and muscular wings. Between them they got the flames going while their giant friend consulted his inner self. As the flickers of orange started to speak, Willman returned from his thoughts, pulling bread and cheese from his pack, he shared it amongst them. Then he gave Tredor an orange, making the little guy bounce in birthday party excitement.

But it was no celebration night, so it was not long before exhaustion crept in and they all slept.

The next morning, everyone awoke refreshed. Little was said as they cleaned up camp before starting the final walk toward the cave. It was only a few minutes into their hike that T.W. started to sing. It was a merry song and one that they all knew. Dreador took the alto part, cuckooing at the right times. This fun passed time easily, until, with weary legs, they finally reached the black silent mouth. Once there, Dreador landed, although he didn't need to - the cave was more than big enough for him to fly in. As his feet touched earth, T.W.'s voice echoed around.

"If anyone wants to turn back, now is the time." The Willman looked around at his best friends. Waiting. No one moved away, or flinched in any form. "Ok then... Let's go!"

They all marched forward, passing quickly from light into darkness, as if all of the candles had been blown out at the same time. It was so difficult to see, Dreador decided to shuffle on his feet instead of flying... *just until my eyes grow accustomed,* he thought. It seemed that they hadn't gone far, when the darkness started to lighten. They could hear a distant noise, which grew in pitch as the light became brighter still. It was strange, for surely there was nothing around them except the hard stone walls of the cave, but the heat of the sun started to warm and the noise continued to grow, until finally, they stepped out of the dimness into a bright summer market place. They were stunned. One minute it was not there, the next, it was. The long narrow street was lined on both sides with stands. Brightly covered awnings protected some from the shining sun, whilst others stood naked. Creatures were everywhere. Some took human form, some animal, some alien. But they all talked. The odor was strong. It wasn't all bad, but it wasn't all good either. There were soaps and lotions and herbal mixtures that gave off a nice scent. Then there was something else in the air that was a bit rotten. Willman looked to his left, seeing a sagging bench dripping with pastries of different kinds. It smelled good in that direction, so he moved that way. He stepped forward, using a coin that he pulled out of his pocket - it looked just like the one the woman next to him was paying with. He learned quickly. More coins jangled in his pants. He pointed, "the whole tray, please." The pastries were still warm. They ate immediately - hunger hot after their journey.

After satisfying their stomachs, they carried on down through the market. They had not gone far when they noticed that the stand they would pass next - which was covered with a blue awning - displayed rows and rows of heads. Human ones! None were decaying, but all had different expressions; some joyful, some horror, some hurt, some anxious, some even laughing. From this stall came one of the not so nice smells. One of the smells they had wanted to avoid. Willman noticed though, that people bought the heads too, just like the pastries. He watched as they placed a scented hanky over the hair to camouflage the odor before dropping the heads into a shopping bag along with other purchases. A puzzled expression crossed his brow. Tredor was aghast, the little monkey just hung on tighter to his friend's hat. They moved on. The next few market stalls, on either side of the road, sold usual wares - like saucepans, vegetables, flowers and soaps. Some sold magic potions that were in small lime green bottles. There was a large stand that lorded several spaces - it was attracting a lot of attention. Many were around it. Tizzie pushed forward, through rows and rows of legs - it was worse than getting to the front at a concert. Willman followed. They could hear a voice shouting out prices for its wares. Their pushing eventually got them to the front.

*NO! NO! Cannot be!* The Willman was not happy with what he saw.

For sale were live creatures of all sorts. Most trapped inside small cages, crammed, crunched and shackled. In one, was a young Delfar. Tredor gasped as he watched his tiny mirror image cling in desperation to the cold rusty bars. It took only a second for T.W. to toss several coins in the direction of the tender. The cage was thrown aside and the young monkey scrambled up trouser legs, shirt buttons, ears and hair until he was perched next to Tredor. They hugged and chittered, the poor little guy telling his new friend all about it.

In another cage was a creature that moved slowly, it eyes sadder than sadness. Its soft sloped back a shell that housed its living self. The neck stretched out long and pendulous when it saw Tizzie, a fizzle of interest lighting its face for probably the first time in at least twenty years. It's size matched that of Dreador, being more than large, and wisdom oozed from the gentle face, even though it lived in a cage that did not fit.

"That one! Coins for that one!" yelled Tizzie, pointing, his face crimson with anger.

Willman threw over ten coins. The tender just shook his head.

"That's a joke! This one is older than old. Many coins."

This meant nothing. More coins grew in T.W.'s pocket. He tossed out five hundred more, his thick fingers releasing the money into the air which scattered at the feet of the tender, tinkling a rich tune.

"Ha! All yours, my friend! And good riddance."

Tizzie ran forward to unlatch the cage. Not that it mattered. The creature inside had been in there so long it could no longer fit through the door. It simply stretched out its long neck through the opening, flicking its tongue toward the tiny, pointed eared man. It was soft, gentle and moist, but it knocked him over anyway, it was so strong. Tizzie laughed. He jumped back to his feet, managing to get past the protruding head to the cage opening. Once there he could see wounds that he had not noticed from a distance. He was livid. He ran back to the stall tender to tell him what for.

"You evil, no good, piece of cursed alien flesh!" He spat out at the creature before him, using language he had never used before. "And on top of that, YOU ARE A... A... A STINKER!"

Then he kicked the thing before him, which had a human body topped with the head of a fly. A dirty fly. He didn't just kick once, but twice.

The tender was stunned, but only for a moment. His tongue lashed out, venom on the tip, but before it could strike the livid little man, Willman's hand yanked Tizzie backward.

"TWO HUNDRED MORE!" he yelled, just in time.

Willman held out the coins, his palm full of gold. Now this was the tender's language. The nasty creature nodded his acceptance while sending a scathing look at the pointed eared atrocity before him. T.W. stepped forward and with ease broke the bars of the cage, tossing the broken metal aside. Their new friend stepped slowly into free space, its four large scaled legs moving stiffly, lumbering forward with the huge shell of time on its back. It licked Tizzie again, knocking him onto his back. The pixie just laughed, rolling in the dust, until the muscular tongue curled underneath, lifting him back to his feet.

Before they all moved on, away from this market stand, Willman whispered something into the hole in the side of the tender's head whilst handing over a large leather bag full of coins. The antennae above the bulging eyes curled in glee. Sticky fingers grabbed the sack of money, its head nodding as it did. Then they left, Willman and his friends. As they walked, not looking back, they heard the opening of cage doors, the clinks and the clanks, the scurrying of feet and flapping wings. A bird the size of a moth appeared, fluttering between them, twittering gibberish, but really, he was saying, "thank you." Willman smiled to himself, his heart toasty warm.

Eventually, when they came to the end of this place, they were standing in a square. A fountain was in the middle, and in the middle of that was a statue. The statue was small, shapely and woman like. The place felt peaceful so Tizzie moved to sit on the small stone wall surrounding the fountain. His new friend lumbered toward him.

"NO!" Yelled Tizzie, hand out in front, seeing what was coming, but he wasn't quick enough. The tongue appeared anyway, pushing him backwards. Tredor rolled around laughing, his monkey legs kicking the air, pointing his bony finger as he watched his friend disappear with a splash. His new son gurgled, tittering, with one hand clamped over his mouth. Tizzie floated to the surface, grappling to get his short legs to stand under him - water dripped from his brow as his sodden clothes leeched to his slender form. He wagged a finger at the giant beast before him, until finally his humor got the best. He could never be mad at this kindly looking soul. But before he said anything, he glared at Tredor, who was still rolling in mirth. His look only made the monkey laugh more, so he turned back to the thick-tongued creature. Spitting out water, he asked.

"What's your name?"

"T H E L M Aaaaa"

"How long in the cage?"

"F i f t e e e o r m o o o r"

Tizzie's brow furrowed as he slogged out of the water, ready to race back up the street to confront that no good for nothing fly headed beast. Willman saw what was about to happen and stepped in.

"We don't act in haste, Tizzie. It will get us nowhere. Patience is the key."

There was a silence, before a voice said, (which was not Tizzie's).

"Wise words young man..."

T.W. looked around, trying to find the source, as did Tizzie, Tredor, Dreador and Thelma. Then the words were said again, followed by the sounds of splashing water. It was the statue climbing down from its towering base, crossing the watery space between them. It was only moments before Thelma's eyes lightened with recognition.

"O h m i y, L i l l i a n n n. H o w w w n i s e t o o o s e e e y u u a g e n n n. H o w w m e n e e e y e r s s s?"

The statue responded as she waded.

"Too many, Thelma. Glad you are free of the cage. Rotten bug eyed keeper you had. Hey, Willman. At last, you are here. I saw your coming reflected in the waters. Tizzie. Tredor. Dreador. Too meet you, nice. Could hardly stand still waiting - you took way too long."

She curtsied then, her stone form cracking. Dreador was the first to bow back, his feathers rustling. He sure did like this kind of woman.

Reaching the fountain edge, Lillian creakily climbed out, over the low rock wall, not pausing in her talk.

"We must go. I am done with this place. Let the

water scatter without me. Follow. I know of a shelter."

The menagerie walked with her as she led them through a maze of narrow streets, just wide enough for Thelma and Dreador to pass. Then they crossed through golden fields until they reached a large barn structure. Inside was enough hay to bed an army. There they rested and ate - it was warm and comfortable, with moist humid smells of home. This was the place they chose to stay, not for just one night, but for the many more to come. Eating. Sleeping. Dressing Thelma's wounds and sharing stories. The stories were the best. Thelma's memories were long and slow, but so full they could have been told slower still and been all the more rich for it. Lillian's were sad.

"I was at Tunkatee Commons, the witches gathering place," she said, "when a fight ensued. My daughter, Tombhra, was taken from me - she is still alive, but not living. Another witch died during the brawl and I was entombed in this stone form then placed atop the fountain in the square. Over time, I learned to loosen my prison. I found movement again, day by day. First I lifted a toe, then a finger, a foot, then an arm."

She told them she had taken to nightly jaunts, practicing, but always returning to her place at the fountain, for there she learned much. Now she was done. She needed to find her daughter, and from what she had heard, this group might be able to help. The Willman sat still, intent on her story. Tredor listened in between swinging from beam to beam, high up in the roof, teaching his new son all of his talents. He swung half the night, a pendulum hypnotist, but it disturbed no one, he was so silent.

CHAPTER EIGHTEEN

# THE SHIPYARD AND THE MOAT HOUSE

Every few days, Willman ventured out. He wanted to go alone but Tizzie would not allow it - nor Tredor - so these three often went back to the bustling market together. On some of the visits nothing happened, on others there would be some strange encounter or another. One time, on reaching the edge of the market, Willman decided not to go there, instead he veered off down a side street which meandered on a ways, reaching crossroads, which he crossed, and street corners at which he turned. Until eventually they reached the shipyard. It was no normal shipyard. It was like the shipyard of the dead. Bodies trudged along, headless and alone, unloading lumber and crates full of wares. Black beasts with beetle heads slashed whips across their naked backs. Some fell and crawled, but none were allowed to stay down. They could not die, so if they did not stand and move again, the lashings became worse.

*What was this place?* The Willman was transfixed. He had never seen horrors like this before. It was at this moment that a body near to them raised its hands up to the place that its head should have been. And screamed! Except that the scream was silent. It was the most terrible thing to ever be seen. Then the whip cracked down, the contact emitting a moist sound into the air.

Tizzie ran first, but T.W. was not far behind. Tredor

gripped onto Willman's hat tighter than Tarzan hugging Jane. They only ran a short ways, before they were back in the main hub of buildings and the shipyard seemed light years away. Finally, their breathing slowed and their hearts stopped pounding. Perspiration beaded on the big man's brow. He was hot. His muscles flexed. As Willman inhaled again, his massive form growing, a middle aged woman passed by. Her head cocked to the side at the sight of this great male. Hmmm, she had a daughter his age who needed a man. Her mind scrambled no further, nor was she shy. Her palms rubbed together in a sinister way as her throat rumbled an evil chortle.

"Hello, young fellow. You are new here, I think. May I welcome you to my home for a fine night of dining?"

Her manner allowed no refusal, besides, he was curious. Introductions were made.

"Come! You may freshen at my house - looks like you need it. Bring your... friends... with you." Her sneer was not missed by the group.

The threesome followed this woman - her perfume suffocating. They turned north, then south, then west and north again, until finally, they reached a home of riches. A moat encircled this place with crocodiles idling on its shores. The bridge across was high and safe. A guard let them in. He had the skin of an eel and eyes to match. The door crashed shut behind. This bridge led to a large courtyard, which was encircled with doors. The woman flapped her hand in the air toward them. Royalty - waving dismissal.

"Pick one... Go clean yourselves... party in one hour..."

Their eyes only followed the wave of her hand for a moment, but when they turned back, she was gone. So they stood in the courtyard. For there was nowhere else. Each door was of a different color and size and shape. Tizzie picked first. His favorite color. Pink! With a hexagonal shape. The door opened easily - no creaks, no squeaks, no straining hinges. Inside was a room, small, dome shaped - with nothing in it. The three stepped inside. The walls were smooth, like leather. There were no windows. Willman was just about to say they very well could not clean up in here, when the door closed behind them. Gently - but firmly. Tredor clutched T.W.'s hat so hard it actually hurt. The giant said nothing, until he could no longer stand it.

"Tredor! Calm. Stay calm. You're squeezing my brains out."

They waited. Nothing happened - except they could not get the door open again. The domed ceiling was as smooth as the walls, the floor as smooth as the ceiling. There was nothing in it that was frightening, even when the walls and ceiling started to shrink in. Just their own fears - strong and silent.

"Sit. Close your eyes and sit. Be calm." Said Willman.

They did - all three of them. It seemed only a while before they felt the room return to it original size. Then the door opened on its own, the sunlight streaming in. T.W. hushed the others.

"Do not rush. Rise gently. Slowly we leave this room."

So they did, finding themselves in the courtyard

once more, with no more choice than before.

Tredor picked next - a jungle-green door with a triangle top. Willman went first with the Delfar on his hat, sensing for anything wrong. Finding nothing, he motioned for Tizzie to follow. This room was much better - it had a sink, a bed, sofa and many windows. There was even a table with appetizers and drink. Tredor was hungry. He scurried between his friend's shoulder blades before leaping down - he wanted to munch on the fruits of rainbow colors. T.W. stayed him as he tested the food first, smelling, sensing, finally tasting.

"OK Tredor, it's safe, go ahead."

Tredor dove in. Head first. His pink face was soon smothered in sugary sap. Meanwhile, Tizzie stood on a stool in front of the sink to rinse off, scrubbing at his cheeks, then poking in his ears and finally curling his eyebrows. While his friends were busy, Willman moved over to one of the windows. He looked out. He knew he was facing toward the courtyard, but what he saw was not that, it was a graveyard, full of protruding bones. He moved to the next window, in this one he saw a galaxy of exploding stars. In the next, he saw Chetsy crumbling. Still he did not panic. He ate a little, then he washed. He felt clean.

The door opened easily allowing them entry back to the courtyard, except this time there was another way out, not just the hundreds of different colored doors. This time, before them were steps, steeply climbing to a grand entrance above. So they went up the steps.

Once at the top, they found more guards - with skins of eels and eyes to match, that walked around in a stooped way, with trays full of glasses full of drink. Inside was merriment and dancing. Dancing! Something Willman always found hard to resist. That is when the woman reappeared, with her daughter at her side.

"Ah ha... Willman... let me introduce... my daughter... please... dance!"

The daughter had the face of a beauty queen, with the innards of a devil. The Willman danced, but his feet were not into it. Looking into her vicious eyes was worse than looking down a well full of tiny cretins shackled with heavy irons, pleading for release, all clawing at each other, chewing and spitting, stomping and climbing to get out. Her shallow soul dried up all movement his body may have had. He did not dance, just swayed back and forth like a tree about to be slain. Tredor stayed with him, even though he was terrified as he looked down onto the rootless hair of the skeletal bitch in a skirt. He clung crazily onto the floppy hat brim, not willing to leave his friend's side. Tizzie stood on the edge of the dance floor, never far away.

"What a strange place this is." His feet trudging to the music.

"Do you love me?" she asked, trying to cling to him, her fingers becoming tentacles.

He was struck dumb, but only for a moment.

"I don't even know you," he said, holding her away, gently pulling on the roots she was already growing into his skin. He flinched, feeling the prickling over his body as he inched their bodies apart. He narrowed his eyes - *what was this? How could she try to grow into him?* - he questioned as his body tingled at the narrow escape of her suffocating hold.

"What are you doing!" she cried as her feet became still, not believing that he had stopped her courtship. No one had managed to stop her before - no matter who it was. Once her creeping sinews entered the skin of the other, it was always the end. They had no chance - they were hers! Even if later she cast them aside - the poor bastards no longer had a choice once she had set her seed - their lives were destroyed, their bodies laying sodden in the rotten dungeons below the moat, still moaning at their lost chance at her beauty, their minds chewed apart by the maggots of her evil soul. No one that touched her in The Dance could ever leave, to tell of her secrets! She just could not believe that he had stopped her - *just what was this!* Her mind stormed. Stomping her feet, her heels clip clopping on the stone floor wailing a tune of their own - her anger carried her on a flight of thunder, until her departing body disappeared behind one of the large Roman pillars that held up the domed ceiling. Shortly after her disappearance, as Willman floundered near the edge of the dance floor not sure what to do, the lights dimmed. Everyone became silent. All dancing ceased. Bodies and faces turned in the direction of the vast gaping hole that the Eel Men always seemed to come out of - and out they came - at least fifty of them - stooped, holding large upright poles in their slippery palms. Atop the poles where heads - stuck firmly onto the spiked ends.

They were the human heads from the market place!

Some of these heads were laughing, some grinned,

some smirked, some wept, some were angry. But all talked, telling of what they were doing when their heads were taken. The crowd in the dance hall was enthralled. Never had they seen such a huge display all belonging to the same household. They clapped and cheered. What a show!

One dour looking man, who had never danced a step in his life, or ever smiled - called out to the nearest... "And what were you doing when you received the beheading spell - which of course, you so fully deserved!" His words chortled into space.

This comment caused waves of laughter.

*"How funny!"* everyone said.

The head had no choice. Once asked, it had to answer - loud and clear, instead of just able to mutter on, with, hopefully, no one paying any real attention to what it said.

"I, was... I, hum, I was fiddling with my best friend's wife." The head said with a big wide grin, even though he was sadder than a fly caught in a trap.

"Got what you deserved then, didn't you!" said the dour man - not thinking about his three mistresses. He was having so much fun he carried on.

"Hey you! You! The one laughing so hard. What were you doing?"

"Me? I was at my father's funeral. Someone had just told me a funny story about something my dad always did. It made me laugh instead of cry.

The head should have stopped talking, but it didn't.

"Felt great at the time. But not now, even though I

keep on laughing. I want to weep, but am not able. Shouldn't have gone into the bathroom on my own after that story, should I - then I wouldn't have been beheaded, hey?"

The head pointed its question directly at those close by.

This one had a little spunk to it. A few people backed away.

*What if it got too much spunk... found the shipyard, somehow reunited with its body, remembered them...*

Despite the small fear involved, the crowd was enthralled. "WHAT FUN! How funny!" everyone yelled out, as they listened some more.

The Willman did not like this place. While the crowd was distracted by the talking heads, he nodded to Tizzie.

"Let's go!"

They raced down the flowing stone steps. Once in the courtyard, T.W. soared to his giant size, scooping the pixie into his arms. Tredor dropped from his perch on the hat to hold on to T.W.'s bright green bow tie, feeling much safer there. Willman ran toward the drawbridge which was being lifted as quickly as it could to stop their escape, but it was slow. Too slow. He raced onto it, his giant legs pounding a drum, even though the bridge was half way into the air, he leaped... a magic giant leap, his muscular legs lifting him. As his feet left the rising boards, he heard the woman roar...

"KEEP HIM HERE! KEEP HIM HERE! HE IS OURS! FOR MY DAUGHTER!"

As he landed on firm ground on the other side of the moat, he heard the crocodiles gnashing their teeth and he heard the pounding of chasing feet, shoeless, with eel skin flapping madly. He did not stop to look back. Moving fast and furious, leaving no trail, running through the streets, turning left then right and right again, until finally he found the square with the fountain. From there, he found his way back to the barn.

That night, they shared with the others what had transpired. Lillian wanted to hear more about the windows through which T.W. had looked - especially the one with the crumbling Chetsy. They talked at some length - time seeping by.

Later... Willman dressed Thelma's wounds, which were still gnarly and prone to infection. He cut away parts of the dead flesh as gently as he could. Afterwards, he gently rubbed in a salve that he had made from herbs growing behind the barn. The great lady never complained, just closed her eyes against the pain. Once he was satisfied that everything looking clean, the flesh pink, he rested again, listening to his family around him. He heard everyone as he sat, but his memory was in the shipyard - his face stern, as the images flicked across his mind.

CHAPTER NINETEEN

# THE LITTLE MAN SIMON

A few weeks later, Dreador decided to stretch his wings, taking off with a mighty flapping sound.

"Don't go far!"

"I won't, Willman. Just a shoooort fliiiight," his words stretched and faint as he disappeared into the distance.

Dreador never felt more free than when he was flying - the wind whistling in a way not heard on the ground, it was such a happy tune. The sun felt better, the clouds looked prettier - even the earth was a nicer looking place. He flapped his wings a couple more times, then glided, catching an uplift of air. He closed his eyes. Floating. How a giant creature could be so graceful. When Dreador opened his eyes again, adjusting to the glare, he looked down. Below, he saw the pool in the square, surrounded by buildings of all sizes, then the long bustling market place. To the north was the shipyard, teeming with misery, then an ocean of water stretching to the horizon. Dreador circled, veering away from the shipyard, not wanting to go near, but he did want to see the other horrible place that his three friends had visited. He soon found it - it was easy to spot - the moat standing out like a halo of darkness. He swooped down to take a closer look, seeing the strange creatures that Willman had mentioned scuttling around like ants. They were doing something, but he could not figure out what. He needed to be closer, so he folded his wings in and dropped lower. Now he could see. Not one of the creatures looked up, for they were after something on the ground. Dreador saw a shadow dart across the courtyard. First it ran this way, then that - like a trapped rodent. It was small, no more that ten to twelve inches as best he could make out. It was then, that one of the eel men leapt onto the running form.

"GOWP HUM!"

The thing that had been captured - screamed.

"Help me! Help me!"

There was no hesitation. Dreador knew enough from T.W.'s description - this place was not good. That meant the thing captured was really in need of help. He was older now and knew how to dive. So he did. His huge body barreled toward the group of rubbery slobs. Dreador flexed a few specific feathers, knowing what was needed to accomplish his task. The feathers stuck out at an angle from his body, catching the wind in a way that made a loud 'DRUMMING' sound. It was very impressive! The group beneath were now aware of his presence - they scattered, afraid of what was falling out of the sky - surely it was a bomb - afraid of whatever was making that incredibly LOUD sound. Dreador slowed his body at the last minute, landing stealthily next to the screaming creature. He grabbed the thing in his beak with no time for explanations, then took off fast. He heard a woman yelling, loud, and angry.

"YOU IDIOTS! YOU LOST OUR PRIZE POSSESSION!"

Her voice faded away as he flapped his wings, taking them further away from the hostilities. How he wished he could tell the crying creature that he was safe, but he knew that if he opened his beak, the thing would fall to its death. So he waited, heading straight back to the barn.

Willman was beside himself, marching back and forth, wearing a groove in the ground - there was no earthquake needed to do what he was doing.

"Where have you been? I've worried myself crazy!"

The Carmedgeon stretched his neck to place the now silent thing onto the ground - it lay curled up on its side - fast asleep. Simon, it seems, had enjoyed the ride.

"What is that?" T.W. bent forward, to get a better look.

Everyone moved into a circle, looking with amazement at the little sleeping man.

He was tiny, only twelve inches tall, with two very human legs, although they were double jointed, and spindly at that. His ankles swiveled, knees and hips the same. The concave chest, with two large nipples that hung like pendulums above a Buddha belly, was a sore sight. There was no covering on the creature - no clothes, no cloth, no cloak. Between its legs, hung a long limp penis that drooled from its tip when fear was at its height - it was parchment paper dry as he slept. The arms attached to the chest were long, clingy looking, as were the fingers on the end. Above the skeletal chest was a skinny neck - turkey like in its length. On top of everything, sat the most beautiful looking face ever seen. Lush lips set below an angular nose. The eyes so green, they shone through his closed lids. After traveling the map of his body, that is where everyone's stare rested - on the most wonderful face they had ever seen.

T.W. stepped gingerly forward, lifting the tiny thing into his arms. Simon still slept as if rocked by a lullaby. Everyone moved back into the barn, whispering questions coming from every direction, all aimed at Dreador who shuffled along behind.

Once inside, they seated themselves with fixed eyes on the mesmerizing face as T.W. placed the sleeping form onto a small bed of hay, near to where he himself sat. Next to the little man he placed some bread and cheese for when he awoke. Then the conversation started. Dreador explained everything that had happened, his eyes lingering mostly on his giant friend, until T.W. gave him what he needed.

"You were very brave, Dreador. Thank you for saving this tiny creature."

Dreador blushed, the ends of his feathers turning a sunset pink.

As the talk continued, Simon awoke but he did not open his eyes. Instead, he listened. He needed to know if this group were friends or foe? *Should he make a run for it?* It didn't take long for him to decide, the feeling here was so peaceful. He rose from his laying position to sit cross-legged, nibbling on the food laid out before him - his magnificent eyes moving cautiously from side to side to take in the strange gathering. None of them payed him much heed - their talk continued, although Tizzie did offer some water, and Trevor skittled over with a piece of fruit.

*How strange...* Simon thought... *they do not seem disturbed at all by my appearance.* He humphed to himself while chewing on the most delicious juicy mango, its sweet nectar drizzling down his chin. *They probably don't like me. That's why they are not looking at me... hmmmph.*

Willman had already given a shake of the head to everyone when he noticed Simon stirring - just wait, the shake said, don't pay attention to him - don't rush him. He knew that Simon would speak, when he was ready.

Simon did not speak that night. But he did feel safe enough to curl up close to the big guy. He snuggled under the hay, feeling the heat of the large man. Thelma was on the other side. Her huge form a mountain towering above him. Her head had disappeared inside her shell. *Hmmph, where'd it go?* Simon wanted to get up to see where it had gone, but he was not ready to expose himself that much yet. So he went to sleep.

The next morning, his curiosity got the better. He woke, before anyone else - or so he thought - but actually, T.W. was watching him through closed lids, his pupils wide and seeing behind the skinny screen. Simon glanced around, peeking through the straw before crawling out. Then he tiptoed around to the front of Thelma. He couldn't see! *Hmmph!* He was too small! He tried jumping on the spot, his spindly legs launching him higher than a power ball, but it was not enough.

"Hmmmfff!"

He jumped again. He could see nothing.

"Hummmffffff!"

His exasperation was overwhelming - *just where was that head!* It was then that he felt the hand curl around his body, a shawl folding him to a warm bosom. He had heard nothing coming but was not shocked when it happened - there was something comforting about the palm that enclosed him. T.W. lifted the small form, high enough so that he could see into the front of the shell with the gnarly head tucked back into the folds of skin. Simon was amazed. He turned his head one hundred and eighty degrees to look back at the big man that was holding him.

He mouthed silently... T H A N K S.

The Willman mouthed back... NO PROBLEM.

Then they both grinned, wide enough to eat cheese.

Not long after this, everyone awoke to the start of a new day.

Tredor and his new son, Trevor, hung out near to Simon. But it was Thelma who eventually managed to get Simon to spill his story. She played a game of hide-and-seek, putting her head inside her shell, then out... in... out. It made Simon laugh - he sure did feel comfortable. Finally he relaxed enough to talk. All ears were his. His story was an unusual one, telling of the people whose heads were taken, never to be reunited with their bodies - their lower parts trudging in hell at the shipyard, with whips and screeches from rubbery beetle lips. The lopped off forever living heads were put up for sale at the market place, most purchased by the rich and wicked who loved to hear the stories they told. It was great entertainment to hear of such suffering. But not for the heads, it was an eternity of reliving the same thing, over and over again. Some of the heads went insane - they were left in the dungeons on top of short poles, gibbering away, experiencing occasional moments of painful lucidness.

"I guess I was one of the lucky ones. A nice witch bought my head. The nice ones don't usually buy us because they don't want to support the evil activity. Well, she thought I was beautiful. She felt so sorry, that she tried to make a new body for me, but the beheading spell seems to affect any attempt to put things back together. It worked, her spell, but not in the way she had planned. She had made a body that matched my head - it was really pretty. But it all went wrong. I was left like this. My head shrunk, the body with it, along with the changes you see. Better than nothing you might think. But it is very difficult having your head atop a creature that is not you. So, yesterday, I decided I could not live like this anymore. I didn't care if I died in my attempt. I escaped from the Moat House, making my way to the Shipyard. I wanted to find my body, in the hopes of getting it to follow me to this place I know of - a place with an old man who might know how to reunite us. But I was caught before I could find my body and they took me back to that horrible woman with the evil daughter. She keeps me in a cage for display at special parties. Before they dragged me back to the cage, I had managed to slip free of the Eel Men... and that is when Dreador saw me."

This story left everyone silent. Trevor jumped out of Tredor's arms, chittering, then ran over to hug Simon. Simon cried. The first deep tears for a long time.

CHAPTER TWENTY

# SOPHIA THE OLD ONE

T.W., Tizzie and Tredor often went to the market for supplies. It was always a beehive of activity with vendors yelling out their wares, voices haggling with flurries of hands and claws and tentacles as goods exchanged hands. Red, blue, orange, purple and turquoise awnings covered the stalls that carried wares, from salted fish, dried pepperoni, stacked rounds of yellow, white and blue cheeses, chunks of flesh, yards of silken materials, to copper pans and honeysuckle soaps mixed with sweet lavender lotions. Scrumptious odors of baking pies and candyfloss mingled with the more odiferous smells - weird smells, as if a long line of camels had walked by. It was a city of strange dwellers in full glory. On this day the first thing they did was visit the stall with the creatures for sale. Willman handed over another sack of money. It clanked loud and full as the clamping fingers grabbed, the thin darting tongue flicking close, but not touching. The beady eyes set in the metallic blue fly head bulged at the weight of the leather bag. It was only seconds after the exchange that cages clanked open, followed by rushes of wings and tapping feet. The vendor closed up early with a heavy smirk - a day's work already done. Some of his regulars were not so happy, sending scowls and dark looks toward the threesome.

They watched the release, deflecting the ugly comments from the ugly mouths around them, before moving on to pick up various supplies. Eventually their stomachs started to talk. This day they ate from a different place than on their other visits - it was at a small cafe down one of the side alleys. Tredor was the one who noticed it first, bouncing up and down, making the rim of T.W.'s hat flop in front of his eyes to get his attention. The pungent odor of home cooking was pervasive, wafting sensuously out of the lane to dance exotically around them. The place was easy to find. Noses were followed, their twitching tips pointing the way. Outside were small wrought iron tables, intricately woven into mesmerizing lacy patterns. As they took their seats, an old lady appeared at their sides. She patiently waited as Willman produced a large cushion out from somewhere for Tizzie, so that he could sit and eat with ease. Tredor climbed down from his perch, his tiny fingers poking in between the lattice work of the table top as he settled his bony bum into place - no cushion would make him tall enough, so he sat next to the salt and pepper shakers. Once they were comfortable, the crackled dark brown face, trimmed with fuzzy white hair, spoke.

"What's it to be today? Fried tadpoles with mustard dip? Scorched cockroach in a tomato sauce? Blanched rat with potatoes? Orrrrr... succulent shrimp over pasta - with a delightful... creamy... butter garlic sauce?"

Then she grinned. Her face was nice. She was older than old, but warm. Her smile full. Her teeth still all there.

"That was very funny," said Tizzie, actually thinking it was not - his stomach had started to turn.

But now, at the thought of a plateful of shrimp and pasta, it settled. He couldn't wait!

"Six servings!" (T.W. was hungry), "and a plate of fruit... please. Then before we leave, maybe we can order more to take with us."

The old lady bowed, just a slight tip of her body, before turning back into the tiny cafe.

It was pleasant out, the sun shining, making it a warm day. T.W. sat with his eyes closed, face pointed up, his ear tips flexing toward the yellow globe. As he relaxed, he heard footsteps coming toward them. They were trying to be quite, but he heard everything. Sensing no immediate danger he remained still - besides, he could smell who it was, his inner nostrils flaring their warning, putting him on silent guard. Then came the sound of one of the chairs scraping the sidewalk, being pulled out from the table. He opened one eye... then the other - to look. He focused on the evil daughter, who was seating herself, at *their* table. Before she even had time to sit, he uttered the words.

"You are *not* welcome here!"

Darkness boiled in her abdomen, rising to fill her face.

"My mother says we are to be married! I will sit with you!"

Then the dreadful creature actually sat down, her red fingernails drumming a funeral march on the arms of her chair. Willman could not believe how absurd this was. He had only laid eyes on her once, and that was months ago. *Words would be wasted on this one!* He looked at Tizzie, who was looking at HER, THE THING, in disgust, no disguise to his glare.

T.W. closed his eyes again, a plan in mind. Earlier, when he paid for the release of the caged animals, he had noticed a swarm of wasps, four times the size of a normal wasp, crawling around in a glass box. The wooden lid of this box had been opened when he handed over the bag of coins. He now called for their help, sending out his silent message - *I need you now...* It did not take long, only minutes, before a faint droning could be heard, a siren coming closer. Which grew louder - and louder. The evil daughter started to look around, the red of her eyes glinting, wondering... *just what could it be?* Her nail tapping stopped, the swinging of her leg over her crossed knee stopped, as did the pat pat pat of her other foot. Her lips crimped, as if sown tight with needle and thread. Her now squinted eyes stormed, short lashes flailing to cover the alarm she was starting to feel. It was as she swiveled in her chair - her luxurious bottom, (that had sent many a man to the dungeons), followed by her shapely hips, all succulently twisting around... a robust snake ready to charm to death - that the swarm entered the alley, landing on the walls, window sills, on awnings, the ground. Seven of the striped wonders landed on the table in front of her pouting form. From this position they attacked. Landing on her bare arms, her neck, her face... popping stingers, each one making an electric zapping sound - they not only ate her, they took out knives and forks... enjoying the feast. Before the swelling even started, she pushed back her seat - which fell with a crash to the floor - then turned to run crazily up the alley, her tapping heals singing a wild song, her Quasimodo form leaching shadows from the walls. The entire swarm followed, buzzing as loud as they could, a full orchestra in its finale. Her whore of a scream leached into every pothole and sewer drain, as her legs picked up speed. They chased, all the way to The Moat House, never allowing her body to rest, until she threw herself toward the drawbridge, allowing the sloppy black arms to drag her away from the swarming warriors. Her swollen face was her jailer for a month or more as she sat in front of her mirror swearing revenge, her nails tapping again, her leg swinging, her foot pat pat patting. The red of her wicked soul finally exposed as the swelling in her face receded, her eyes slanting open more each day.

Willman sat at the table with his friends as he watched the venomous scourge run up the alley. It caused no humor for him, only a frown on his strong forehead as he saw the visions of evil cascading from the daughter's mind as she ran - visions of her real self. A movie reel of horrors that he hoped would not rerun. He wiped drips of perspiration from his brow, as the aged one moved with grace toward him - it appeared she was not disturbed.

"That was wonderful! Nice work young man! Never liked that one - or her mother. Dessert is on the house... and don't worry, what you saw, is what you needed to see."

With that the old lady placed their food on the table. It was incredible - rich cream, butter, white wine and garlic - melded beautifully with a hint of lemon that made it zesty. The shrimp were large and succulent, with home made pasta that was firm, but tender. To crown everything, freshly chopped herbs adorned the plates. It smelled delicious! Their thirst produced sparkling water flavored with fresh berries poured into cold glasses. Fruit from foreign lands was scattered around Tredor. It was a feast to be savored, slowly, in the warming sunshine. Willman felt himself relaxing as they ate, the food massaging all of his senses.

Once satisfied, they rose, with intentions to go back to the market. Before they left, the old woman spoke.

"Be careful. The one you sent running is cunning. She will not be easily thwarted - nor her mother. She would rather imprison you as her husband than not have you at all. I see you as a kind and strong man - that you have great strengths. Use them well. You are always welcome here... remember that."

She reached her hand out to the gentle man before her. In it was a rose petal of a deep crimson color.

"My gift, to you. Put this in your pocket. You will know when to use it."

"Thank you, wise old lady."

"My name is Sophia. Again, remember. You are always... welcome in my home."

Full and satisfied, T.W. Tizzie and Tredor left the small cafe with bags of food for the others. They returned to the market, picking up the remaining odds and ends needed. Then they headed back to their friends.

They spent many nights, many weeks and a few months living this way - the great red barn their home, talking, sharing stories, visiting the market. Nothing outstanding happened - some small things, but not much to talk about. They stayed for Thelma as her wounds still needed to be dressed daily. She winced rarely, but they all noticed the way her eyes watered during the treatment - the salve finally giving her comfort, her breathing easing as the pain quieted. Her injuries had been there for a long time, with new ones added daily from the beatings she received, but eventually she started to heal - her flesh closing - the jagged gapes of tissue disappearing. At last, her true energy returned and discussions of leaving the barn began.

It was the night after a nice visit to the market that it happened. Supplies had been packed ready for the journey and everyone had said their goodnights. The Willman was the last to lay - Simon, as usual, curled up close. Thelma wheezed, Tredor chittered, and Trevor snored. Regardless of the circus sounds, they all learned to live together with restful nights that were easy to accomplish. Usually, no one awoke. T.W. was always the first to rise along with Tizzie and Tredor - it had always been this way with them and always would. On this night it was dark. No moon had shown its face. They slept tightly.

It was Willman, of course, who heard it - he really was growing into the wisest wizard. He was laying on his back in the way that he liked to sleep. The slopping sound happened twice before he opened his eyes. He heard it the first time, but needed a repeat for a reaction. Now his eyes were wide open. His body on alert.

"Tizzie. Tredor. Wake up. Everyone. Wake up. I hear something not right."

Tredor sat upright - his small form hardly

noticeable. He woke Trevor, hugging him to his side.

Tizzie stood... quietly... slowly.

"What is it Willman? What do you hear?"

He was not sure. He just knew that something was not right. He had heard noises that were not of the night - the night that he knew as peaceful and precious.

"Ssshhhh..."

Everyone was awake now, but no one moved. They all remained silent, waiting. T.W. listened longer, his senses keenly aware. Finally, he knew.

"It's the Eel Men. There are many of them. They have surrounded the barn."

Simon was the first to move. He was livid. Neither he, nor any friend of his was going to be taken by those sloppy black creatures - not if he could help it. Thelma and Lillian were right behind. They all stood to their individual tallness in the barn. Simon was tiny compared to his friends, but his bravery made him big. There was no question about the loyalty of Tizzie and Tredor. And Trevor was now blood. They were united. The Willman rose. He had maintained a height of six feet four for a long time - he stepped quietly across the barn floor, pushing open the great doors that let the night air enter. He could see rows and rows of Eel Men before him, surrounding the barn - a bright green slime covered the earth over which they had moved, casting an eery glow over their gluey bodies. Willman felt his family behind him - all standing firm. He thought for a miniscule of a second.

*Should they fight?*

*Was it necessary?*

He thought of his friends. Of lives being lost. That

is when he remembered the rose petal - it was speaking to him - now he knew what to do.

The Eel Men were immobilized for they had not expected anyone to hear them, they always moved stealthily, capturing their prey easily. Their sloping forms swayed from side to side, rows of seaweed choked by a red tide - they were unsure of their next move. This slight hesitation gave Willman the time needed. He pulled the petal out of his pocket and handed it to Tredor who was at his side.

"Take a bite. Quick."

As the petal was passed around, the Eel Men sensed a problem. They started to move, masses of them, making nasty slopping slithering sounds. They were so fast and slippery that they could easily overtake those before them, they knew that, but they felt a wariness with this group that was unusual. They moved slowly. Willman stepped toward them.

"Tehahe, tunto, zin passentri!" he said calmly, before shooting like a beanstalk to the height of twenty-five feet. Far taller than his natural size. He was a giant, roaring man! The eel men had not expected this. They were taken aback! Willman started to stomp his feet, splattering the ground around him. His friends stood well behind, passing the red delicacy from one to another. The black, sloped back creatures were afraid to come closer, loath to be the first to die. This move bought enough time for everyone, as one by one, after a bite of the petal, they disappeared. Tizzie was the last to take it - seeing what was happening, he yelled up at his best friend.

"NOW WILLMAN! NOW! TAKE A BITE TOO!"

Before he too disappeared, he tossed the last bit of rose onto the ground. The loathsome Eel Men saw their chance, realizing what was happening - they still hoped to be able to take the giant down - especially now his friends had gone. They raced forward, trying to reach the petal before Willman. T.W. simply watched from above - it seemed surreal to him, seeing this mass of slimy creatures clamoring toward the crimson speck on the ground. He reached down just as a sneaky hand creeped toward the velvet softness that lay lonely, but before the slob could grab, his own fingers picked it up, lifting the dripping crimson into his mouth. The last he remembered was looking down at the crawling mass of slime that was starting to cover his feet... it was full of zillions of beady eyes staring furiously up.

When he woke, he was curled in a bed of normal size. He looked around - it was a large room of a strange shape that was full of his friends. Sitting at a table by a roaring fire, was Sophia. Willman smiled, rising freely.

"Thank you, old woman. Your gift and wiseness are appreciated."

"No, young man. Without your wiseness, some of your friends would be dead. To not fight was a choice most would not take - your kind are few and far between. However, you must move on now - the evil woman wants you as the husband for her daughter and will go to great lengths. And... to make it worse... you have the little man. I see in the Telling Flames that you need to save Chetsy, it being the grounds of your forefathers. You must go now. Your lesson here is learned."

The Willman knew what she meant. He turned to his friends.

"This is home to some of you. Stay if you wish."

No one wanted to.

Sophia hugged him then. Another mother.

"Leave now, son. Follow the lane into the market place, go back the way you came, it is the only way back to your village. Quickly! They come!"

"But, you?" said The Willman.

"Believe me. I am safe. Go. Quickly! Before it is too late!"

T.W. reached down, grabbing a hold of his friend, Simon, who he put onto his shoulder. Tredor and Trevor clambered up. They formed a group, Tizzie always by his side. Sophia guided them a little ways, pointing them in the right direction. As they moved down into the darkness of the street they could hear the slopping noise in the far distance - it made them move faster, until they found that the dark of the night became even blacker - the openness of the street becoming walls of rock once more.

They were back in the cave.

CHAPTER TWENTY-ONE

# THE LIZARD MEN

They travelled some way before deciding it was safe to rest - the slopping sound thankfully no longer in the background. Sophia had given them satchels of food and drink. They sat. T.W. made glowing bubbles of light that floated in the air, but no matter how bright they were, they could never see far down the cave, in either direction. They ate sparingly, just in case.

"What now?" asked Tizzie.

"First we relax, then we just keep walking," said T.W.

They all rested except for Tredor and Trevor, who couldn't wait to explore the walls. They scuttled up the crevices, sure footed, not slipping on the fluorescent orange moss that grew in clumps. It was fun! Higher up they found small nests clinging to the wet rock surface - they were made and attached with mud - like swallow nests. Trevor was young and curious, so he reached one of his tiny hands in through a small round hole that was in the center... as he did so, he looked at Tredor, his eyes sparkling, mischievous - he stretched his arm out - *wattsy in herey?* He soon found out! He yanked his hand back, chittering and squealing, his eyes startled. *Bitey thingy!* He hung on to Tredor, both arms around his neck while twisting his head around to look at the nest. As he squinted his eyes at the nasty mud brown dome, a head poked out of the dark hole with round blue eyes and a long yellow beak - the Thingy hopped out of the nest onto the nearby ledge, flapping its hairless bat like wings in the process. It sat a while, preening its white feathered body before pecking toward Trevor again. Trevor pulled one of his arms free from around Tredor's neck so that he could slap back at the horrible pecking thing... but it just made the Thingy peck more. Tredor grabbed his son's wrist to stop him. Once Trevor stopped slapping, he no longer got pecked.

"I think he's telling you to keep your hands out of his nest, Trevor!" yelled Willman, his laughing voice echoing out of sight. "You'd better come down!"

They started on their way soon after, the floating lights leading the way - everyone was eager to reach daylight so that they could get back to the village. Despite this desire to be free of the dark, Willman was fascinated with his surroundings. He hadn't noticed the flowers when they passed through the cave last time. Walking over to a small clump, he reached out his hand to the violet bud - as his finger touched, it opened... unfolding slowly to reveal a circle of delicate white petals trimmed with a deep red. The center was a startling pink, with fuzzy stamens that unfurled in glory. At the end of one stamen was a caterpillar that changed into a butterfly before his eyes - it was the same coloration as the flower. As the beautiful creature fluttered away, the flower closed into a bud again.

"How fascinating?" He touched another bud - it opened. A new butterfly flew. He watched these amazing creatures as they fluttered towards areas of the orange moss. Once there, they laid small eggs the size of peanuts. He noticed other eggs then, only bigger, they seemed to be growing on the moss as if it fed them. One large egg, now bigger than a lemon, had a crack in it.

"Interesting," he muttered, walking over, leaning forward to see better, his brow frowning like a master chess player. As he stared with eyes of a hypnotist, the crack grew longer, then wider, until the shell fell apart. Inside was a tiny bird, with white feathers, a yellow beak and bat like wings. *Hmmmmm?* As he contemplated what he was witnessing, a *Thingy* flew down from the roof of the cave to the newborn - it pecked at Willman - stubborn in its attempt to be rid of him.

"OK. OK... don't worry," he said, stepping back.

The bird fed the baby then, something syrupy that was white... red... and pink. His mind churned. *The butterfly? Amazing - dying to feed her young.* Willman turned his face towards his friends.

"Did you see that Tizzie? Now... how?"

But before he could get the question out, he saw a bird fly from one nest to another, relieving itself on the way. As the excretion plopped to the ground, a small plant grew - with violet buds.

"Tizzie, Thelma? Did you see that?"

Willman was mesmerized. He watched in fascination as occasionally one of the birds would land on the ground, gently touching a flower bud, which would slowly open, releasing the butterfly.

It took a while for the group to get started again - the cycle of life just witnessed had brought much calm. As they moved along, they were careful not to step on any of the flowers.

Despite this fascinating reprieve, they still walked for days, much longer than their first time in the cave.

"How much further do you think?" Lillian asked while looking at Willman in the hazy light. Before he could answer, a noise came to them, stopping all in their tracks. It was a watery sound, full of splashes - amidst the splashes they could hear the flopping of feet on wet rock. Was it The Eel Men? Had they come all this way just to be back in the same place?

"Let's turn around," whispered Dreador.

"No. You hold here. I will look. I don't smell The Eel Men or feel their presence. Wait here," said Willman as he moved silently forward, his feet barely touching the ground. As before, when they had finally left the cave to enter the market place, the darkness started to become lighter. It was a soft, but bright light, like an emerging dawn. Eventually, he found himself on the edge of a high cliff. Dropping to his hands and knees he crawled forward to look over the edge. Way below was a big fluorescent green pool full of swimming creatures, some of which were resting on the banks basking in the brightness - others were diving from rocks into the deepness. The creatures had four legs with a body fashioned after a large iguana, but from the shoulder up they had a human neck and head. Even though they ran around on all fours, as a lizard would, their forelegs had human hands - but these hands were not covered in soft pink skin, instead, the fingers and palms were scaly and coarse. He studied for a while, seeing that these creatures could sit upright, placing their tails for balance, using their hands to caress each other and to offer flapping fish to those laying on dry land. As he watched, his glance noted a long flight of steps cut into the rock to his right. The steps led to the pool. Sensing no danger, he rose from his kneeling position and walked down the steps in full sight. Now the Lizard Men saw him, this grand man that walked into their den... they stopped swimming, they stopped diving and stopped laying peacefully. Those in the water floated, with eyes watching. Those on land lay rigid - planks with beating hearts. The movie was on pause - who was this? As T.W. reached the last step - his sturdy stride his message - he sent out his honest greeting.

"Greetings. We come as friends, lost in the cave. We had to leave the market place to flee The Eel Men. My name is Willman. My friends wait above."

The mention of fleeing from The Eel Men immediately made him and his party their friends. One of the smaller of the creatures moved forward, his wizened face grinning in delight.

"Gleetings black. Anylone stalked by thosell mangy black bluzzards are fliends of ours. Bling your fliends down. Join usll. I am Malamandor, the Chief of the Lizard Men."

Willman called for his friends, who came openly. Thelma had the most difficulty getting down the stairs as they were a bit narrow, but T.W. used some salty broadening magic to make it happen, until finally, everyone was by the pool. Introductions were made and many conversations followed. The chatter was wonderful, resembling clanging pots in a happy kitchen. During all this commotion, the Lizard Men were told of their adventures and what The Willman needed to do in Chetsy in order to save his race.

Malamandor knew of his mother, Theadora, and of The Jebber - he expressed his great respect for them and the village. During all the talk, Tizzie sat silent. He noticed that although they had initially thought all of the creatures were male, some were in fact females, with pretty faces and long hair - their scales polished a deeper red than those of the males - he sighed at their beauty. Then his nose twitched, the smell of fish was slight, but it was there - after a moment he decided it was not ripe, just nice - made him feel at home. As his eyes explored, he saw that beyond the pool were holes dug into earthen mounds - it seemed that these were where the lizard men slept. He found these creatures fascinating and enjoyed sitting, listening, finding out that Malamandor's race went back many years - they had lived in this cave for a timeless age. From the stories told, it was obvious that the Eel Men were afraid of these scaly beasts. They never came from the market place into the cave, although Malamandor said that the black slimes were strong and willful. Occasionally, the Lizard Men went to the market themselves, taking a short route that only they knew of. After all, they did need to keep up on news. When they went to the market it seemed that the Eel Men stayed at the Moat House, not venturing out. Not only was Tizzie fascinated, but so was T.W.

"Why do the Eel Men fear you so?"

"Beclause ofll our diet," replied Malamandor... "ofll fishll and Eel Men!" He smirked, smacking his lips at the same time. The rest of the clan were listening, they hawked and clacked their throats in laughter.

That night everyone slept soundly, for the Lizard

Chief had offered to lead them out of the cave. He had said that they could not go out the way they had come in, but it would be close enough so they would not need to enter the blackness again to get home. Of this everyone was thankful - even though the dark place had given safety.

It was just a short stay but one that they would always remember, for they now shared the secrets of how this race had lived in harmony for many years. Living simply. Needing little. There was much to learn from this. The next morning, Malamandor, along with thirty others, led the visitors to daylight. A few of the Lizard Men moved on ahead, while others stayed in the rear. Malamandor said that they never travelled alone as one never knew what might happen, anyway it was at least a half a days walk, so precaution was best. They left the poolside early, so when the unusual group emerged it was a bright and sunny afternoon - the Chief stepped out with Willman, both squinting their eyes in the bright light. After a few moments of adjustment, with black pupils dilating in and out, Malamandor turned.

"My fliend. Anytimell you are in needll, you may call on usll. It hasll bleen a pleasure. Howlever, I havell one flavor to askll beflore you glo... rumors tlavel flast you knowll." He grunted then, before continuing, "may I see you in your gleat size? Or is it justll a myth?"

T.W. smiled.

"My pleasure," he said, stepping away.

Then he grew. And grew. And grew. He let it happen slowly this time, like a rose bud opening to bloom, for he saw the joy it gave to Malamandor.

First he grew to his natural fifteen feet, before stopping for a short while, letting the lizard men know that his true size was indeed not myth. Then he shot up to twenty-five feet in height, finally not taking his time - he was like a firework in its glory - his breadth even more massive than Godzilla. The Chief and his clan were mesmerized.

"STOMPLL YOUR FLOOT! I WANT THE PLEASLURE OF KNLLOWING HOWLL THE EEL MEN FELT!" yelled Malamandor.

T.W. obliged. Once! And once was enough! When he shrank back to six feet plus, Malamandor was nowhere to be seen, until finally, Willman saw him poking his head out of the cave, his lizard scales reflecting the light. From the distance, Malamandor looked thoughtful - which he was - then the fine fellow sat up on his hind legs, bowing his head low, respectfully.

"Flarewell Gliant! Glood luckll!"

The Giant nodded back...

"Farewell, my scaly friend!"

# CHAPTER TWENTY-TWO
# KELLY KEEN

The town was a beehive. Kelly Keen was whipped... *but not as whipped as I was when I was laying in the morgue.* She laughed... *still, can't wait to get home, finish my book,* as she loaded another tray with chocolates. *Or should we go out?* At this thought, she grinned. She had never had so much fun in her whole life. Seventy-one and feeling like this again. Lithe, attractive, buoyant and full of sex. The spirit that had been trapped inside the mannequin, who was now inside Kelly, was the spirit of an attractive thirty six year old. Her name was Tombhra. The two spirits - Kelly and Tombhra's - coexisted well, like bread and butter. Kelly's sense of humor had always been dark, now this new enlightenment allowed her to be darker still and she was loving it. Tombhra was happy too, no longer stuck inside the immovable body of the mannequin out of which she had been able to see, think, feel every emotion - but unable to even so much as twiddle a little finger. It had been an impossible way to live! Every day and every night to be stuck in whatever place the shop assistant had placed her - her view limited to whatever direction her head had faced. Sometimes she got to stare at a rack of clothes, the same rack, day after day after day. *Good god, she would go crazy!* Sometimes she was next to the cash register, the smell of dirty money invading her nostrils, the clinking of the drawer vibrating in her head, the headache getting worse, not being able to lay down in a calm silent room with a damp cloth placed gently on her forehead. Some days she was faced toward the dressing rooms. That was better, she could usually get a peek in through the side of the curtains - they never could close tight enough to give total privacy. Tombhra found most of the peeking funny, people struggling with too tight jeans, sweaters too large, or too long. *And the colors they chose. They looked like walking corpses or a decoration at some Christmas party.* She sighed and laughed at the same time. She wanted to offer her help so badly - she was good at the fashion thing. Sometimes though, she would get a peek at someone's titties. There were big ones, small ones, pointy up and pointy down ones. It nearly always made her giggle, but mostly she got a craving right in her crotch that was hard to bear. It was worse though when she was outside the men's changing room - sometimes she got a glimpse of a bare bottom. It could be smooth as a baby's bum or hairy as an orangoutang. Made no difference, she liked them all. It was times like that she thought her lifeless body would just melt into a blob on the floor.

If she concentrated really hard - although it didn't always work - she found she could move the eyes of the mannequin, but it took so much of her strength, that once, she had lost a hold of space and nearly disappeared - so she didn't do it often. She only tried it when she thought there was a chance of someone seeing her that might help her escape this solitary hell. But alas, no one ever saw her. And after all the effort it took her too. She would cry silently after that, usually for days. It had been six years since she had been entombed inside this dried up carcass, and as strong as she was, she didn't know how much more she could take.

She'd been thinking along these lines again, just a few days ago, when she had sensed an unusual presence out the door - it started to fill the shop, wafting in from the outside. It was as if the shop had become a giant mug and a magic brew was pouring into it. The brew was full of the greatest of well being, of colors abundant with life as it swirled. She breathed, filling her mind and soul with the strength. The mannequin was facing away from the door frustrating her to no end - she wanted to see what was coming! Tombhra could not see it, but she could feel the shop door bulge wide as in stepped a casually dressed woman with long ebony hair and a handsome face. The smile was contagious.

"Concentrate. Concentrate," Tombhra whispered. "Do not miss this opportunity. This is surely someone that can help." Then she put all her energy into the mannequin's eyes.

"Afternoon Theadora," said the shop owner, welcoming Thea as she stepped through the doorway.

"Hi Tammy," she responded in a warm voice. She hadn't been in the shop for a while, even though it was one of her favorite places to buy clothes. She liked the warmth of the environment, the styles, and most of all, the owner, whose policy it was to let people shop in peace - never being pushy and always pleasant. Shopping was not her favorite pastime, in fact, she had put it off for as long as she could, but she needed a couple of sweaters. As she moved toward the shelf full of colorfully folded garments, a body stepped out from behind a large rack - one that held an assortment of party dresses. The thing stepped right in front of her.

"Why, Theadora," it said, "fancy seeing you here!"

She groaned inwardly, a woman of tremendous patience, but there were a few who could test it - the person standing in front of her was one of those. It was Brendan, nosing around in the women's section. *Probably sniffing the clothes, instead of buying them.* She wondered who had recently tried on anything in the surrounding racks. *Well, Brendan will figure it out... he seems hot on some female track.* Problem was, no matter whose scent he was on, when he saw her, his tracking took a turn.

"Nice sweater," he commented, while looking at her breasts - even though he was wearing sunglasses, she could still see the direction his eyes pointed.

"Thanks," she uttered trying to pass him. He blocked her move well. She tried again. He blocked a second time - a rugby move he'd learned in school. She sighed.

"How's work?"

"Just dandy," he enthused. "Want to go for a coffee?"

She had tried the coffee thing quite a few times before because she actually did think he was a nice guy inside, he just didn't seem to be able to get the niceness to move out and stay there. The times she had said yes, she had ended up walking at least two steps behind while HE talked at her about what HE was doing. She'd had to trot now and then to keep up. He didn't seem to need any responses and when they made it to the coffee house he usually made some underhand comment. The last time it had been in front of the new young female helper.

"So, are you actually going to get your wallet out to pay," he'd voiced in a much too loud way, insinuating that she was a tight wad and he was the forever giver. Last Theadora remembered from a couple of years ago, was that she had loaned him money. She hadn't seen it return yet and had decided a long time ago to let it go. Before she could open her mouth to respond, he continued, "never mind, I'll buy". Then he smiled serenely at the young lady behind the counter. The brunette glowered through a stack of coffee cups at Theadora, as if to say, how can you make this endearing man pay – again - even though she had never seen them before. Brendan hummed with glory.

The last time she had said yes, to obediently trot down the street after him like a kid following the ice cream man, she'd decided to come to a dead stop in the middle of the sidewalk, just to see if he noticed. He didn't. She could still hear him rattling on a hundred yards down the road. She had wondered what he had thought when he reached the coffee shop, only to find she wasn't behind him. She now wondered if this was a payback offer or if he had really forgotten all about it. Knowing Brendan it would be the latter, he would get far more glee out of her being subservient, two steps behind, than anything else - well, she just did not feel like it today.

"Thanks Brendan, but I can't."

Brendan looked crestfallen, hurt beyond belief. He turned toward Tammy as Theadora picked up a sweater.

"Don't expect her to pay for that," he chortled, "she probably doesn't have her wallet with her anyway." Then he marched out the door without a glance or another word. Theadora heard him calling to someone on the other side of the street - a loudspeaker on full volume - the whole town probably heard him. She sighed. Regardless, she liked him, it was just that... he didn't quite get it. She was thinking this as she moved over to check out some scarves, when the mannequin caught her eye.

"Oh... nice. One of the old ones," she commented.

"Yes, found it in an antique store down in the city - more life like than the ones they make these days," responded Tammy. "Its great fun to dress her up."

Thea put her hand out to touch the face, her fingertips grazing the cheek. At first touch she flinched, a strange tingle had rippled down her arm. She looked at the mannequin, cocking her head an inch to the side, full of curiosity. Just as she turned her head toward Tammy with a comment on her lips, Tombhra managed to make the eyes move, to the side and back again.

Theadora missed it!

It happened right then, when she turned her head toward Tammy.

Tombhra was about ready to burst, she just could not believe the timing and try as she might, she could not get the eyes to move again. She started to panic.

She was going to miss her chance!

"Interesting creature." Thea's hand hovered in front of the face before she moved away, placing sweaters and scarf next to the till. "I'll take these please."

While Tammy wrapped the colorful garbs in tissue paper, Thea glanced back over her shoulder, she had a strange feeling that she needed to look at the unusual figure again. Her feeling was right - as she watched, a lonely, solitary tear slid down the mannequin's cheek, leaving a trail of sorrow all the way down to the jaw line, where it dropped, exploding as it hit the floor into a million tiny pieces of golden sparks. *Oh... my...* She walked back, reaching with her hand again to gently trace her finger down the mannequin's face, easily finding the line of loneliness the tear had left. The same tingle she had felt before, but much stronger this time, warmed her arm as she did so. She smiled to herself then. *Aah. I feel you now.*

"Don't worry, gentle spirit," she mouthed, keeping her back to Tammy.

Tombhra was standing in the chocolate shop with Kelly, remembering how it had been. She didn't have to wait long before she found herself inside a real, live, moving body. Wrinkles or not, it moved, talked, walked, kissed, hugged and best of all, had a wicked sense of humor. She thought about the days leading up to the transformation, they had been some of the most stressful ever as she waited patiently, looking out the eyes of the mannequin at the rack of dresses she had now been placed in front of. It had been torture, thinking she knew that the nice woman could help, but not really knowing. What if she was stuck here for another six years - she didn't think she could take it.

The night it happened was a night full of stars, the whole sky was a kaleidoscope of brilliance. She was snoozing when a sound brought her stark alertness. *What was that?* She heard it again, a crackling of fire. *Huh? Building on fire... no no... please not...* She sniffed, smelling. *No smell. What then? Hear fire crackling....* The sound grew louder as heat invaded. *What? What is happening? Please don't let me burn to death! So hot!* She started to fidget harder than she ever had - desperate to escape the heat - causing the mannequin to topple backwards, crashing into racks of sequined dresses that spit silver dots across the room as their tassels tangled with the flailing arms of the dummy gone mad. As the heavy body landed with a thud, Tombhra's spirit hissed out, becoming a ghost of gold. She floated freely above the toppled figure until she felt the heat again, its white hotness enveloping her shimmering form. Then she blacked out. She remembered nothing more until she was nimbly climbing out of the drawer in the morgue - the one she made open with the strength of her will.

Her memories were making her hot again, so she pushed them aside. Instead she thought about now.

"Let's go to The Green Cow after work," she whispered wickedly to Kelly.

Kelly fought the urge to grin.

"OK," she chortled back, forgetting the half read book at home.

It wasn't long to closing time. Kelly had gone round to the other side of the counter for the umpteenth time to spit and polish the glass front of the display case - she finished shining away the zillion finger prints that people insisted on leaving there. Everyone had to point. Not only point, but to press their fingers onto the glass in the process, sometimes smudging fingerprints to point at something else in the case. It drove Kelly nuts - it was so rude. She stood back to examine her work, hoping it was for the last time today. Just then the door tinkled open, letting in a cacophony of voices.

"Aah no, sounds bad," she muttered.

Behind the voices came a man, a woman, and five kids. All of the kids were fat except one, who was wiry as a coat hanger. The father of the kids was thin too, just like the one kid. Snap in half thin. The youngsters invaded the shop with a Viking charge, pushing chairs out of the way, tipping over sugar pots, making syrupy castles, adding a little honey from the containers to make a slurry that was easy to lick up. Kelly looked on with horror and fascination which gradually turned into one of those pissed off looks she could do so well. She turned toward the woman, not the wiry guy since he tended to hide behind the bull elephant that was his wife.

"Can I help you?" chirped Kelly in her pissed off voice.

The woman should have seen it coming - the pinched face and chirping quality saying it all. Besides, anyone who let their unguided hoard of demonic little bastards do what they had just done, really ought to know to get out while the going was good. But instead of apologizing and leaving - The Biggness said.

"I'll have a coffee."

"What kind?" Kelly chirped again, now on remote control.

"Just give me a coffee!"

"What size?" Kelly offered, pinching her face a bit more.

"A sixteen ouncer! Or bigger!"

"We only have eight or twelve ounce," Kelly delighted in saying.

"Fine. Give me two of the biggest..." the woman snarled. "And," she said, pointing with her finger before putting it firmly onto the glass, "I'll have one of those," then the finger smudged in a line to another location, "one of those," finger smudging again, "one of those. AND," she bent down to kiss the glass with extra large, lipstick encased lips, "four of those little babies!" Then she stood up in triumph.

Kelly froze, harder than an icicle. She could have tolerated the rudeness of the five brats, but this was just too much, she had just finished cleaning that glass! The finger was still there, leaving a giant print. Kelly could not help herself - the words just came out.

"DID YOU KNOW THAT YOUR FINGER IS TOO FAT!"

Before The Bigness could make a response, she continued.

"IN FACT, IT IS SO FAT, YOU PROBABLY COULD NOT STICK IT UP YOUR ASS EVEN IF I TOLD YOU TO!!!!!!"

Kelly stood perfectly still. She smiled a tight lipped smile at the big buxom beast whose face had turned a bluish color, her large lips trembling as they worked on letting a response fly - when something started to drip out of Kelly's right ear. Whatever it was that was dripping, and with some volume, was awful looking, with a funny color to it and it definitely was not normal. All else was forgotten.

"What the hell is that goo dripping out of your ear?" The Biggness asked.

Kelly raised her head to respond, just as her glass eye started to roll in its socket, a tumble dryer gone mad - green then white, green then white - turning around and around trying to find its way out. It was at this point that the wiry husband peeked his head out for a look. His mouth clacked open and closed like a venus flytrap. Kelly waited as Tombhra whispered the answer inside.

"Oh! That!" she finally said. "Its embalming fluid... always happens when I get a little... umm... upset... something to do with when I was in the morgue."

Tombhra snickered inside Kelly's head. All of the kids and the big bitch - not the husband, he had dissolved into his wife's back - looked on with a slowly dawning fear - comprehension starting to form on their faces.

"Uummh..." muttered the woman, starting to smell The Smell - a nasty kind of smell - she felt like she was trapped inside a bag full of rotten oozing shrimp that had been left to steam in the afternoon sun. "Uummmh, think I lost my appetite," she said, grasping a handkerchief over her nose as she quickly backed out of the shop, tripping over the skinny guy, telling him to "MOVE IT!" He yelped in pain when she stomped firmly on his foot. The kids didn't move, mesmerized by the increasing amount of goo that dripped from Kelly's ear and stunned by the growing smell.

"PEUW! WHAT'S THAT STINK!" yelled one of the little fat bastards.

"NOW!" yelled the woman from outside, "NOW!"

The kids, able at last to do something they were told, ran toward the door leaving their dishevelment behind.

"No guts, you guys! No guts at all!" yelled Kelly.

The piece of wire kid stopped in his run - a look of fear mixed with awe.

"Whoa, mum. No guts, mum. Does she mean us... or her?"

His mother slapped him across the head.

"Shut it - get moving!" before she turned for one last look. That is when the door shut! Not gently at all. It banged! Her hippo face stretched wide as the booming sound burst her eardrums. No one had touched that door - she could see Kelly still standing behind the counter. She quickly moved away, hoping to put a continent between them. Finally, Kelly's perfectly still posture moved, exploding with glee. Her mirth was the highlight of her day at this point. The tavern was to come later.

"Tombhra! You are wicked!" She chortled, not minding having to polish the glass one more time. She paused for a second... "I'm not really full of embalming fluid... am I?"

Tombhra giggled, giving her assurances. Kelly felt better - the goo disappearing as quickly as it had arrived, like a snail sucking back into its shell.

## CHAPTER TWENTY-THREE

# THE MOUTH BUG

On the other side of town, something else was happening.

Jimmy was almost nine now. He stood on his own in the playground, hating to be around anyone these days. He didn't feel good. *Please don't make me go out tonight!* He had been to see Better B. so many times he could not stand one more visit. His onetime schoolmates were running around laughing. He was so tired. He noticed other children not doing anything - they looked pale. *How long have they been like that? Don't know, can't remember much anymore.* He was glad it was recess so that he didn't have to do anything. Everyone was just waiting, passing time, one more class then the final bell would ring and the school would empty out like a foaming bottle of champagne. But the other kids were waiting for a different reason than he. They wanted to go home to eat and play. He wanted to go home to bed. He knew his time was running out. Soon he would be inside the lifeless painting that Better B. hung on her wall - a momentum of the soul that was.

On the back side of the schoolhouse, not known to the little gremlins running around like a herd of dwarfs, a creature appeared. It was jet black, smallish in size, hovering about six feet above the ground. Its ten hairy legs protruded from its gnarly body, with one large blinking eye in the front. Under the eye, was its mouth, with two rows of broken brown stained teeth. It was a Mouth Bug. A bug that thrived and survived only in the folds of a child's mouth - the inner cheeks being the food it craved. A delicacy beyond compare! It could smell children! *Lots of them!* Its nostrils flared as it started to chomp its jaws. Moving forward, it zigzagged around the building, then into the trees at the edge of the playground where it waited - patiently. It's teeth gnashed together, each pointed razor edged fang grating against the next, making a noise like a fingernail raking over a chalkboard. Lizzie was the first to hear it - and the first to see it. She had been playing catch with her friend and had missed - she ran after the ball as it rolled along the ground toward the small group of dogwoods. It was when she bent down that she heard it. *What a strange sound? What is it?* Her spine shivered as she lifted her head to see the nasty thing, right there, hovering, three feet in front of her face. It clacked its teeth.

Jimmy had been watching Lizzie from the other side of the playground. He saw The Bug at the same time, except he knew what it was. Better B. Better had taught him all about them.

"Keep your mouth shut, Lizzie! Keep it shut!" he yelled, running toward her. He clamped his own lips then, as tight as they would go, tighter than a centipede's bum hole. He didn't want a Mouth Bug! *No way!*

Lizzie was too frightened - she couldn't help it. Her mouth opened so wide a giant watermelon could get lost. She screamed! Then screamed again!

"YAAAAAAOOOOOOOO!"

"YAAAAOOOOOOOOAAAAOOOOOO!"

The Mouth Bug itself screamed, but in ecstasy as it darted forward, not missing its chance, entered the drooling cavern of Lizzie's mouth, instantly burrowing with its legs and chomping with it's rotten teeth - hard, into the mucousy folds.

"Hhuummph, yhuumph, yum, yum."

Lizzie's lips where now tightly closed, glued shut by excretion from The Bug. The chomping noise carried on. Loud and munching, followed by a sickly, high pitched voice, squealing with delight. Lizzie started to cry, big horse sized tears that welled up then drooled down her cheeks. A thin stream of saliva trickled out of one corner of her mouth.

Everyone in the playground looked, but no one moved except for Jimmy. He ran up to Lizzie, taking her hand.

"It'll be ok, really, it will."

She did not believe him. She just did not. They stood holding hands while a group gathered, keeping its distance - the gentle sigh that had mooed around the playground only minutes ago, was gone. In its place was a fistful of fear.

# BACK IN THE OTHER PLACE

## CHAPTER TWENTY-FOUR
## OUTSIDE THE CAVE

The motley crew waved farewells to Malamandor before sitting to bask in the sun, glad that they would not have to enter the cave again. They were not sure where they were, but Malamandor had said it was not far from home. The open meadow stretched before them - in the distance was a stream.

"Maybe it's the same one that runs through the village," Tizzie said hopefully. After a good rest they decided to head in that direction, the skittering of the water over the pebbles making a jolly sound as they grew closer.

"Which way now?"

Willman nodded, his face pointing.

"Downstream."

After several days of following the flowing water, Tizzie was deep in thought... *I thought Malamandor said it would not be far.* He was grumpy. He was fed up of all this walking. It was at this point in time that Dreador flew back to them. He had been sent ahead to scout - but not far! He landed elegantly.

"There's a large house up ahead with a vast garden and a courtyard full of pigs, cows, sheep and horses. I saw an old man outside, stooped, with a pipe in his mouth."

T.W. took in this news. He sat thinking while

everyone splashed around in the warm water. *Should they skirt the house or stay on course?* He decided they should rest until the next day, hoping he would then have an answer. That night, they made a small fire that they all huddled around, it being chillier than usual. Lillian talked of her daughter. She rarely mentioned her, but everyone knew that the subject was always on her mind. Later, Thelma slowly told of her time in a foreign land - her stories were always fascinating. This way, they spent the evening. Simon fell asleep first, close by his big friend. The others were not far behind.

The next morning was clear... in weather... and in mind. Willman made his decision - the tightly knit group moved on toward the house. As the building came into sight, just as Dreador had described, a blur of cloth came from behind a tree - it had a staff in its hand which it used to crack onto the back of T.W.'s legs, sending him falling to the ground. Quickly, Dreador moved in front of his brother, flapping his wings - madder than a goose - at the attacker. The staff was attached to the old man who stood, his bent frame leaning on the tall pole that was now planted on the ground before him. He was laughing, his long white hair floating in the breeze.

"You must be more aware than that my son, if you are to battle the wicked witches and save your people. I am but a grizzly old soul and look at you sniveling on the ground."

This brought T.W. to his feet, although his legs were burning in a far more incredible way than just the thrash of a staff should cause. He wondered about this for a minute, making no hasty actions. It was obviously a magic staff. Besides, the old man was not acting threatening now. It was then that the ancient male turned his head to look directly at Willman. T.W. stared at the eyes before him in disbelief. They were the eyes of his grandad - The Jebber. But? This person was not he? Who was it then?

"Ha! I see recognition, Willman. You are faster than I give you credit. Be it known that I am Hayban... your great, great, grandfather. It is no mistake that you are here. Come! All of you."

T.W. did not hesitate. His recognition of his own kin was verification enough, but before they walked, his thoughts wandered - *why had no one told him of Hayban.*

"Because you were to find me yourself, son."

*You can read my thoughts?*

Hayban let out a bellow of a laugh.

"Of course, my son. We are kin. How do you think you always know where Jebber is?"

Hayban turned his back then, walking toward the farmyard.

"Come!" he called over his shoulder, "let us eat!"

Trevor was the first to move. He loped after Hayban, jumping at the last minute to grab onto his trouser leg before scuttling up his behind, then his back and onto his shoulder. He chittered, telling great great granddad a story.

Hayban bellowed.

"Well little one, the Thingy wouldn't have pecked at you if you'd kept your hands to yourself!" He rubbed the tiny monkey, gently with one finger. This made Trevor fall into a trance - he fell forward, his face landing in Hayban's ear. His gentle snore tickled, making the wise old man chortle. *Nice little fellow, aren't you?* He kept his finger there, making sure his new friend did not fall.

Willman soon caught up. His surprise now behind him, but he still did not understand. *Why weren't you at the village? Mother did not mention you? Nor Jebber?*

"Ah son, you needed to find me. It is the only way to learn the strength of our bonds."

Willman thought on this as they crossed the barnyard. The pigs squealed in delight as Hayban passed, his stooped form petting them as he went. Stewart, the border collie, was close behind, never letting his master out of sight - but when several black geese wobbled toward Simon, their pecking beaks having ideas of a snack - he headed them off, herding them expertly out into the field. As the geese moved away, Lillian reached down to pick the small one up, placing him safely on the back of Thelma. Although Tizzie was two feet taller than the little twerp who was now grinning at him from the giant shell, he'd had enough - *why should Simon get to ride and not me* - he clambered up the old dome of time that was worn with age, the indents forming many small saddles for each of them to sit in. Now he grinned back at Simon. *About time I got to rest. My legs are killing me...* then he stretched out, a sigh oozing from his lips. Thelma felt it all as she mashed her toothless mouth together, glad to be of assistance. Tredor was riding on Willman's hat as usual, his silver ponytail bob bobbing with each loping stride.

The menagerie reached the front of the towering

house, the double wooden doors belching open to allow entrance. Of course, no one had to push, turn a knob or anything to get in. The doors just opened.

"Welcome! To my home," Hayban said, as he stepped in, his dog hot on his heels. They entered to smells of garlic, fresh basil, roasting parsnips and boot polish, and were greeted by a few chickens that flapped out of their way - there was even a baby pig that lay snoring in a rough hay bed close to the fireplace. He led them through this small kitchen, his staff clopping the ground as he headed toward a brightly painted red door that opened to another, bigger kitchen - one with a long table made of oak that stretched down the side with chairs surrounding it, like pawns in a game of chess. Trevor, with no manners yet, leapt off Hayban's shoulders to land on the long table, over which he scurried toward a lick-smacking bowl of fruit. Lillian moved to a small round table that sat near to the fire, glad to take the weight off her creaky legs - she placed her rough hand over the worn worm eaten wood, feeling comfort in its age. Tizzie the pixie was the first to climb into one of the armchairs that was stuffed full of feathers, with Simon right behind, snuggling in with him. The fire roared its welcome. Thelma had plenty of room to lounge. She stretched out, her shell feeling the cool of the slate floor, her legs and neck appreciating the warmth of the flames. Finally, Dreador took his place quietly by the window, looking out at the yard that teemed with life - chickens, geese, ducks, two pigs, a calf and a donkey.

The black-leaded oven, flanked by thick maple

counter tops, was smoking in the room - despite the red on white "No Smoking" sign - but even though it smoked, it did at least smell heavenly. Hayban grabbed the heavy iron handle so that he could look inside - whatever was in there, spit, hissed, crackled and popped.

"Hmmm, looks good." He let the door close with a clang. Then he turned to the sturdy chopping block that was heavier than a sumo wrestler and started to dice freshly picked vegetables - a fresh tarty smell started to invade the area. Sitting silently in the middle of the floor, was a worn, warped trapdoor - leading to the cellar below. Hayban nodded toward it.

"Fetch some wine, son."

*Wine? Hmmm? This was a new one...* Willman lifted the ancient beast of solid wood, pulling on a wrought iron ring in order to reveal the stone steps that led down - he disappeared beneath the floor to return shortly with three bottles - he placed them on the counter. Hayban bellowed his laugh.

"Fine choice," he said, picking up the bottle of single malt that his boy had brought into the light. "Not quite wine, but it'll do! Here - your first. Enjoy." Then he uncorked the other two bottles for everyone else to savor - Thelma had to use a straw, but she minded not one bit.

It turned out to be a merry evening, so Willman decided to wait to share his grizzly stories of the shipyard and the Moat House. After food and much talk, his great great grandad showed where their family's musical side came from. He raised his bent form from the old rocking chair, using his staff as an aid to reach the large mahogany chest tucked in the corner. The lid opened, he reached in, lifting out a guitar full of rising dust that danced in the chinks of light.

"Well, now. Hmmm. Strings would be nice."

Everyone chatted as Hayban brushed the instrument clean. Underneath the messy armor was a fine musical instrument - it took little time to replace the worn strings.

"Now... let's see..." He started to hum, strumming as he did so. Eventually his picking fingers came back, followed by his golden deep voice. His missing digit made no difference - he had learned to do without. Willman joined in, warm and rich. They sang well into the night. Thelma bobbed her head, Dreador shuffled his feet and Lillian danced for the first time in years. Tredor, Trevor, Tizzie and Simon simply boogie woogied on the table top - they couldn't stop laughing.

Eventually sleep came. Thelma wanted to lie where she was - she was so tuckered out - so Hayban placed a thick wool rug beneath her shell. The two tiny monkeys snuggled together in one of the large armchairs, while Lillian was shown to a soft wool bed. Dreador was the only one who did not move, he simply tucked his head under his wing.

Willman and Hayban retired to the smaller kitchen so that they could share more words - of course, Simon and Tizzie followed, each curling up on an ottoman in front of the fire - next to the baby pig - content to be in the same room. It was late into the night before Hayban fell asleep, his large armchair becoming a bed. Willman never took his sight off the line worn face until finally, his eyes too, shut. As everyone snored, chewed and sputtered, Stewart slinked onto the end of Hayban's bed, resting his chin on his master's leg.

Despite the long night, Willman and Hayban rose early. Tizzie too. They left the others to sleep in. Outside, it was a glorious morning. The sky was a rich velvet blue as the sun said hello.

"Come, son. Let me introduce you to the Grey Ghost."

Great great grandad led the way across the yard to a small barn. He pushed the doors wide, causing moths to scream at the light before fluttering off to another dark hole. Willman peered in behind the ancient one. *What was that?* Whatever it was, was long and grey with two white eyes and a silver smile. Hayban stepped forward to lay his hand on her.

"Ah. Haven't driven this old dear for many a year. No need here... Hop in son. Your first driving lesson."

The others woke to weird grating sounds that they had never heard before. Lillian creaked over to the window. *Oh, how funny. I've seen pictures, but never the real thing.* She watched as the stately Bentley moved out of the yard following a partially worn lane.

"You should see this, Thelma! I do believe it's a motor car!"

Tizzie was sitting in the backseat, watching his friend move a stick around that was stuck into the floor - at the same time, T.W.'s knees moved up and down as if he were riding a bike - they lurched forward, then came to a sudden halt, which threw

Tizzie back into the seat, its soft earthiness cushioning his body. It wasn't long before Willman got the hang of it - even with the bumps in the lane the ride felt smooth. He was grinning from ear to ear, as was Hayban.

"Good job! Quick learner, aren't you?"

Everyone in the car was happy, but Stewart was upset - he was not sure what to do. He ran behind the slow moving vehicle, barking, moving from this side to that, not understanding why IT would not do as IT was told and go back to the barn. IT was frustrating. Hayban's elbow had been resting on the open window - he now flicked his hand back at his dog.

"Don't worry, boy! Don't worry!"

An hour later, with The Grey Ghost safely back in the barn, Hayban put his arm around his great great grandson's shoulder. He squeezed - despite his stooped state he was still a strong man.

"I have much to teach you and little time to do it. You are a quick study son, so I think we will manage."

CHAPTER TWENTY-FIVE

# LESSONS WITH HAYBAN

The next few months were spent at the farm - it was a crazy, sometimes fun, sometimes sad, time. Most of it was spent around T.W. who took many lessons in magic and in the history of his kind - his skills were fantastic, turning out to be tenfold of what his great great grandfather had expected. Hayban was a wise, kind and gentle teacher - Willman thrived in his presence, for although his magic abilities where strong, gentleness was his guiding factor. Hayban was mesmerized as he watched such beauty unfold, especially on this day.

They were in the meadow near the large farmhouse where Hayban was teaching his kin the art of relaxation. The green grass swayed in the gentle breeze as scents of lavender floated in the air. Hayban was fascinated. He had never smelled lavender in this area before - there was none growing here? The scent grew stronger as Willman relaxed more - it took a few minutes before Hayban realized – it was coming from Willman, seeping from his pores! It was just after this thought, that Hayban saw a flitter of silver in the long grass. He looked more intently. *This could not be.* The flash of silver again, then another... more sparkles in a different place. Great great granda was thrilled - he knew what they were! The silver flashes increased, until finally they came closer. Moving through the grass blades, he saw tiny beating wings - creatures flying in all directions - the silver of their wings glistening in the sunshine.

*Fairies*

It had been many years since he had seen a fairy but he would never forget.

*Wonderous fairies*

His heart slowed. His soul smiled.

The fairies stayed at a distance, enjoying their dance in amongst the green fronds to some music only they heard. Willman still sat, cross-legged. Finally, one of the fairies moved away from the rest. Coming nearer. Hayban held his breath. The fairy made no straight line, taking her time to enjoy the ladybugs, butterflies, earth and wildflowers. She drew close. Close enough for Hayban to recognize her. My goodness, it had been so many years.

"Jazz! How wonderful."

Jazz fluttered near, flittering her fingers in acknowledgment at Hayban before landing on Willman's knee. T.W. opened his eyes then. It was the first time he had ever seen a fairy, although he instantly knew what she was - after all, he was born as part one. The shed wings of a fairy that had been gifted to Theadora in preparation for his birth were no mistake. The fairy kingdom had known he would be a part of them, even before he was born.

"Hello Willman. You called?" Her small hand gently stroked his knee.

She was the one who had shed her wings, giving them to Theadora. It took many years to reach the stage of shedding and once the wings were shed, the fairy was grounded for months while her new wings grew - always though, they came back bigger and more beautiful than ever, with diamonds glinting in the web of silk they were spun from. Fairies actually had the choice whether to go through this, but most chose not to because their first wings were beautiful enough and the thought of not flying for so long while new ones grew, was more than they could deal with. Jazz hadn't minded though - her grandmother told her she would help give birth to a great wizard if she sacrificed - that her family through the ages had helped birth the giants. She had felt no different than her mother, grandmother and great grandmother before her. Their races were intertwined. Besides, in a way, she had enjoyed running around on the ground, climbing trees instead of flying up into them, digging in the mud and generally making a mess of herself. When she had wings she could do none of that. It had been a good choice, she thought, as she now sat on the knee of the one she had helped birth.

Willman lifted his hand level with his face, holding out a finger. Jazz fluttered up, landing on his perch.

She was *brightly stunningly beautiful.* Silver in her grace.

Without a word, she fluttered from his finger to his face. She gently leaned forward from her place in the air, to plant a small but wondrous kiss on his lips. The tingle shivered down his spine.

"l o v e  y o u"

"l o v e  y o u  t o o"

They spoke no other words. There was no need. She lingered before flying away, into the distant grasses, to play a while, before finally, all of the silver sparkles slowly disappeared.

Willman watched, a smile playing on his lips. In that short time he knew everything he needed.

Hayban sat perfectly still. He had been born of fairy's wings too, but nothing like this had ever happened to him. He looked in wonder at his son as he thought of him. Could he sit here so peacefully if he knew the existence of his race had been placed upon his shoulders? He thought not. Willman was different.

It was some time later before T.W. moved again - his muscles flexed, his abdomen breathed. Together, the two returned to the farmhouse that was so much like the house in the village, and, the one in Chetsy.

That night around the fire, stomachs full, Willman broached a question that had been on his mind for some time.

"How are we born, Hayban? Bunting alluded to it, but I didn't get all the details."

The old one slapped his knee.

"Thought you'd never ask... well, let me see... since we are three feet tall at our birth and our mothers are never giants, obviously the normal way isn't going to work, is it?"

Lillian cringed at the thought, but held her tongue. She was just as curious as T.W.

"Of the fire, son - of the fire. Our mothers are always strong witches. They spend years gathering the ingredients that will meld together, giving us life - as each ingredient is gathered, it is stored in the cellar. You already know that Jebber gave his finger. An absolute must to pass on our own traits." He held his hand up in front of his face and grinned, the empty slot a sign of a new generation. "Then fairy wings for love, kindness, gentleness; a dragon's skull for strength; the Dittermore's tongue for wisdom; a pixie's head for beauty..."

Tizzie went beet-red, "A PIXIE'S HEAD!"

"Ha. Ah, ha. A joke, Tizzie! Just a joke!"

Willman reached his hand out to point at his friend.

"I wouldn't want to look like you anyway, Tizzie."

Tizzie scowled - but only for a second before he decided it was actually quite funny.

"I wouldn't want to look like you either, you big galloot!" he said, pointing back.

Hayban bellowed again, slapping his leg in mirth. Then he told of the other things needed, before adding.

"And of course, your mother's love - followed by her strong magic once everything is cast into the fire."

"And I just step out of the fire, no burns, nothing?"

"You've got it! Well, uuhmm, must admit, if your mother didn't love you and have great strength, you could be burned to death... and, ummh, mmmh, well, Thea smolders in her abdomen for about three days. Heard it's a bit uncomfortable." He grunted then. "Well - you know, hurts a bit and all that." He stared at Willman as he thought about the pain, his lips clenching in a downward grimace. Willman's lips did the same before he asked.

"My father?"

"Never a father. Our birth requires only a witch daughter of a giant."

"OK, my grandmother?"

"She passed giving birth to Theadora. I'm sorry."

The final question, Willman asked gently.

"And my great great grandmother. Your wife?"

Silence fell on the group as Hayban looked down,

his head dropped low. Finally, he lifted his face - the sparkle in his eyes strong and bright. After all these years - he was still in love.

"She's visiting her sister. I needed time with you alone. When you finish your job in Chetsy - then you will meet."

*I have a great great grandmother!* Willman was ecstatic. Tizzie clapped his hands in glee and Dreador shuffled his feet from his very favorite spot by the window.

"What about his great grandmother, Jebber's mother, your daughter?" Lillian asked, her mind working quickly.

"Hey, yes? Where is she?" T.W. was on the edge of his seat, expectant. Hayban had not alluded to her at all. Everyone was waiting for the answer, but the old guy just fidgeted before saying.

"Later, I think. When you come back. It's a long story."

"B b u t..."

"No buts! Later."

CHAPTER TWENTY-SIX

# THE DOG AND THE BEAST

Two more months passed - far too quickly, Hayban thought. It was getting near to when the motley crew would leave. He would miss his great great grandson, his friends and the many nights around the fire sharing pickled peanuts and hot baked potatoes. On this particular day the light was leaving, the fine flecked sun filtering through hazy clouds. Hayban walked with Willman across the cobblestones, deep in conversation, the grand barn flanking one side, allowing the pungent odor of horse manure to sing its song. Following them, as always, was Stewart, his black nostrils sniffing, his eyes keenly set on his master's face. It was then that a shadow crossed the falling sun, bringing darkness into their lives - it swooped over the shingled roof, falling to earth with death dripping from its beak. It moved fast and cunning - a ginormous leathery beast with flapping wings of doom. Beneath its body were daggers glinting with hatred, aimed at the trotting dog as it dropped from the sky - with a final plunge, the talons dug deep into Stewart's unsuspecting wagging body, lifting him from the ground like a pea on the end of a fork. Hayban screamed far louder than Stewart did - louder than dolphins scream that are caught in a net! Moving at great speed, he cast his staff upward, knocking the vicious claws out of his friend. Stewart fell to the ground with a hard thud as the dark creature withdrew its weapons of death, flying off into the distance, cawing loudly about its lost meal. Hayban fell on his knees next to his friend who was yelping in pain, a gapping wound in his abdomen spurting blood, his guts spilling onto the ground - the yelping turned to a soft whimpering - a heart wrenching sound, a torture that he could do nothing to stop. Then the black and white furry body fell limp in his arms. Gone!

Hayban cried so hard his shoulders heaved, his salty tears mixed with his dog's blood. *My best friend!*

"No! No! No!" he yelled at the sky. "Nooooo..." he whispered, smothering his mouth into the still warm fur.

Willman stood still as Hayban wept.

Slowly he closed his eyes, standing tall in the yard.

His friends were gathered near the barn. They watched in silence.

It was only moments later when Willman's eyes opened - but he no longer saw this world, even though he looked around. What he saw were hazes of grey, white and blue. Reds and burgundies. Greens and lavenders. The buildings had fuzzy edges, the flowers shifted in and out of focus. Horse heads were big then small, their eyelashes were longer than long hair. The sky was white then pink. There was that faint smell of lavender again. His friends he could not see at all. Nor could he see his greatly grandad. He could hear him crying though. He looked around the yard - searching.

Then he found it - the thing he was searching for - the shape of Stewart. The form was not running. It was not moving toward him, or away. It was not lying down. It was simply standing, looking lost. He moved toward it, down the tunnel that his vision had become. He moved toward the lost shadow.

"Ts s s s s ... t s s s s s ..." he sissed, "t s s s s..." It was a soothing sound to the shape before him, for it did not run away, although it looked around once as if trying to make some decision whether to stay or not. Willman moved closer and closer, until eventually he laid his hand on the shadow's head.

"Stewart? Do you wish to go? Or stay?"

The shadow looked up with pools for eyes, the look of love for his master swimming there. This was a spirit not tired of his life or his duties. He wanted to go back. The giant creature in the air was a mistake, not meant to be the end of his life. Willman felt it all.

"Come follow me walk back it is up to you."

The shadow turned to look away only one time before following. It traced behind him, not faulting its step. Willman could see nothing - too much haze and fog with the ground swirling around his feet. *Stay steady,* he told himself, until finally he reached the side of the stooped and weeping old man who was still cradling the ripped body of Stewart.

He spoke gently to the grey shadow.

"Step back inside... it is up to you... take back your body... but only if you wish."

Stewart whined, a low mournful sound before lifting a paw... then another... and another.

Willman placed a hand on the broken form in Hayban's arms, the wounds closing over as the blood dried - then the young giant fell, his energy depleted, passing to the earth at the feet of the ancient man.

As T.W. fainted, the hairy beast in Hayban's arms stirred, at first emitting small whimpers, then yelping as his body twitched and jerked, until finally the muscles relaxed so that he could reach his long canine neck to lick the wrinkled chin that hung over him. Tears streamed down Hayban's face as laughter beat away his sorrow. He hugged his dog as if he would never let go. Then he reached a gentle hand out to the giant lying before him - he knew now what this kin of his had done. *You amaze me son.*

A few minutes later, Tizzie and Tredor, breaking from the spell that had held them, ran across the yard. They cradled their friend's head until he came back to this world. Stewart helped him come back, his licks bigger and better than ever. When T.W. opened his eyes to the wet sloppy kisses of a dog, the stroking of his cheek by a monkey, and the slapping of his face by a pixie - all he could do was smile. This was life and he loved it.

## CHAPTER TWENTY-SEVEN

# BACK TO THE VILLAGE

The final weeks passed quickly. The group gathered in the courtyard while Willman stood with Hayban at the enormous entrance to the house - the door towering above them - their giant forms only visible in their hearts.

"You have learned well son. Your talents are far greater than any wizard I have known in my time. Hold on to your gentle side. That is what makes your magic good. I'll really miss you."

Hayban placed his hand on his great great grandson's cheek - a touch that was gentler than any whisper of love. Willman reached up to place his own hand over the wrinkled one, both taking a moment to look into the others eyes. With difficulty, Willman turned away, his own lashes wetter than his grandad's. He joined his friends and as they left the yard, the farm animals mooed, clucked, snorted and neighed - but before they moved out of sight, Willman turned to wave to his kin - *have to look one more time, just in case I never see him again...* His heart felt heavy. Hayban waved back. Stewart barked happily by his side.

"I'll miss you. See you soon! I will see you soon!" This hopeful echo bounced back and forth between the two.

It took only a day to reach the village. Of this T.W. was glad. *Not far to reach Hayban,* he thought. He would be back, he knew! He hoped. They made their way to the dinosaur house where Theadora and Jebber were sitting on the stone wall - they had sensed the homecoming. Tredor was not with them as they approached the waiting couple, he had veered off to his home in the trees with Trevor - he couldn't wait to see his wife and introduce her to their new son. He wanted her to love him, just as much as he did.

Jebber grinned when he saw Willman.

"You look great, son. Time away has treated you well."

They hugged each other, Jebber thumping him on the back - a little too hard in his enthusiasm - T.W's voice vibrated tenor as he responded with a thump of his own.

"Good to be back," he turned his head, grinning, "missed you ma." Theadora smiled, she was more than happy to have her boy home.

Introductions were made as Thelma lay down on the grass, lapping up the warm rays - it wasn't many minutes before she munched on some of the giant blooms. Her face lit up.

"I theenk thaat I laike thes plais."

That caused everyone to laugh. Lillian sat next to Theadora. They became instant friends - it did not take long for her to share the story of her daughter. Simon of course, stayed close to Willman.

"Keep an eye out for Tombhra please. I cannot go through the mirror like this, but I sense she may be on the other side. Maybe in a while I will loosen up enough to pass for a mortal. But not yet."

Theadora assured her they would.

The evening turned into a restful one, although Jebber was sad that he had only the one night with his grandson, but there was no choice, time was running out. Bunting had given several updates during Willman's absence. The people of Chetsy were being bewitched far too easily.

The next morning - much to Simon's disgust - Jebber escorted Willman and his daughter to the room that housed their mirror.

This time, Willman took his mother's hand – then they stepped forward, dissolving once more into the glass.

# BACK IN CHETSY TOWN

## CHAPTER TWENTY-EIGHT
## EVIL MAGIC

They had been back for two weeks, both missed the village and their friends - *it's hard to be away,* thought T.W as he strode across the kitchen, stepping over the cellar door and out into the crisp morning breeze.

"I'm going into town," he called to Thea as she worked the garden. He walked across the lawn to the barn that housed the Grey Ghost. "Hey old girl."

He lovingly petted the gleaming Bentley, taking a moment to admire her lines. Hayban had sent her. He pulled the door open, she was comfy inside, the leather of her seat molding to his contours, but best of all, he could smell Hayban's boot polish trapped inside this small space. *Hmmm.* He started her up. *So quiet, old lady.* He drove down the driveway, saluting to Thea as he went, then passed through the guardian trees that breathed in to let him out. "Thank you, Ladies," then bowed, respecting their majestic honor before turning onto the road that headed into Chetsy.

He parked carefully in the small lane behind Chetsy Chocolates - before walking away he stood to admire The Ghost again. *So beautiful...* It was moments later that Brendan showed up, headed for his shift at The Green Cow.

"Coming for a drink?" he asked, "I could tell you about my escapades in Italy." He chortled, thinking about women in gondolas eating ice cream and him. His eyes misted as he became Brendanonni Maddisonni. For the moment, Brendan of Chetsy was forgotten, as was T.W. for that matter. Brendanonni sighed, walking away in a daze.

T.W. just smiled to himself. A whiskey would be nice but he had things to see to. A visit to Mary Jane first, a good source of information there, then afterwards, a coffee - he wanted to people watch. Felice had done well finding the den of evil on the corner of Main Street but he needed to know more. He turned toward the barbers, looking forward to seating himself in the ancient brass chair with the thickly cushioned seat that had been passed from father to son in the barber line, and now to Mary Jane the only child. He was deep in thought and hadn't gone far when he felt a sudden flush envelope his body - one button on his shirt popped off as his body started to grow, the seams on his clothes ripping apart. *What! Someone is trying to break my holding spell!* His body scorched! Quickly, he uttered the incantation needed to retain his small size, fighting off the stray spell.

"Zes. Tey tummo! Tey tummo!"

*This will not do! What if I am seen?* The seams of his clothes loosened into place, his bow tie no longer a noose about his neck. He walked with his thoughts, *strong forces, more wicked than I thought - they need our identities.* Just then he felt the heat returning, stronger than before - it was so intense that he ducked into the meandering alleyway that connected the lane to a quaint arena of shops. A vicious wind followed, stalking, knocking him to his knees as a bolt of lightening flew in behind, hitting him with a zip and a zap. He was flung forward onto his face as his clothes became instant rags hanging from his now fifteen foot frame. Pain struck, curling him in agony, a tendril of grey smoke trickled from one ear. He writhed on the floor as the spell clawed at his innards, burning him from the inside out. He groaned. But still he held himself. *Stay calm. Stay calm.* He started to chant, scraping his knees on the red brick as he pulled himself up. Theadora heard him, she knew his agony - she started to chant with him from the tall house outside of town, the spell traveling across the meadows, over the rocks, toward the alley in which her son was being overcome.

Willman, now huge and on all fours, was dripping words from his mouth as Theadora's voice floated in a whisper about him - this is when Carly Jones turned the corner to enter the alley. He was headed to his very own pottery shop, the one he owned in town. In his hands he held his prize, an exquisitely painted plate that he had finished the night before. He wanted to display it in the storefront. Upon seeing the strange creature in the alley, writhing and gasping about, with weird words echoing around, he dropped the plate, which smashed and scattered like confetti.

He ran! In the opposite direction to the nightmare. *Going home! Don't need this shit!*

"D a v e e d!"

He had only travelled ten paces before he felt Able leave his shoulder, making his running feet stop - he turned to see flapping wings headed back the way he had come.

"NO ABLE! NO! THIS WAY!" He watched in horror as his parrot flew toward the giant. *NO NO no no no!* "ABLE*!* Come back!" He wasn't going to leave his bird in this mess. He ran back down the alley, giving a wide skirt to the sweating, writhing creature - he kept his eyes averted as he passed the frightening man. Able landed on a small bush, five steps further on.

"Oh, thank goodness! Up boy!" He put his arm out toward his faithful friend.

But Able didn't hop up - instead he flew again, this time landing on Willman's bare shoulders. He squawked! Doing a dance. Squawking louder still!

"SHIT ABLE!" *Holy beJeezus, I just can't believe this.* "ABLE! COME HERE!"

That is when the giant lifted his head so that Carly could see his eyes. They were big pits of kindness and warmth. Even in his obvious agony, he looked nice. Carly had no idea why, but instead of reaching for his parrot he fell to his knees, placing his hands gently onto the giant's sweating forearms. Then he too, started to chant.

"Te adis mey, tutenenki, sia diy. Te adis mey." Carly said, having no idea what he was saying or why.

Smoke still curled out of the giant's ears, a few wisps were now coming out of his stomach. The wind started to howl again, slashing at the bushes, at them - lightening bolted sending worms scurrying. Still Carly stayed, holding on, chanting.

"Te adis mey, tutenenki, sia diy. Te adis mey,"

never letting go, until finally, the wind calmed and the crackling ceased. Carly looked at the giant before him as the smoking stopped. "Oh, thank goodness," he said. He watched in amazement as slowly the great man unfolded himself, rising into the air. Tyrannosaurus rex! Then, just as slowly, the big beast shrank back to acceptable human size, his clothes in tatters. Carly was speechless, until the giant spoke.

"Thank you, my witch friend."

"Huh?" Denial was Carly's strong point - after all, he had lived that way his whole life. *Got a crazy dick here!* Then he thought he'd better respond, just to keep the crazy dick in line, but before he could, the zillion pieces of his shattered plate flew together making it whole. It hovered in the air, waiting for him to take it.

He hesitated before the love of his art got the better.

"Well, shit!" He grabbed the plate and ran, without looking back. He raced down the final stretch of the alley, around to the front of the buildings and into his store, entering with a slam of the door behind. Luckily, Able managed to get in first, perching himself in the corner. Mandy, with his curly white hair, just made it without getting flattened. Carly plonked down at his table, placing the plate carefully out of the way, a sigh of relief hot on his lips. After a few moments he looked at the plate, which instantly took his mind off what had just happened - it was gorgeous, adorned with different characters sitting together at a picnic in the woods. There was a badger, a mouse, an elf and a hedgehog. He looked adoringly at his priced piece before picking up a small cup he had been working on - he started to paint. Thankfully, he was lost in his work in an instant. He was not aware that in the opposite corner of the shop sat the very same badger that was on his plate. The badger was drinking a cup of tea with the hedgehog. The mouse his very self sat under the table holding an iced drink with a tropical umbrella and straw. The elf was still sleeping, curled up in the plate. Carly didn't see them. He couldn't see them. Not yet anyway. He buried his head in his work.

Back in the alleyway, T.W. was recovering himself. He covered his sweating, muscle bound body with clothes picked out of the air, along with his bow tie that he found stuck in a bush. Once dressed he stood a while, thinking, regaining his composure, placing the strongest of strong protective spells about himself. *Nasty. Nasty. These are some very nasty, wicked witches.* He thought about Carly, hoping his mind was not too abuzz - he would visit the pottery shop later. Then he took a deep breath before striding out of the alley to go about his business.

## CHAPTER TWENTY-NINE
# BRENDAN'S BIRTHDAY

Better B. Better was in a jovial mood. It was the day after one of Jimmy's visits. She didn't feel depressed at all. *I need to do that more often,* she thought, smiling to herself at the memory, unconsciously rubbing her hands together in that sinister, gleeful way. She turned toward Seteeva Haar.

"Look after the shop, Seteeva, I'm going for a gander, see what's up or down in this little piss ant town."

Seteeva had the 'high' smile on her face - not unusual, her pipe never got cold.

"Sure B.B." she yelled, doing a chortling choke at the same time. "Send some more suckers this way, will ya, so's I don't get bored."

Better B. left, banging the door behind her, then headed down the street. She had to walk several hundred yards before she reached the outskirts of the town shops. On the way, she passed some gardens that filled a few vacant lots, then a dilapidated wooden structure that could have passed as a small chapel. After that came the main framework of the town, the living, breathing core of Chetsy. She made her way to Lance's Coffee House, making a slight sniff of repulsion as she entered. She could smell that bitch Felice. This made her wonder where the other witches were hiding. She wrinkled her nose, tighter than a toffee nosed lady - the coffee shop disgusted her, but she needed to keep an eye on things.

Besides, half the town came here, it was good for her own business to be seen. She needed to seem nice, if she wanted to hide what she was really doing in Chetsy.

At the counter she ordered a coffee along with a piece of homemade carrot cake. While she waited, a cushy armchair positioned by the window called to her. Once seated, she eyed Victor, who was helping out.

"Better B.!" he called, as he put the large cup on the counter next to the doily decorated plate with the tall slice of cake - it tottered like a kid on a new bicycle. Better B. rose. She threw more than a few dollars into the tip jar, making sure that Victor was looking when she did. He smiled. She knew how to make people like her. Sitting back down in the armchair that was tucked away in the corner, she sank into the cushions, becoming mostly invisible. She people watched as she pretended to sip the brew - her stomach had a hard time with the Taste magic that Felice used - it was sweet and sickly and turned her guts inside out. She looked around, noticing that there were two groups of tourists gathered at the counter - they were of no interest to her. There were the locals though, some with kids stuck to their hips like ticks. She recognized a few of the little brats and had to stop her hands from reaching forward toward them, her eyes glazing as her lips formed a kissing pout. She automatically started to suckle at the air, a baboon baby gone mad. Finally, she dragged her wits back. It took some will power, but she managed to pull her eyes away from their small bodies, only to see a few people sitting alone, tapping away on their laptops. She was Miss Poised again. *Not much going on.* She set her cup down on a small table and was about to rise when Brendan threw himself into the accompanying armchair.

"Hi," he crooned, "mind if I join you?"

"You already did!" snorted Better B., a slight snarl on her lips.

Brendan, now totally in the Brendanonni moment, was not phased in the least.

"Coming to The Green Cow tonight? There's a birthday party for me," he smirked, smiling to himself. "Lots of friends coming."

Better B. had the letters N. O. on her lips, when she thought better of it. Maybe it would be a good idea, she thought. Maybe, just maybe, she might discover something important.

"OK," she retorted, curling the snarl into a smile.

"Its a date then," chortled Brendanonni with a gleeful glint in his eyes. He was up and gone before Better B. could comment on just what kind of date it was not going to be.

"Crap!" she said out loud, "maybe I won't go."

But as the day wore on, with not much discovered on her walkabout town, with little happening at the shop and the temptation to call Jimmy out of his home again tonight, she decided to go. Two nights in a row might be too much for Jimmy, he had a big soul, but he was getting weaker and she needed him around a bit longer yet. She couldn't afford any suspicions just now.

Seteeva was elated.

"Thank you, Jeezus," she cried loudly, "a break from the monotony of being a wicked witch working in this goddam shop..." then dashed off for a few puffs on the magic pipe before they headed to The Cow.

It was a cozy pub, overlooking the bay. The view out was spectacular - some days the water swayed to a gentle ballad, others it splish splashed, a kid in a bath - at other times it did the Jitter Bug. And all the while, ducks, geese and seagulls gathered - Lords and Ladies mingling in a watery mansion. Salty air and seaweed breezed through the open windows. The wide planked fir flooring creaked as worms chewed away on beams that ran across the ceiling. It was only six thirty when Seteeva and Better B. arrived - but the place was packed. They recognized most because they were the suckers that came into the shop. Better B. scoffed with disdain as she looked around. In one corner sat a few people from the old folks home, most of them had a shot of some sort, along with a smile on their faces. There were also several business owners recognizable by the tight grip on their wallets - at least that is how she saw it, as they had not come into her store. Mary Jane was sitting at a small table. Next to her was someone Better B. did not recognize. She stared intently at the female form but got nothing back. As she stared, the form looked up, across the room directly back at her - she flinched, not understanding why. Thea smiled to herself as she turned her head back toward Mary Jane and the conversation at her table. Better B. continued to look at Theadora but still got nothing, so she shrugged, letting her eyes continue their tour of the pub. She noticed T.W. but scanned quickly over him. It was only his male form that she noticed and she needed no distractions like that tonight. The wizard in him was completely hidden.

After a few minutes of looking around, the gruesome couple moved toward the bar that ran along the length of a short wall. It seemed there were two empty seats just for them. They hopped onto the high stools, Seteeva's feet hitting the bronze kick plate as she scrambled up, a leech trying to get a hold. They looked for a few minutes at the hundreds of bottles lined for inspection, their own faces staring back from the mirrors behind the glass shelving - it was a bowling alley full of skittles that they did not want to knock down. A beer tap creaked, bringing them back from their reflections. They ordered - quickly. Better B. guzzled down two glasses before steadying her pace. Seteeva kept up - a bad combination along with the smoking of the smoked root. An hour or more passed with people milling around, sharing jokes, chatting, catching up. During this time, Kelly Keen arrived. She always attracted attention! Everyone thought she had died, at least that's what the rumor had said, but then, there she was, large as life four days after supposedly being carted off to the mortuary. Not only larger than life, but full of more life than ever before. Obviously the rumors had been wrong. And obviously, Kelly was not dead, she said so herself.

Kelly waved to everyone when she walked in. Tombhra looked around, quivers in her spine, at all the male bottoms. Six years locked inside the mannequin had left her feeling deprived. *Delicious!* Licking her lips. As they sidled toward the bar, she managed to coddle a few of those lovely bums. Tombhra let out a musical laugh, while Kelly giggled.

"You're making my crotch all hot, you'd better stop." Kelly whispered this out loud, by mistake, instead of talking to Tombhra in her head. As she said this, she had been squeezing past old Harry Tomb.

"Kelly!" he cried, "I didn't know you felt that way about me. Here, let me buy you a drink!" and followed her, like a dog after a bitch in heat.

Tombhra still did not behave as they pushed their way through the crowd, but Kelly just winked at all the young males that glared, startled, in her direction. Tombhra was having a blast - and so was Kelly. Not too long ago, she'd been lying in a morgue, so what the hell, if she had to come back she was going to have more fun than she did before, live and let live, she was going to do whatever Tombhra wanted. Tombhra really wanted... well, she really wanted... but she realized the difficulties involved in getting some young buck to look her way, and all because she had a few wrinkles - if only they'd give it a chance, they would be in for a surprise. The thought alone made her laugh again - it tinkled bright and clear - it didn't make her sad at all, she saw the humor in it and was glad to have what she had, no longer being stuck inside the mannequin. Besides, old Harry here looked like he still had a twinkle in his eye. Go with the flow was her motto. She liked Kelly - why not give her a good final ride before the boat went down again.

As Kelly walked to the bar with old Harry panting, hot on her heals, something made her glance to her right, catching Theadora's look that was aimed in their direction. Kelly wasn't fully sure what it was about, but Tombhra smiled inside her head, so she waved anyway - if Tombhra liked Theadora, then so did she. Next to Theadora was a big handsome guy. Tombhra hadn't seen him before - she sucked in a breath. The big guy had caught her attention, just something about him. Willman looked up at that precise moment. Their eyes met.

She no longer wanted to coddle anyone - just him. She wanted to... She let out a big sigh. Tombhra pushed the thought to the back of her mind. She knew it would never happen. Not while in this body. *Let's go Kelly.*

Kelly turned, winking at Harry as she sidled up to the bar next to Seteeva and Better B.

"Who's that?" T.W. leaned toward his mother.

Theadora brought her attention to her son. She told him of her discovery of the mannequin.

"I released the spirit at the same time you were born."

Willman sat in silence - watching. He felt broody.

Over at the bar, Better B. shifted in her seat, something was off, she just did not know what. She sniffed loudly as Kelly moved into place next to her. The sniff was scoffing.

"Something wrong?" Kelly asked.

Better B. was just about to comment on what a hideous smell was emanating from her and that maybe, just maybe, she should bathe once in a while, when Kelly said, with that pinched expression on her face that she did so well.

"Pooh, what is that smell? Oh. Oh. I see! It's the brewery gone stale sitting next to me," and started to laugh - her hyena coming out.

Seteeva and Better B. started to fume. *Smell! Smell! It was not they that smelled!* On top of that, the hideous odor that was invading their nostrils had NOT gone away and they simply could not understand why every one else was NOT shrinking away from this godawful, unbathed woman. In fact, not only were people not shrinking away from her, they wanted to give her a hug and a kiss. As a final show of defiance, in unison, they hitched their bar stools to the left, like a move in a line dance, both breathing a little easier as they did so.

It was then that Brendan arrived. He waltzed into the pup from the veranda that overlooked the bay, the ancient french doors closing behind him. He had a manner befitting a king, although he had left his crown at home. He scanned the room as he entered, turning his head languidly this way and that, until his eyes landed on Theadora. By instinct, he meandered that way.

"Happy Birthday! Happy Birthday!" he met along the way, but he fought on, until finally he reached her side.

"Happy birthday," he tried to whisper.

"Same to you, Brendan," she mouthed. *He was alright sometimes,* she thought, he'd remembered at least that their birthdays were on the same day. He went to grab a chair from the next table so that he could sit next to her, but before he could, her hand nestled his wrist.

"No." she muttered, " I hear you have a date."

Brendan looked confused. He confused himself as much as he confused others. Theadora nodded in the direction of Better B.

He snickered.

"Oh."

He'd forgotten. But now it came back to him, what he'd said at Lance's Coffee House.

*Hmmm?* His dick started to rise - *she must have come for a reason - i*t poked at his fly trying to pull his zipper down - give it a microphone and it would have blasted out a song. Puffing his cheeks, he sauntered over to the bar, making passing conversation on the way. Eventually, much to Better B.'s chagrin - who had been watching him make his move like a knight on a chessboard - he made it.

"Hi," he said, adjusting his jeans at the same time.

*Crap!* Better B. downed the glass she had in front of her... as did her pipe-smoking friend. They ordered another one. Brendan himself went behind the bar to serve as he struck up a conversation with the two - their monosyllable answers, interspersed with glances around the room, made no difference to him. Their indifference was different, that's all. *They hadn't got up and left - had they?* In an instant he became Brendanonni - he scootched around the end of the bar, his chest broad, his buttocks twitching. Better B. and Seteeva gave a pissed off glance - they weren't going to leave just because of this idiot. So they stayed in their seats as he inched forward, pushing between them, knocking Seteeva's arm, spilling drink onto her blouse - she glowered at him but he didn't notice - then he smooched a little closer toward B.B. *Oh boy! She is so into this!* His dick did a jiggle. She hadn't slapped him off, so he moved closer still, his thigh rubbing on hers.

Finally, she could stand it no longer.

"Just, what do you think you are doing, Brendan?" after he was almost sitting on her knee. Seteeva started to giggle.

Brendanonni made his move, his tight dick-a-roony now dictating. He leaned his head to whisper in her ear - taking quick, short, breathes.

"Hey, lets go to my place. I have a gondola set up in my front room." He wasn't kidding either. He loved Italy!

Seteeva heard what he said, causing her to blurt a laugh out. The whole room looked their way, which made Better B. groan. She directed a glare at her friend telling her to shut it, but Seteeva just shrugged her shoulders and smirked. Brendanonni tried again.

"My place. Do it in the gondola and all that stuff," he muttered sexily, his jeans feeling too goddam small.

Better B. could stand it no longer. She leaned forward, putting her lips to his ear. He was tantalized. Her breath tickled - he quivered, shivering in anticipation.

"Brendan", she husked, "it's been soooo long since I went home with anybody," she paused, wetting her lips, "it's been soooo long... that, well, well, my pussy is just glued shut..."

Brendanonni choked on his beer! It splattered down his jeans, which were now loose and baggy. He couldn't believe it. Brendan returned instantly, sticking his hands in his pockets.

*A glued shut pussy, was NOT, repeat, NOT, in the Italian vernacular.*

The wicked witch tried to look innocent but her glare made him back away in infant like steps, until, nodding once, he said, curtly.

"Thanks, Better B." Then he smirked to himself. It only took an instant, before it dawned. "Hey, I never thought of that, that's so funny, maybe you should try to 'BE BETTER!' " Then he roared with laughter at his own joke. He was never floored for long. The problem was he didn't know how near to the mark he was. He was in the danger zone.

Better B. Better looked at him with disdain, which she quickly disguised as hurt. *Later, I will punish him for that.* She lowered her eyelids, hiding her darkness before turning back to her accomplice. Brendan grabbed the opportunity to escape, turning to Harry and Kelly, inching in their direction, even though Harry was occupied with the bartender. Tombhra saw him coming - ooh, she wanted to coddle this one so bad she had to keep her hands clenched on to the edge of her seat, even though the big fella was still on her mind. It was just that she had been in that damn mannequin for so long! She did refrain from hands on, but could not stop herself from leaning toward Brendan, to whisper sensuously in his ear. He leaned in, eager to hear what she had to say - he'd always had a soft spot for Kelly. Tombhra put her lips close, her words a trickling stream.

"I would like to see your gondola, Brendan."

His head bolted up. *My God! With Kelly!* Not quite what he had in mind.

"I, err, I, umm."

"Y e s?" asked Tombhra, ignoring Kelly's pleas.

"I, umm, well... I think... the gondola sank," he said in a somewhat relieved voice and a now slight upturn to his quivering lips. He backed away, mouthing the word *'sorry',* then was off in a red head flash.

Tombhra had found all of that quite thrilling, sitting there enjoying the little surges she was getting thinking about what she could do to Brendan in his gondola, but then Harry quit talking to the bartender and came back to Kelly. She came down off her Brendan high - besides, if she was real with herself, she knew the big guy was now filling her thoughts, but of course, that could never go anywhere. Could it?

## CHAPTER THIRTY

# SETEEVA'S LITTLE DEMONS

Better B. was mad as a hatter - that stupid dimwit Brendan had really pissed her off. She and Seteeva staggered home together, ignoring any of the town morons, (as they thought of them), that were out and about. The eagle nosed used furniture proprietor had her gingerbread house on the mountain, but she hardly ever went there. The crooked house on the corner was more her home. Seteeva's too.

The pipe sucking witch fell through the door first, throwing herself onto one of the couches - she pulled her feet up as her buxom bottom sank, the worn out springs singing an off key song. As her body relaxed into the plushness she yanked the 'FOR SALE' tag off, putting a line through the *$249* before writing underneath *New Price - $649* she grinned at her handiwork, knowing the morons would go along with anything. All the while, Better B. paced back and forth.

"You should calm down, B.B.," snorted Seteeva, taking a big drag on her pipe, slowly inhaling, then, just as slowly, exhaling, puffing out demons that were trapped inside smoke capsules the shape of big water bubbles. Each bubble contained one demon - the bubble it's cell - the contorted shape floating across the room. In the first moments, as the globes emerged from the pipe - at the start of their journey - the demons thought that their time of incarceration was over. Then, when realization dawned, knowing they were not to be released after all, knowing they were heading for their demise, the demons started to writhe in agony! Some of them even cried out in despair just before they disintegrated. It was a painful noise, this screaming - tooth extraction without anesthesia.

But not to Seteeva Haar and Better B. Better! It was more like a gong of pleasure.

"You really are wicked, Seteeva," Better B. retorted, "those little bastards had their hopes up that you were setting them free. What on earth made you come up with that sick little trick?"

"Can't help it," she muttered, grinning. " It just relights the smoldering pleasure of when I trapped them in the first place. Heck, B.B., I have to keep myself occupied somehow. I'm bored all to hell. When, flip-a-dickin-trickin - just when - are we going to do more than set the seed for greed in this town. I feel like I'm living just outside someone's goddam asshole. It stinks here!"

Just then - one of the smoke bubbles hit the wall. But it didn't disintegrate.

The demon inside stopped screaming, looking up slyly - expectation of release on its face. YOU PICKED ME, the sneaking smirk said.

Seteeva replied with a smirk of her own, cocking her head to one side.

"Are you kidding me!" she hissszzed at the demon, the 'ssszz' sending a stream of molten liquid toward the bubble. As the steaming liquid hit, a terrible burning smell filled the room. The demon screamed before it died. Howling in pain! Then the smoke bubble disintegrated just like all the others. A raucous laugh followed. Seteeva was in hysterics.

Better B. just shook her head - that's not how she got her kicks. She started to think of Jimmy and a few of the other kids that visited her on a frequent basis - and to top it, Alice had come into her domain as well. She rubbed her hands in delight. Greed was not the only evil she was bringing to this town, but she hadn't told Seteeva yet. She wasn't sure if she would.

This thought allowed her to relax for the first time that night. She remembered back a few days to when Jimmy had come rushing over the road. The school grounds being opposite her shop, he'd felt safe to come, seeing her arranging plant pots that were for sale in the front yard. She had told him after all, the last time he'd seen her, that if any of the schoolchildren got in trouble or needed help, she was here for them - no matter what it was. Besides, Jimmy especially knew about Mouth Bugs and he knew that only she could help if ever there was one around. She'd given him one of the magic cookies after explaining all this too him. As he chewed on the cookie, everything she said became clear, he knew then what Mouth Bugs were, where they came from, he knew all about them, he saw it in his head as he ate the cookie.

"Lizzie has a Mouth Bug," he gasped as he reached her side.

She grimaced at Jimmy, her eyes expressing deep concern. Inside, she was laughing so hard she thought she would burst - The Mouth Bug was one of her better creations yet. Then she slipped a small gold coin into his hand.

"Go back to Lizzie, give her this. She'll be able to

open her mouth again. The Mouth Bug will stop chomping and screeching. But! And this is a big BUT! Make sure you tell her she has to keep a hold of the coin or it will start chomping again, much harder the second time. You tell her the coin came from me, quietly so no one can hear or I won't be able to help. Tell her when I call for her she must come, so that I can get rid of the Mouth Bug for good. Tell her not to fight me. OK! Got that Jimmy?"

"Got it," gasped Jimmy already crossing the street, dashing across the playground to Lizzie who still stood crying. Everyone was circled around her. He hadn't wanted to go to Better B. but he wanted to help Lizzie.

The chomping sound was loud - rare steak chomping loud. Everyone was quiet, what on earth was it? A small ripple of fear moved through the group. Jimmy sidled up to Lizzie - no one had noticed his absence. He went to hold her hand again, this time slipping the small round coin into her palm. He bent forward to whisper in her ear - keeping his lips as closed as he could, but still able to talk - he didn't want to take any chances of the mouth bug jumping ship.

"It's a magic coin, trust me - don't say anything or it will stop working. Don't drop it."

The instant the coin touched her cold clammy skin, the chomping stopped - Lizzie now knew all about Mouth Bugs too. She opened her mouth taking in one big breath. She gripped her hand tightly. *No one, not no one, was going to make her open her hand,* she thought ferociously. She couldn't bear the thought of feeling that thing chewing away inside her cheek again. The noise it made had been really loud inside her head. She started to sob just at the thought of it.

Just then Jimmy leaned in again.

"I got the magic coin from Better B. Better. She's going to help - when she calls, go to her so she can remove the Bug. It's still inside you, it just went to sleep."

Lizzie sobbed even more.

"Don't drop the coin," he muttered, "or it will wake up."

Her knuckles went white, her grip tighter than a pythons.

One of the teachers moved.

"Let's go to the medical room, have a look in that mouth, hey?" Miss Reeves was relieved to notice that the swelling had already gone down.

Lizzie stopped crying at the click of a switch.

"I'm alwight weally," she said.

Still she went - she would just refuse to open her mouth. She knew - absolutely knew - that the only person that could help her was Better B.

CHAPTER THIRTY-ONE

# BRENDAN'S NIGHTMARE

Brendan was having nightmares. He never had nightmares, only lovely dreams. It was starting to affect his sleep. That's something he didn't like - sleep was important to him. He tried to think when it had started - was it just after his birthday? Seemed like one minute he was having his normal Italian dreams -walking in Rome, driving through the countryside, stopping for sheep in the road, visiting vineyards, watching olive picking and then, finally, the Venice part. He had never made it to Venice during his real visit to Italy, but his imagination was far better than the actual thing. The Venice part of his dream was always his favorite - that's where he purred along in a gondola with a pretty Italian lady at his side. They would stop somewhere, climbing out of the long sleek boat to meander down an alley to a small restaurant, the exquisite aromas of baking bread, sizzling garlic, pungent basil, escaping into the night air. It was heavenly. He could smell it all, even in his dreams. Brendanonni would turn to the gorgeous woman at his side, opening the door for her to enter. After a romantic dinner for two - sitting at a rustic table, low lighting, soft music and a glass of wine - they would drift back through the narrow streets to the gondola where they would float off into the darkness, lips finding each other, caresses and love filling the night. He loved that dream. Absolutely loved it. LOVED IT!

But now! He put his head in his hands, sighing heavily. He was barely able to think about it. The thought alone sent shivers down his spine. He always woke in a sweat after the nightmare, actually screaming out loud once.

That is when IT had nearly caught him.

That is why he had screamed out loud.

He could run really fast in his dream, but this one time it had almost not been fast enough. He thought about it. The dream went well enough for a while - the part that had changed was after the romantic dinner, when he stepped out of the restaurant door. He would look up at the sky to see the stars, the moon was always full - his attention would come back from the glittering sky to the beautiful lady at his side, but in the nightmare she would be gone. Usually, in his good dream, she was there to take his hand, smiling lovingly into his face. But she was gone. Gone! Gone! Just a nothing! In the nightmare he would look around anxiously trying to find her, stepping away from the restaurant feeling disorientated, not knowing which way to go, which way back to the gondola. Always, he went the wrong way. Always, ending up in the same back alley feeling lost and alone. In the alley were several tin trash cans, and as he walked down the narrow cobblestone path passing the first one - it started to shake. Rattling with a strange intensity. Even though he knew he shouldn't - but he just couldn't stop himself - he would move toward the trash can. He knew he shouldn't open the lid, but he had no control, his arm reached out, his hand grasped the handle, yanking the lid off in one quick movement.

At this point the can stopped shaking, but he could hear a little smacking sound coming from inside. That's when he would lean forward to look in. That's when he screamed for the first time in his dream, after which he turned and started to run.

In the can was a woman's pussy, it had two sets of black wings, and IT was making that smacking sound. As he started to run the pussy flew up and out, its wings drumming loudly as it chased him down the alley. As he passed each receptacle that lined the way, the lid would fly off and another pussy would emerge, hovering for an instant before joining in the pursuit. In most of his nightmares he would reach the gondola making a huge, insane leap for safety. As he was catapulting toward the sleek boat he would wake up. Sweating miserably. Once though, the nightmare had been a bit different. He had fallen during his mad run - landing sprawled out on the cobblestones. Quickly regaining himself, he jumped to his feet, but his big mistake was to look behind. There, not two feet away, hovered one of the giant pussies - its wings beating rapidly - holding still in the air. He was unable to move. Rigid with fear. Then he heard that little smacking sound again, the one that he had heard after he opened the first can lid. He watched in shocked horror as the pussy lips started to part, exposing a set of pearly white teeth - three on the top row and two on the bottom. Long, narrow teeth that started to gnash together, the lips smacking side to side. In this instant, Brendan thought he was going to die. He managed to turn, his legs moving into the fastest run ever. He felt a hot gush of air on the back of his neck following by the horrible gnashing sound. That's when he woke up screaming. His legs were still moving when he woke - he even put his hand to the back of his neck, just to be sure.

The dreams had been bothering Brendan so much that he'd told Mary Jane about them yesterday during his haircut. He'd started out a little shyly, but Mary Jane had a way of making him comfortable, so it wasn't long before his whole nightmare deal was out in the open. She had a hard time keeping a straight face, but Brendan's fear was more real than a cow with a horse's head, so she had concentrated on making it a more serious occasion. She guessed, for once, that he was not being flippant. As Brendan was leaving, he threw one last comment over his shoulder.

"As far as I'm concerned, there are two kinds of pussy - the flying kind and the none flying kind - personally, I prefer the latter!"

He sounded a little irritated, she thought, watching him march off. For Brendan, that was not a good sign.

Later that afternoon, T.W. came in for a haircut. Although Mary Jane was really good at confidences, this time she was not. She'd bit her lip afterward, not sure why she had told someone else's secret. It was just that T.W. had asked her if she'd heard anything different lately. It was the way he'd asked, and she had just simply answered. He hadn't really said anything in response either, just nodded his head politely. Most guys would have started laughing, she was sure. He acted as if she had been telling him something else, something far more serious than about nightmares and flying pussies. She pondered this for a while, but soon moved on in her mind, as her hands zipped away, scissors in hand, like some snapping turtle at a ball.

## CHAPTER THIRTY-TWO
# CARLY WAKES UP

Willman and Theadora drove into town together. Parking in the usual place, they climbed out into the waiting sunshine.

"Hmm, lovely," sighed Thea, her face taking in the radiant heat, its warmth stroking her worry. She looked at her son, her hand lifting, tenderly touching the side of his face - she noticed that her family line had passed down nicely. For now she smiled contentedly, but she knew strife was to come. The time was drawing near. T.W. felt her concern as he placed his hand over hers, then he leaned down, planting a kiss squarely on his mum's cheek.

"See you later, Thea".

She was headed to Lance's to meet with Bunting - he was off in the other direction. Before they parted, they stood together, putting fingers of senses out, feeling for any errant spells floating around. This time they were prepared - they had strengthened their magic armor, pulling their invisible cloaks more tightly around. When they were sure that there was nothing that could hurt them, they went their separate ways with plans to meet in two hours.

T.W. sauntered down the lane before turning into the red-brick alley that zigzagged its way through the arena of quaint shops. The sun had brought the tourists flocking, the place was a droning beehive. As he passed through the crowds, more than one head, and not only female, turned to stare. He was stunning to look at - even shrunk down in size he was big. As a last minute decision he turned into Chetsy Chocolates - he had resisted for as long as he could. The door was propped open letting a warm breeze enter. There was one person ahead of him, ordering a mocha along with a scone - TO GO - otherwise the place was empty. He waited, eyeing the display of colorfully adorned hand made chocolates - sultry Latino's dressed to kill. He knew which he wanted.

"Next," said Kelly matter of fact. She had not looked up from the till.

"Two blackberry truffles, one salted caramel and an espresso. Please."

Kelly looked up at the same time that Tombhra did... *W i l l m a n...*

She couldn't believe that he was here. She had watched him walk by so many times.

*Kelly... help?*

It's ok. Stay calm.

"Take a seat Willman, I'll bring them over." Kelly had found out his identity after the night in The Green Cow. Otherwise Tombhra wouldn't let it rest, she couldn't stop thinking about him.

He stepped over to the small table in the corner - his mind had never left her eyes since that night.

*Hope she chats for a minute can't stand it anymore.*

Behind the counter Kelly and Tombhra had a discussion. Neither one knew what to do.

*Don't know what to say don't go over he won't like me don't go stay here he'll leave...*

Stop Tombhra, you're driving me bonkers. I have to

serve the guy.

Tombhra started to palpitate.

Hey, my body is old you know... stop that!

*Sorry Kelly it's just I don't understand why I feel this way...*

You're in love! Now hush.

Kelly made the espresso machine hiss before she arranged the chocolates on a plate.

"Here you go," she said, placing everything before Willman.

Before she could let go of the plate, his hand rested gently on her wrinkled wrist.

"Sit for a minute. Please. We need to talk."

Kelly nodded emphatically, ignoring Tombhra's pleas. She slipped her hand into his.

"Yes we do."

As she sat, the door swung shut and the closed sign lit up along with the three inside. Kelly was not disturbed as HE told his story. After all, she was the one that had been in the drawer at the morgue, so if anything, her story should be the strangest. She listened intently, as did Tombhra. All the while, their hands had not let go, nor did they want to.

Eventually the three dragged themselves apart.

Willman exited the shop carrying a smile light as snowflakes. He stepped into the sun-flooded courtyard where artwork winked like gems in a goldmine, tastefully placed in amongst the bushes, hiding in the cradles of small trees. Flowers were in full glory, spilling over rims of planters, trailing like satin drapes that flowed from some Sheik's bed. The fountain talked, dancing a fox trot with a blushing lady on his arm. The small shops lined this surreal, busy courtyard. Townsfolk meandered back and forth, but now they were not family groups or twosomes anymore - they walked alone. Single, solitary - sludging along. Willman was not happy about what was happening in Chetsy. The community wasn't tight anymore. People that had been friends for years were bickering. *And over what* - he thought - *just possessions!* Thea had given him the history of everyone in the town, he knew who people were before he even saw them. He now watched Terry, the plumber, walk right by Steve, his life long friend - they sneered growls for recognition. Willman had heard it was something to do with an old pistol that they both wanted. He sighed again. How far were people willing to go? Too far it seemed. It was originating in the used furniture store, he knew that much.

He stepped away from Tombhra, moving quickly toward the pottery shop, thinking that Carly would be there today and not at the cabin. His spirits lifted at the thought.

The mouse with the tropical umbrella cocktail was wearing a fire engine red waistcoat today. He looked up at T.W. as he entered the shop. T.W. wiggled his fingers at the mousey, the mousey grinned back - *'bout time you came* - he mouthed at the big guy. Over in the corner, the badger and the hedgehog stopped chatting. The badger removed his green bowler hat, holding it gently to his chest as he bowed slightly. The Willman bowed in response. Able, the parrot, called out to him, and Willman replied.

"Hi, Able."

Of course, he could see them all.

Carly was distracted from the urn before him - he was decorating it for the ashes of a dear friend. Something dimly registered in his mind as he came back to this world from the land his painting put him in. *Hi Able*? It struck him as odd that someone acknowledged his parrot, and by his name. As his head came up, he leaned back to see who his customer was. He was so utterly shocked, and frightened, to see the man giant standing there in full real glory, that he slithered from his sitting position to crouch under the table. From there he tipped his head sideways, peering up at the creature that he had decided some time ago was all in his imagination. This couldn't be happening. He brought his hands up to his face, pressing his fingers into his eyes, massaging the closed lids. After what seemed like minutes, he removed his fingers, cocked his head to one side again and looked out.

"Damn! You're still there!" he spoke louder than he had planned. "Go away!" He put his fingers back over his eyes.

Hi, Carly," said T.W. in a casual voice.

"Agh!" groaned Carly, as he took his fingers away from his eyes, immediately sticking them in his ears.

"Look Carly, we have to talk," the voice said to him.

Carly started to sing - loudly - fingers still stuck in his ears, eyes clamped tight shut. If he couldn't hear the creature, if he couldn't see the creature, then maybe, just maybe, it would go away.

After a while, he knew he must be safe, he hadn't heard anything else - he stopped singing. Nothing.

Then he unplugged his ears. Nothing. He opened his eyes, warily looking back out from under the table. The Willman gave him a little wave.

"Shit!" the big jerk was still there.

Just then, he felt something brush his knee that was planted firmly on the pine plank floor. Instinctively, he looked down to see what it was. The mousey waved up at him. Now, finally, Carly could see him - he had a conniption. He banged his head on the underside of the table as he scrambled to get out, making it jiggle a crazy dance. This caused the urn that had been sitting on its surface to tumble to the floor, but before it hit, he saw it arc gracefully back into place on the now still table. Having escaped the confines of the underside of his wooden sanctuary, he stood upright, rigid as a plank. First he looked at T.W., then he cast his eyes downwards to glance at the mousey, he looked back at T.W., then down at the mousey, T.W., the mousey. The mousey did a finger wiggle wave each time. T.W. The mousey. T.W. The mousey. T.W. Both of them kept doing the wave, like he was some kind of idiot or something, which actually, he thought with a little shock, maybe he was? Maybe he was an idiot, like one of those people that suddenly goes off their rocker, loses it, becomes a dithering loon overnight. Poor Carly, everyone would be saying, heard what happened to Carly, carted him off in a straight jacket. He could hear it all now. Carly started to hyperventilate, when finally, the final straw happened.

"Heck Carly, just relax, sit down and relax before you have an attack."

Carly looked around.

"Who said that?" Dread in the question.

"I did!" yelled the badger from the corner.

Carly looked - saw the badger - and fainted. A big dead faint.

T.W. caught the falling body with invisible arms, lowering him gently to the floor. Then he changed the 'open' sign to "shut' without leaving the spot he was standing on. *Don't want any interruptions.* Then he sat down on the floor next to Carly and waited.

It wasn't too long before Carly stirred. First he moaned - a coming back to this world moan. His eyelids fluttered open. Then he moaned again because he saw that the creature was sitting next to him. Panic attacked. He felt his breaths starting to hitch, his breathing coming in shorter sharper efforts. His windpipes started to sqeeze.

"I can't breathe," he gasped, as he lay flat on his back.

"It's in your pocket!" yelled the little voice of the mousey.

"What?" his voice rasping, thin and airless.

"In your pocket! Quick Carly, hurry up!"

"Yaack! Kurry huup!" Able yelled.

The Badger dropped his bowler hat - it landed on its rim, rolling a crazy eight on the floor - and scurried over to Carly to poke at the bulge in the thin cotton shirt.

"That, in there. Your whizzer!"

Carly wanted to say something, but his asthma had seized his vocal chords, squeezing everything tight. His mind still good, even if it was crazy - made him reach for his inhaler - all the while he felt a furry hand calmly stroking his neck. He put the whizzer to his lips and sucked, taking in a mouthful of relief. His lungs stopped shrinking, his airways quit tying his breath in knots - he puffed again. Finally, his gasping eased, he felt like he was back on earth, even if the furry mitt was still petting him, and now, a small black nose had started to root around in his ear. That got him sitting upright.

"Good job, Hedge!" yelled Badge, "that got him going!"

Carly looked at Willman sitting next to him. He looked at the mousey. He looked at the badger, and the hedgehog. Able flew over and sat on his knee. Carly looked at the parrot with sudden realization on his face. All these years of suppressing his knowledge of what he was. He'd gone on and lived his life as if it was perfectly normal to have all the strange things that happened, happen to him, on top of which, a parrot lived with him following him wherever he went. He had ignored David when he said he couldn't see Able, and now couldn't see Mandy. Why had he never wondered how Able managed to get to all those places. All these years - how many had it been? Carly thought about that. *Forever*, he answered himself. *Forever*!

T.W. broke the silence knowing that realization had just dawned on his friend.

"The Willman." He held out his hand to Carly.

"Carly Jones," Carly said, as he took the big hand in his, giving it a firm shake.

Without releasing his grasp, T.W. pulled Carly to his feet, as he himself rose effortlessly from the ground, his body floating upwards. Carly shimmered up after him.

"It'll take some getting used to," Carly offered, knowing now, that he really was a witch, "but I think I will manage," and started to laugh - a real nice bowl of jelly belly laugh.

"Looks like party time!" a little voice came from under the table to echo around the room.

Instantly the mousey's drink was full again with a new multicolored tropical umbrella garnishing the glass. The party began with a gentle chant that seeped out of the walls, it started to fill the room, growing slightly louder, and slightly louder still, until little cracking sounds became interspersed in the chant, lots of little cracking sounds. Carly looked around in total bewilderment as he watched tiny fissures appear in every piece of pottery in the room, the fissures growing bigger and bigger until out of each crack popped whichever characters were painted on that piece. From rabbits to owls to more mice and badgers, hedgehogs, pigs, crows, to fairies and elves, even fish that started to swim around the room through the air, their tiny wings beating like a hamster's heart. It was a party alright! Everyone was celebrating the birth of the real Carly. It seemed to go on forever as enlightenment smiled. T.W. just waited, allowing him to catch up on who he really was. A mirage of images and thoughts cascaded through Carly's mind - his body felt the tremors of his own magic that he could now fully see and feel. He was surrounded by all of the magical creatures that had filled his life so far. They all let him know in their own way just how deep this really went. The place was a hum of magic memories, a jostling of space and time

- but nothing can go on forever, not even something this good.

A sharp rap on the door jolted the dickens out of everyone, the door even rattled as the impatient person outside grabbed the handle, shaking it with some ferocity, even though the 'shut' sign was right at eye level.

"Bah! A customer!" blurted Carly, who before this time was eager for everyone to walk in. Business was business always. And he loved to share his art. But not now! "Bah!" he said again.

The impatient person outside put his face up to the glass, cupping his hands, trying to peer in.

Action was needed. All of the creatures knew that. The chant in the room started up again, beginning as something quietly distant then growing in volume as everyone dashed back toward their fissures, dashing back to their lives on the other side of the cracks, shouting out merry farewells as the crackling sounds started again. It took only a short while. Then all was quiet. The place was empty. All the cracks had closed, each piece of pottery nicely in its place, each merry hand painted character colorfully intact, no person ever knowing that a simple plate, mug or jug, could open the magic entrance to that other world where these creatures lived. T.W. and Carly looked around the empty room. It had all happened so quickly.

Then a small voice lifted up from the floor.

"Oh no!" it exclaimed.

Both T.W. and Carly looked toward the mousey under the table.

"Oh no," the mousey groaned, as he pointed up.

Their eyes followed the direction of his tiny paw. There, high in the room was a fish, still gaily gliding between the beams of the ceiling. There was not one more chant left, not one more cracking sound. The fish had missed her window to get back to her own world. The mouse, the badger and the hedgehog were supposed to be here - but not the fish!

Believe it or not, after all this, the impatient guy was still outside, but now he was rapping like a hammer in a forge, demanding entry! The audacity. Then he stopped knocking and pushed! With a nod from Willman the shop door flew open - and in he fell, the scraggly, unkempt, stinky fellow, staggering forward, almost landing on his mangy knees. It took a few reeling steps before he managed to regain his balance and stand up tall - that is, tall for a rodent. His mustard yellow, tweed sports jacket hung crooked - tugging on each front corner, twisting his scrawny chicken neck inside his slime lime polo shirt, he removed the dirty look that had been on his face, replaced it with a smile, and said.

"Howdy." He hated being locked out of a shop that really should be open. Now he was in he felt better, even if he didn't want to buy anything. He looked around, his little piggy eyes darting here and there. "Could have sworn?" He muttered under his breath.

"No swearing in the shop," retorted Carly trying not to laugh. Even though this annoying person had interrupted his moment of emergence from his self made cocoon, he had found his entrance to be extremely amusing. Carly couldn't believe the rudeness to stay peering in for so long and to actually start knocking was beyond him. *Couldn't he read!* The fact that the buffoon was ignoring his comical entry made it even worse.

"Could have sworn what?" egged on T.W.

"Well, you know," the little man seemed a bit more coy, "thought I saw, umm... things... you know, flying fish, queer things and all that." He tugged on his sports jacket again, fidgeting his feet on the hot tin roof at the same time.

"The only queer thing in here is me!" quipped Carly, "unless you like guys too!" he said, suddenly clapping his hands in anticipated delight, grinning mischievously.

The impatient guy looked a little shocked.

"How dare you," he blurted, as he backed toward the shop door, which unbeknown to him was now closed due to a magic nudge from Willman. One more step back and his foot hit up against the door. "Aggh," he gargled turning, grasping and grappling with the brass knob, which kept slipping in his sweaty grasp until he managed to yank it open. He twisted his head over his shoulder, glaring - he managed a huge HUFF in their direction and marched out, the same evil look returning that had been there before he had painted it over with a smile. They watched him leave, thoughtful expressions on their faces - a frown scarred Willman's forehead.

Just then, they heard the laugh of Bunting echoing down the alley, gushing like a gurgling stream in through the shop door. Behind the laugh came, of course, Bunting, and with her, Theadora. As they stepped over the threshold they both sniffed as one. One of those sniffs that actually makes the nose bob up and down - rabbits on hind legs, nostrils twitching in the air... danger - beware!

"Pew," scoffed Bunting, "who was that?"

Theadora simply looked at her son with raised eyebrows, creases growing on her face, a jigsaw puzzle of concern. He raised his eyebrow back at her. He had not unlocked the door for the stranger to come falling in by mistake. He had his suspicions - he'd just needed to see if they were founded.

"We'll talk later," he murmured. Everyone nodded.

Bunting, sensing the change in Carly, marched over.

"About time you came to your senses," she quipped as she gently punched him in the shoulder. "I've been waiting years for this. You've been such a deny artist. A really good one." She laughed. He too. He was so happy - he knew he had come home. Just then, they heard a little glugging sound high up in the rafters - all of their faces turned up like sunflowers seeking warmth, to see the fish, still there, flying happily around, darting in and out, enjoying an invisible coral reef. Carly threw a peanut into the air - the fish opened its mouth, emitting a swirling, sucking sound. The peanut, instead of falling back to earth, was pulled into the vortex, shooting through the air to enter the botox fish lips. As soon as the peanut was gone, the glugging sound came again. Another peanut went in the air, phwoooomp, sucked in. Gone. It took a half bag of peanuts before the fish seemed happy to just swim around again.

"Can't believe how hard that thing can suck," commented Bunting.

The Willman broke the fascination first, adjusting

his bow tie, making sure it was straight.

"Shall we go for an early dinner?" he asked of everyone, "The Green Cow OK?"

Without a word, they moved in unison toward the door.

CHAPTER THIRTY-THREE

# THE MUCKDEANNE

"WHAT DO YOU MEAN? YOU LITTLE CREEP! YOU WENT WHERE?" Better. B.'s voice was way louder than when she and Seteeva were in the shop with customers.

"YOU'D BETTER NOT HAVE BLOWN OUR COVER! YOU STUPID CREEPAZOID!"

The little creep turned out to be the impatient guy that had been at the pottery shop door. This little rodent now stood inside the used furniture store, head bowed, twiddling with the dull tin buttons of his greasy jacket. His dirty fingernails chewed and spat out. When he looked up, his beady eyes settled on Better B. He did not look remorseful - in fact, he had a stupid grin on his face to match his name. A creepy grin, for a creepy guy.

Seteeva was sitting on the couch with her pipe for company - watching.

"I'm tired of waiting," he creaked out in a squeaky voice. The impatient guy, the creepy guy, was in fact, a Muckdeanne. A Muckdeanne, who could only replenish his magic abilities by sucking on the souls of young children. Souls sucked over time, gradually draining the child of life. This particular Muckdeanne was even more disgusting than most. Better B. was his daughter. He'd left her when she was five years old, but only because her mother had made him. In order to make his magic stronger, he'd been sucking his own daughter's soul, because at the time, other little children were scarce. He had to do what he had to do, in order to survive, he told his wife before she started to beat him with a horsewhip. When Better. B.'s mother had found out, a battle almost to his death had ensued. In the end, this nasty slime of a Muckdeanne had crawled from the house never to be heard of again until two years ago, when he had turned up on his daughter's doorstep. She was alone, her mother having died ten years previous at Tunkatee Commons, a regular witch-gathering place on the other side. When Better B. had seen her slithering father, she had wanted to kick his ass and smoke his hide, but a small part of her was also glad she had some family left, someone to belong to. She opened the door wider and let him in. And in he'd sneaked, crawling on his belly - that's all he'd been doing ever since - creeping around her house, around her mind, around her things. He no longer wanted her soul, it was of no use to him now for she was no longer a child. But she could get him children, couldn't she? He asked. Over and over. The festering boil of a sneak was no longer strong enough to do his own dirty work. To begin with, Better B. had refused, out of respect to her mother. But, like father, like daughter, in the end, she started to lean his way, his persuasions seeming more and more logical to her.

In the end. Yes. In the end, she agreed. "I'll bring the children to you. Teach me how to do it. You get some. I get some." He was so hungry, he readily signed up.

Now here he was, sniveling away like the creep he was - and in front of Seteeva too. *Damn it! Now I will have to bring her into the picture,* thought Better B. He had never come out of their gingerbread house before without her permission - he had overstepped her line, and with what outcome she wondered. Things had been going remarkably well - children with Mouth Bugs all coming to her for help, thanks to good boy Jimmy. At first, she would only call them to her on the nights she allowed her father out of the house, inviting him down to the used furniture store to start the feeding process. At first, that was, now she kind of had the thing down for she had tried a few times on her own - not the most successful to begin with, but somewhat. The kids had suffered more than they should, but she was not worried about that. She'd gone through it, why shouldn't they? Anyway, she felt she was successful enough that she would keep on doing it without her father. She'd even got the greed thing going with the adult populace at a nice pace and had now started a few other mind twisters on certain people in the town. All in all, she had a good start on destroying this goody, goody town without anyone suspecting anything. The more goody, goody she destroyed, the more powerful she became. On top of which she would be rid of 'the village'! But now, to ruin it all, here was her greedy, no good for nothing, two-bit soul sucking father, showing his putrid side. AGAIN! She was furious! And then, to top it, Seteeva started to blow her bubble encased demons as her stupid father continued to pull on the corners of his stupid coat, slathering as the gibberish spurted from his mouth. Her furiousness just grew!

"OK. OK." Seteeva said, standing up from the

couch. She had watched the last bubble burst against the wall, applauding at the ability of the encased demon to exude such a loud scream before its demise. It had given her some glee in her somewhat boring, present world. However, interestingly enough, the boredom seemed to be slipping away.

"You are who?" she asked, drawling out the 'are' as she strutted toward the sniveling little man.

Seteeva could be overwhelming if she so wished, her laid-back attitude disappearing when she wanted something badly enough - and now, she so wished. She could feel how furious B.B. was. She could feel something else too, but she couldn't quite grasp it, so now she really wanted to know what it was. She stepped closer to the sniveling thing that still stood near to the door. She came toward him from the side, noting the sticky looking earwax lodged in the folds of his enormous ears. As she moved to stand in front of him, she studied his face. He tended to breath through his nose. In his right nostril was a big gooey piece of snot stuck to one of his thick nose hairs. As he breathed, a booger appeared, then disappeared. Appeared... disappeared. For a few moments Seteeva was mesmerized by the repetitive action of something so gross, until finally she was able to shake herself, mimicking a dog after a bath, breaking the hypnosis caused by the continually reemerging booger. Now she could speak again.

"Who are you? What are you?"

The poor excuse for a man started to rub his hands together in a turning motion - to say he was agitated would be an understatement. He glanced at Better B.

who now had a thunderhead hovering directly over her beet red face.

"She's my daughter," he said, recovering with a sly smirk.

That did it! Better B. erupted.

"I'm not your daughter you stupid man! You may be my father! But I am not! Repeat! Not... your daughter!"

At this point she raised her arm, pointing a long thin finger at him. A bolt of lightening shot across the room hitting him squarely in the chest. He dropped to the floor. Deader than a doornail.

"Holy Shitarroony, B.B., you just killed your dad!" yelled Seteeva, as she bent forward to look at the crumpled figure. The creepy guy just lay there - flat out. His jacket was all disheveled, one leg bent backward in an awkward fashion, his polo shirt riding high over his big pot of a belly exposing the fuzzy hair that lined his black gooey out-button. Just as Seteeva leaned in closer to confirm his death, the piece of snot appeared. Then disappeared. Appeared. Disappeared. She quickly pulled her head back. "Drat! Guess not! Looks like he's breathing again. Too bad, dirty looking sniper!"

"Yeh, too bad." The shock made B.B. start talking. "He's a Muckdeanne, weak little asshole he is, but harder than all get out to kill. My mother tried, but he just crawled off into a ditch somewhere. Now he's crawled back out to me."

She walked over to the still unconscious figure, gave him a good kick in the ribs, another shot of lightening, then busied herself around the shop waiting for him to regain consciousness. Seteeva sat back on the couch.

"A Muckdeanne, heh? When were you going to tell me? I'm not too interested in that kind of activity."

Better B. stopped what she was doing. Holding still for just an instant too long. Seteeva caught it. She jumped up.

"You WEREN'T going to tell me... I think you had better start coming straight."

Better B. became a ramrod of forged anger, then she swirled around.

"Don't talk to me like that, you piece of witch ass!" She hissed, dropping into her crouched attack stance, arms waving like tentacles in front.

Seteeva's eyes narrowed, her stance also dropping to crouched, ready for a devilish dervish. She hissed back.

"Witch ass back! Wanna fight?"

The moment was long. Both witches hissing and spitting, fingers pointing, dancing to a slow beat from hell. Black pupils, slits in a fortress, shooting arrows, pouring boiling oil.

It didn't take the crooked nosed witch long to realize composure would be a better tack, although it was difficult for her. Letting all hell let loose was more her style. But she had been getting a lot out of this relationship with Seteeva and knew it really would be in her best interests to continue. She glanced at her father as she thought this - *hmmm, what to do, feel unsure,* she really didn't need him anymore. Sure, she could do with a few more soul sucking lessons, but it wasn't imperative, she could make do with what she knew. Seteeva, however, was another matter - she wanted to keep her around. So, hands down............ *daddy, has to go!*

Better B. slowly unfolded, standing up straight.

"Nah, don't wanna fight... Want to help me deal with the soiled clothing laying on the floor there. Any thoughts?"

"Yeh," uttered Seteeva wickedly, happy at the turn of events and happy to straighten her arthritic knees. "First though, when did he last have a child, I want to know how strong he is?"

Better B. knew the answer without thinking, it had been a while, that's why he had ventured out of the gingerbread house without her permission. He was getting weak, and hungry.

"Long enough for a dead man to walk," said Better B. gleefully.

They both looked at each other and giggled - their partnership back on track.

Behind one of the couches was a wooden, ornately carved, super large trunk. The lid of the trunk lifted to reveal ample, but moldy storage space inside. The space was plenty big enough for creepazoid. Better B. had already danced around to the lovely piece of furniture, opening the lid with a quick glance at Seteeva, who in an instant, was with her - she answered Better B.'s look with one of her own. Then they both started to laugh insanely. A sanatorium full of Crazies.

"You take his shoulders!" Seteeva told B.B. as she grabbed his feet.

They didn't need to do this - they could have cast him in with magic. It just felt better to toss the sagging heap in. Then they went to work. First they sealed his lips shut with the gum of a slug's liver.

This they followed with a numbing lotion made from ground black leeches and a dead man's tongue. They slathered his prone form. He was a gooey mess. Finally, they bound his wrists with the intestines of a rotten dog. Should last a while they both agreed, weak as he was. Wait till he comes too, they thought, hoping it gave him a heart attack when he found he was locked and bound in the dark trunk. Quickly, they banged the lid so that Better B. would not have to deal with any guilt if he did open his eyes. If he got to look at her, he could start his creeping tricks with her conscience. Not that she had much of one for most people, but he was her blood. The lid had a latch, which they secured with a padlock and a magic spell.

"All done," Seteeva crooned, "let's go to The Green Cow to talk."

And so they did. Arm in arm - in allegiance once again.

## CHAPTER THIRTY-FOUR

# THE GREEN COW

Carly, Bunting, Theadora and Willman had wandered over to the pub after making sure the fish was happy. They were sitting comfortably around a small round table tucked into the corner. T.W. had a single malt before him, as did Thea. A fine bottle of zinfandel sat between the other two. They were heavy in conversation. T.W. had explained about the impatient guy at Carly's pottery store.

"What's a Muckdeanne?" asked Carly, still trying to catch up on all the witchy things he had suppressed for so many years. Bunting started to explain, but as soon as she did, his inborn innate witch sense kicked in. He immediately knew all about Muckdeannes without further help from Bunting. He wished he didn't.

"YUK!" he exclaimed a little too loudly. "Are you sure he was one?" he asked turning to T.W. knowing as soon as he did that it was a pointless question. He could remember the smell too - now he knew what it meant.

"Do you think he is with anyone?" asked Bunting.

"Well, no other Muckdeannes for sure. As you know they travel alone. But I sensed a witch he didn't like and yet for some reason is unable to stay away from. So that witch is here," mused T.W.

Just at this moment the door opened, the slight wind blowing in the trash. It was Better B. and Seteeva still laughing joyously about tossing creepazoid into the trunk. As they moved over to their favorite spot by the bar, Better B. saw Carly Jones. She knew it was his shop her father had visited. She knew what her father had seen. However, she did not know that there had been another man in the shop because she had gone on high boil before he had reached that point in his story. And now, he was locked away, so he still couldn't tell her. What she did know, was that Carly Jones was a witch, well, at least according to her father. He'd never seemed like a witch though - she hesitated - whenever she'd been on her rounds of the town, checking things out - he didn't do witch things, or act witchy. She pondered this. Still, her father had said...? She glanced at the other people around the table, recognizing Theadora from Brendan's birthday night. Again, she wanted to stare, but could feel nothing. The big handsome guy was something else though, she wished she could get something from him. This time, unlike the night of Brendan's birthday she took her time looking. *Yes sir!* She thought with some glee. *She would most definitely like to get more than something from him!* With some effort she reigned in her thoughts, concentrating on the problem at hand. Nothing from him either. *Cute bow tie,* she thought. *Of course, anything would look cute on that body.* Her final glance fell on Bunting, just as she let out a peel of laughter. Some confusing feelings coming from that direction. *Maybe that's why she's out with Carly. Both of them witches?* She continued to move toward the bar with Seteeva, climbing up onto the stools to seat themselves side by side. She nudged her friend, tossing a look like an ice cold fish toward the table in the corner, filling her in with a whispered voice about her father's visit to the shop. They were soon interrupted.

"What would you drunks... I mean... uhmm... ladies like to drink?"

Better B. looked over at Brendan, noting with some delight the dark bags under his eyes and the drawn look to his face. *He sure does look pale,* she thought, a smile starting to play on her lips. *Looks like he's been losing sleep.* The smile lingered as she thought about the nightmare spell she had cast his way. The way he looked was enough for her to hold her tongue at his 'drunk' remark. They placed their order, downing the first round in seconds, piranha's at a party, asking for refills almost immediately.

"Refill? So soon? How unusual..." muttered Brendan, loud enough for them to hear as he replenished their empty glasses.

Better B.'s lips quivered. *Screw you Brendan... but not in the way you were hoping...*

Back at the round table, the arrival of the two evil ones had been noticed. They blanketed themselves thicker than ever with their disguising spells, buried inside a goose feather mattress. They immersed themselves in idle chatter, even though their minds were on the two seated at the bar.

It was sometime later when the inhabitants of the round table rose, watched with some curiosity from the bar seats - beady eyes following the group out the brassy door. It was sometime much later that Better

B. and Seteeva themselves, left. The trash blowing out of the pub the same way that it had blown in.

CHAPTER THIRTY-FIVE

# SETEEVA AND THE FLYING FISH

It was busier than the streets of New York City inside the small shop. Seteeva had managed to cause a holocaust and all over the small oak desk sitting in the corner. The more cookies the customers ate, the more they wanted the desk. The intense need growing in each person. Greed begetting greed. Yelling! Screaming! Venomous comments spewing forth. Vile, spit and malice was singing its awful song. It was evil at its best. Seteeva was loving it. She had been a little bored with the whole process for a while, but that was while it had been in its birth. Now it had a foothold, it was just a hoot. She stood looking on, laughing at the hideous scene before her. These people were really ready to kill each other over a desk. *What incredible fun,* she thought, hoping the cretin, Sheila, would jump on Desmond and claw his eyes out. She couldn't help herself - she started to yell and jig around - a cheerleader at an execution.

"Un-fucking-believable!"

One of the customers actually heard her above the din. "What was that?" he asked incredulously.

"I said," said Seteeva, wearing a cheshire cat smile, "it's an un-fucking believable desk! I want it too!"

The customer's eyes bugged, seething anger dripping from his lids. If Seteeva wanted it, he thought, she'd probably get it, what with her working here and all. That just made his behavior worse.

Seteeva snickered, enjoying the moment, watching,

even though she badly needed a smoke. Finally, she gestured across the room to her partner, playing charades, taking big huffs from an invisible huffer, letting B.B. know where she was going as she walked out the door. Her plan was to go out back, have a puff, then return. She ducked under the drooling wisteria archway, headed for the bench that snoozed under the languishing weeping willow. There she sat, pipe in hand, stuffed full to the brim with the smoked root that she loved to smoke so much. Huffing and puffing away, a thought occurred to her. *Maybe I should visit Carly Jones' s shop - see what I think of the situation.*

Puff.

*Yes.*

Puff. Puff.

*Good goddamned idea*!

So off she went, forgetting to tell her friend, who was still in the midst of World War Three.

Seteeva had not eaten that day and the root was a new batch. Strong! Potent! She left the safe confines of the hidden garden to meander down the lane into the heart of town like some drunk escaped from the local tavern. She veered one way, then the other, tripping easily. "Whoopsie!" She snickered, righting herself each time. Several people gave her a wide birth, but they still received a toothy grin. A couple of times her tongue lost its numbness and her lips opened.

"Gleat dlesk in the shlop!" thumbing backwards toward the eerie house on the corner, "tink yud luv it!"

She watched as they ran in the direction her thumb

pointed. *Hope there's room in there,* she thought wickedly, her mind working better than her mouth. That's when she had the exciting thought of bodies piling up and what they could do with them? *Huh huh - if there are enough I could make a dead man's pickling broth.* This left a smirk on her face, until another thought dug its way in - *oh oh, the little sneak is still in the trunk - wonder if he's awake?* The thought brought her to a stop, standing still in the middle of the road, fingers to her lips. *Hmmm... Maybe I should go back?* Her hand fingered her coat pocket, the one with her pipe in it. *Maybe another puff first - I could duck into the alley over there... Yes,* she chirped inside, *good jackass idea.* She headed for the quiet alley that cut through to the next street, disappearing down its narrowness.

Some time later, she emerged at the other end, weaving from side to side. Giggling. She gave more toothy grins as she made her way toward Carly Jones, forgetting altogether her previous thoughts. On the way she passed Chetsy Chocolates. The smell that came out of that place pulled her up short. Not the smell that would pull regular people to a halt - the smell of chocolate, coffee and freshly baked scones - but some other weird, nasty, smell. If she were a dog she would roll in it. But she wasn't a dog and it was ghastly! She glanced in the door to see Kelly Keen making a coffee for some big guy with his back to her. She wanted to go in - to investigate further - but the smell mixed with too much smoke was making her gag. *LATER!* She said to herself, as her stomach gave a little heave. She moved away quickly, steadying herself as she went.

It wasn't many minutes before she reached the pottery shop, glancing in the storefront as she approached. There were several people inside. The door opened with a jingle. *And a jangle.* She stepped over the threshold. Carly sensed her presence before he actually saw her - his years of denial had not made his witch strength any less. While he answered questions from the clientele present in his shop, he sent out a mind telegram to T.W. telling him of Seteeva's visit. The telegram was coded and blocked. She had no access to it as she meandered around, picking up this and that, oohing and aahing, the pipe making her invisible - or so she thought. After thirty minutes her irritability rose. Would the other customers never go away, she wanted to be on her own with this queer moron so she could see who he really was. He was hiding behind everyone in here - it was driving her crazy. She wanted to know, AND RIGHT NOW, if he was really a witch or not!

Finally, there was just one person left. Seteeva recognized her as one of her own regulars - one that could get manic easily over the simplest items. The stupid woman was looking at a turquoise teapot with a mermaid painted on the spout. *Hmmm?* Seteeva wasn't too sure about the mermaid thing on a teapot. *Still, everyone to their own taste.*

"Nice tleaplot, I wouldn't mand thlat!" She leaned toward the woman. "Ya shnow what?" whispered Seteeva in the woman's ear.

"What?" the woman whispered back, her curiosity her guide.

"Gleat likkle desk at the shlop - you shud glo

look... yer fliend, Magglie wants it!"

"Maggie wants it! She told me earlier she wouldn't touch it with a barge pole... Ooh that bitch!"

With that, the woman moved faster than a cowboy in a bullfight. Grabbing the teapot she flung too much money toward Carly, then was off, eyes glistening with shear want, malice not far behind. All Seteeva saw were flaps of skirt as the woman darted up the lane - her own irritability diminished at the gleeful thought of one more person ready to hate over a chunk of wood. It was just too easy to make these people into demons.

She had been standing close to the shop window watching the exit of the woman whilst Carly stood watching her from behind. Carly was no fool. He knew why she was here, but he guessed they were going to dance the two-step for a while.

"Can I help you?"

There was a slight pause before Seteeva turned toward him. She didn't say anything, just cocked her head to one side with, she thought, a look of pure innocence. Too Carly, it looked like someone had poured acid on the Mona Lisa.

"Lice plates - I wike them... who's the alertist?" said Seteeva before her mind spoke to her saying, *Jeezus Seteeva girl... what has happened to your tongue, why don't you just shut up.* Then her mind went on vacation again and her voice came back, "Nicey plates, artertisty?" She crimped her eyes tight - *crap on a lap, Seteeva - get a grip.* Deciding not to open her mouth again, she just grimaced.

Carly stepped out from behind the rustic table, pushing the drawer of the money till closed. Able sent warning, squawking as he flew to Carly's shoulder - "wicked witch!" The badger had been standing with her hands on her hips ever since Seteeva had entered - now she just huffed real loud so that Carly could hear. The mousey yelled, "careful, careful!" as he took big sips through the straw.

"I will. I will," muttered Carly to his friends.

"What wa thlat?" asked Seteeva, forgetting her vow to keep her mouth shut. (She could not see or hear anything other than Carly.) "I will whattle?"

"Oh, I said, I will be happy to talk to you about the artist. Now, ah, yes... these were painted by..." A flowing description of the artist and her talents followed. He almost forgot that it was Seteeva he talked to, so enraptured was he by the beauty of the plates in hand. His speech flowered into pictures as he talked, pleasure filling his face. As he embellished the talents of the artist, the plate Seteeva was holding dropped to the floor. It shattered into at least a million pieces.

"WHOOPSIE..." her face snarled, a weasels mouth.

Carly pursed his lips, a clam closing against poison as another plate plunged toward the floor. It too shattered - along with Carly. Just because he was a witch able to put the plate back together, did not mean that he was not aghast at the lack of respect shown to art. It hurt his kindly soul to see such treatment of something that had taken weeks of loving to create.

He was quiet, brooding, while he decided what tack to take. Seteeva went to pick up another fine piece, destruction boiling in her craw.

Meanwhile, the fish emerged from a giant wormhole in the ancient beam above. It darted to a moist crevice that was gnarled into the enormous round post that held sentry in the center of the room. It hung, swishing its tail, its beady eyes looking down. Its round, moist mouth open, empty, and hungry.

Another plate crashed to the floor, its shattered shards making Badge and Hedge dash for safety. One long, snarly vixen piece chased the mouse away from his martini. The fish watched, then moved, flapping its long luxurious tail, colors of a rainbow scattering beetles and moths. It settled again, balancing silently on a piece of twisted iron that screwed fanatically into the heavy wooden pillar. The crazy chandelier that hung beneath this rusty arm swayed - too and fro. From this perch, the fish watched, waiting. Blinking once in a while.

Carly bent down to pick up the scattered remains of his precious art, his head bowed in sorrow. Bit by bit, piece by piece, his fingers moved, bleeding when pricked by his beloved. He cried silently - *how could she?*

Seteeva was elated as she looked down on the crawling piece of dirt - she wanted to pick up her foot and dig her heel into his spine, breaking it in two! Her heavy black boot lifted, knee bent, her grin wider than an earthquake crevice. She would break his back in half!

Before her bulk could crack down, the fish dropped off its perch, a weight on the end of a corpse, plunging to the depths of a watery grave - it sunk through the air, fast and furious. Once down, it opened its oily mouth, attaching its bruising lips around the bony socket of Seteeva's succulent eye. Leeching on. It sucked. Hard! The eye left its orbit - entering the black hole. The fish swallowed. Gone. Finished. Chum! *Yum Yum!*

*Hmm, delicious, not the same as peanuts, chow mein, pieces of lasagna, crab cakes, smoked oysters, chips or muffins.* But it was satisfied as it dashed back to the ceiling, bolting for a gap in the beams, its luxurious red painted lips still smacking in ecstasy.

Seteeva was motionless, it had happened so fast, her foot was now squarely on the ground instead of over Carly's back. A moan started to escape from her tortured mouth, a siren winding up, her mind a maze of thoughts. *My eye! A flying, fucking fish, just ate my eye!* That is when the full crescendo of sound erupted from her dried out throat, crisp, hoarse, bulging with explosive hate. She clenched her fists, arms ram rod straight at her sides, her head throbbing to twice its size - her mouth opening like a volcano about to erupt.

"I'LL HAVE YOUR PUCKERING, PEANUT BRAIN FOR THIS! ALONG WITH YOUR BLASTED HEAD! YOU HEAR ME! YOUR BLASTED, PICKERING PUCKERING, FUCKING HEAD!" She turned, grappling with herself to get to the door, falling through it with calamity. Outside, the alley was empty, except for Willman standing quietly. He made sure that no one was around to see her, screeching like a banshee as she staggered forward, hand clamped tightly over her lonely, empty eye socket.

CHAPTER THIRTY-SIX

# THE THIN RED BOOK

Felice left Lance's early, her soul weary of witnessing long time friends arguing over some piece of furniture that the evil ones were selling. The malicious hatred spitting back and forth, its leaden poison making dents in her skull. She headed out on her daily rounds, her route passing the Used Furniture Store - she walked by it several times, the creaky house demanding her attention. After three passes and seeing nothing amiss, she felt comfortable enough to move on to her most favorite pastime - the bookstores. First was Melville's. It had been there forever. The current owner's great, great grandmother had first opened the doors more years ago than anyone could remember. It was a small hideout, really small, but with more books than a place three times its size could hold - they were jammed in every corner, every niche, nook and cranny. There was even room to sit, with two old church pews crammed in between the cascading falls of lines on pages. Felice wandered. Sniffing, scouting, feeling with every sense. Nothing! She moved two doors down, to the cramped space that sat beneath the local pie shop. It was long and narrow with no windows - the bookshelves disappearing into nothingness. Felice disappeared too, then reappeared, disappeared, reappeared, as she walked the aisles. Nothing. One street over, smushed in between the bank and the jewelers, was a small square cottage, ages old, with moss for a roof. She entered, after venturing up the crunchy gravel driveway. The blue ocean door swung open. Mustiness filled her nostrils. Books were piled everywhere. *Hmmmm? Here, maybe? Today?* Thirty minutes revealed nothing. She left. Crunching out as she had crunched in.

"Thanks Tony!" she called, looking back over her shoulder.

The next place was the library. *There was nothing there yesterday,* she thought, *maybe I should give it a miss today?* Still she couldn't resist. *Books are books!*

As she entered, her head bobbed in greeting to the bespectacled old hag with a mustache long enough to tickle her lower lip - this was the guardian to the treasures of ink on paper. The old hag nodded back, even smiled as she watched the purple skirt swish immediately toward the rows of books. It was the way Felice always entered this place - with vigor. The expectation and excitement of so many books was enthralling. The possibility of finding a magic book made every day like Christmas. *Quiet in here today? Hmm. No children.* She made a mental note, but moved in anyway - the vaulted, domed ceiling pulling her into the midst of the new and old. To begin, her eyes cast upwards, taking in the beams, cobwebs and rays of sunlight. She did not need to look forward, her body knew its way far too well. The towering rows of books on books closed in over her as she walked each aisle - a bride seeking her groom. Felice shivered. Bookbindings touched her shoulders as she passed, each one speaking to her, telling of their secrets. It was hard to move through. Every book pulling on her soul, its vortex sucking her in.

But she kept on - down one aisle - up the next - down another. As she felt her way through the ninth, something caught her attention. It was on the second shelf up. Low down. Felice bent, knees touching ground, her purple skirt willowing around. She crooked her neck to the side, scanning the book titles. NOTHING! *How disappointing. I was so sure...* Rising, she dusted off her knees before moving on. *Maybe in the next aisle?* Rows later, she sighed, n*ot today, I guess.* The old face of the librarian looked at her, peeping over the high counter top. *Nothing?* ... *No. Nothing, Felice* shrugged back.

"See you later...." she called lightly, passing by the bifocals as she headed toward the door. Her hand reached to push her way out when the strange sensation came again. She held her palm steady, flat on the wood frame as she twisted her neck around. *Hmmmm? Something?* With a steady heart that now beat faster, Felice turned. *What aisle was that? Nine?* It was only a few minutes before she was on her knees again, scanning the titles. Nothing! Again! *No way!* Her fingers pulled out Stephen King's 'The Shining'. She flipped the pages. *Just Stephen.* Looking down she saw rows of *just Stephen.* She groaned, her head lilting slightly. *How disappointing. I could have sworn...* It was then, on her final groan, as her head was tilted to the side while replacing one of the tattered well-read novels, that she saw it. A thin book. Red. Fallen behind the soldierly line.

Her breath left her body.

Carefully she reached in, her hand shaking slightly. *Please let it be...* Gingerly she removed the delicate creature, its thinness a rake in time. *Please let it be...* By now she had sat squarely on the floor, her bottom hidden in the folds of her billowing skirt, its whispers seeping forth through the books of time. *I've found it! Oh my. I have found it!* She did not clutch the book to her chest, nor raise it to the heavens in exultation - she simply laid it on her open lap, weeping quietly. The red book lay quietly. Doing nothing. Just waiting. It would talk in its own time.

"What's that lady?" The kid with the bulbous nose peered over her shoulder. "Gimmee!" His hand slithered forward to take the book.

*Where had this little shit come from?* thought Felice, yanked out of her calming waters like a fish on a hook.

"Hands off, young man!" she said.

"What is it? I want it." He made a quick grab, knowing it was something he should have.

Felice was faster. She hugged the book to her, deflecting his hand as she did so, batting him away like a ping-pong ball. Rising quickly, she looked down at the little punk who was staring at her like a racoon who knew.

"Go pester someone else," hissed Felice as she turned her back. She walked toward the bifocals to check out. The kid traipsed behind. Finished at the desk, she approached the door, his voice following her.

"I want what she had next."

*Tough luck sonny, this book won't be back.* Thirty dollars dropped out of her hand into the donation tin as she passed.

Lifting the flap of her satchel, the book found its home, slipping nicely into place. She couldn't wait to sit down in her room, so that she could digest what she'd just found.

Felice soon left the library behind and was busy contemplating as she walked around the corner. The array of small shops that lined the red-bricked alley with the gay fountain dancing, lay before her. She was in an almost trance like state, when something unusual hit her hard, square in the chest. Her heart beat her like a mad man as Seteeva Haar ran into her headfirst. *Strange. Place is empty,* Felice thought as her awareness returned. Then she cast her eyes down, on to the top of Seteeva's head. She noticed a bald patch that she had not seen before, not normally having the misfortune to be this near. In the center of the bald patch was a small brand, faded green and red, but still prominent. She knew what it was instantly. It was the brand of a troubled set of witches - Selons - she flinched at the recognition. Then her heart did another groan, because Seteeva, not looking up, had simply taken a half step back, then forward again, butting like a bull into the thing blocking her way,

"Get out of my fucking way!" Seteeva muttered.

"Tt. Tt. No way to speak to a neighbor." Felice grinned.

Although Seteeva was living in the horror of the moment - having just lost her eye - something in the voice, and manner, of this, THING, that was blocking her way, caught her attention. She took another step back, a full one this time - her hands were at her sides, her head was bowed - slowly, measuring her pace, she tilted her chin to look into the face of the tall person before her. As Seteeva's head lifted, Felice got a good look at the nightmare. But the nightmare wasn't hers so her humor took over, she just could not help herself, the opportunity was too ripe – after all, this was one of the evil ones before her.

"Oh, hooo... oh Jeezus... oh my, Seteeva, you look like someone just put your head through a meat grinder..." then she paused for effect, holding onto her glee. "Wish I'd thought of it, what an absolutely brilliant idea - who's was it?"

That did it! Seteeva raised her hand to cover the gaping blackness, focusing her one remaining eye until recognition dawned - *Felice, the frickin Coffee Witch! Can't stand you!* Instantly, her other hand screamed into the air, becoming a claw, her finger nails talons as she swiped toward the smirking face before her. She intended to remove one of those eyes to match her own made in hell face, but Felice was ready. Her skirt flapped around her legs as a wind blew down the alley, her hand moving much faster than Seteeva's, grabbing her wrist - twisting it down between them. She kept a python hold as the talons raked thin air, clawing with desperation, wanting to slice like a guillotine.

"Don't try that with me, bitch witch!" she hissed at Seteeva. "Your punishments come according to your life. You're lucky you have one eye left!" Felice pushed Seteeva away from her - forcefully. "Begone you unlucky Selon, I know your sort."

Seteeva was livid.

"I'll have his head! And you - you piece of moron jumbled jelly jockstrap - I will have your frick-a-frackin heart!"

With this, the one eyed Seteeva Haar marched up the street toward the used furniture shop, head held high with not a soul to see. The Willman had seen to that.

Felice watched The Selon's back as it rounded the corner, keeping a watchful minds eye, feeling for any change in direction, any spell coming her way. As the heat of Seteeva's evil distanced, she felt a calm presence behind. She had not noticed until it was close - unusual for her, she was normally so protective of herself, never letting things get too near. She turned, not feeling threatened, just curious. Of course, it was Willman.

"Felice," he said, "allow me to introduce myself, The Willman, son of Theadora. I must add, nice job there, tremendous show!" He grinned.

Felice grinned back.

"Hey there, at last, we meet."

Then they both turned, headed in the direction of the pottery shop. Although it was only a short distance, they talked rapidly, covering much ground, so that when they stepped through the door, bell tinkling overhead, they were firm friends. Once inside, they were instantly alarmed - Carly was leaning over his table sobbing and moaning. They moved with fast steps toward him, concern eating their faces.

"Carly?" uttered T.W. in dismay.

He looked to where Carly's eyes were cast. On the

table lay the fish, her mouth opening and closing – silently - her eyes non-seeing. Her normal brightly colored scales were pale and wilting. Her red lips were white - and not pouting. Her tail flapped uselessly on the wooden table and her wings drooped like limp rags. Carly looked at T.W. as a big fat tear ran down the side of his face.

"She's dying," moaned Carly - then he looked at the fish as her mouth gasped more and more, her belly sucking for life. "I can't stand it," he moaned again, "I love this fish. She helped me, and now she's dying. And all because of that eye!" Carly started to moan like an Italian mother at a funeral.

T.W. wanted to grin, but in respect to his friend he refrained, at least for now.

"She's not dying, Carly."

"She's not?" asked Carly, grasping.

"No. She just has indigestion. Here." He pulled a small silver bottle out of his pocket. From the bottle he withdrew a glass dropper, which he held over the gaping mouth, letting drops of a sparkling crimson liquid fall gently in.

Carly was silent as he watched, not sure what to think. It only took moments, though it seemed like eons, then the fish groaned, after which she let out one huge burp that blew papers off Carly's desk. Her puckering lips became crimson and proud as her wings beat the drum once more - she was up and going, flying back to the ceiling, rushing in and out of the beams, her gay color returning to its magnificent glory, tail flipping and flapping. Carly threw her a piece of cold pizza as he cheered. Felice joined in.

"Careful. Careful. Go slow with the food," said T.W. now grinning widely. "At least we now know that Seteeva gives everyone indigestion."

Although he jested, in his heart he knew that much strife was ahead. Better B. Better and Seteeva Haar were going to be forces to reckon with, especially when they worked together.

CHAPTER THIRTY-SEVEN

# GRAZZELY LAND

That night, Felice entered her room. She ushered Willman in first. The key grated in the lock, dropping back to her waist as she turned toward her friend.

"Sit. Find a seat"

"Sure, Felice. Where?" Laughing he looked around at the books. "Do you have enough?" he teased. There was no empty place to sit. Only her Thinking Chair, so he couldn't sit there.

Felice bustled past him, her skirt rustling against his trouser leg.

"Hmmm? Seat? Where are you?"

'Seat' appeared in the form of a pink upholstered armchair landing between the piles of books that shuffled aside to allow room. She turned to Willman, triumphant.

"Your seat. Sir."

"All yours." He replied. "How about just a table and two chairs?"

"Demanding, aren't you?"

The pink fluff disappeared, quickly replaced by a small desk with two wobbly wooden chairs. Painted yellow.

"Better?"

"Better!"

They both sat.

"Well hurry up, Felice. The anticipation is killing me."

Slowly she lifted the flap of her satchel, reaching in

for the little red gem. Just as slowly she removed it, placing it on the surface before them. Neither one moved. Just looked. Willman sucked in his breath.

"You found it. Unbelievable."

They sat longer, neither one moving. The piles of books sighed. Waiting. The fire wand lit, wanting them to read. Still neither one moved. Until, finally.

"Open it."

"No. You."

"Felice. Open it!"

She did. Lifting the red until all she saw was bronzed parchment. Scrolling handwriting. Tiny painted figures. She read the first words, written in an ancient script.

*"Read me out loud."*

"Go on," said Willman.

"No. You."

"Felice. You're driving me crazy. Read it!"

They both looked at the book. She sighed. "OK! I will."

As she read, the writing rose to meet her eyes, each line zoning in, then out, in, and out. She read, the fire wand growing brighter. As she reached the tenth line the brightness in the room became so white that she could no longer see the book, nor Willman, or anything else. She started to fall.

Falling!

Falling!

**"WILLMAN!"** she cried, her hand reaching, to feel his slide into hers. ***What the hell is happening***

*don't know  just hold on*

***Willman!***

*don't let go of my hand  hold on*

***I won't...  what the heck is...***

Then they were gone.

When they woke they were both laying flat on their backs, their hands still clutched - it was so black they could not see.

**"Willman?"**

"Here."

**"Where are we?"**

"Don't know.  Sssshhh."

They lay in sssshhhhh for some time.  Nothing changed - it was still blacker than the darkest night.

"OK.  Lets go."  Willman pulled her to her feet.

**"Lets go?  Are you kidding me!  To where, may I ask?  Goddam Hawaii?"**

She stood anyway.  Never letting go of his hand.

**"Which way fearless leader?"** She snickered then. ***That's pretty funny... which way?*** It was all blacker than black.  She could not even see her own hand one inch in front of her face.

"Funny, Felice - very funny.  Coming?  Or not!"

He stepped forward - she grasped his hand tighter, moving with him.  They walked, with difficulty, not knowing if each step would hit solid earth.  It was more a shuffle than any walk.  In this way they inched along.  Forever it seemed.  He heard it first.

"Hear that Felice.  A stream!"

She nodded, silently, with no thoughts.

"FELICE!  Do you hear?"

**"Yes, yes.  I hear."**

Inching further, and further.  Not knowing, in the pitch dark, will I walk into something?  ***It is so***

***goddam black! Can't see a damn thing!...*** Felice thought, snickering again, although it didn't feel funny at all. ***Nerves. Just nerves. Keep walking.***

"Keep walking with me Felice. Almost there."

***Almost there - to what!*** She was holding on so tight to Willman's hand, that when he tumbled over the cliff edge she went with him.

Their screams were silent - suffering a mother's grief.

Time slowed.

They fell forever into nothingness.

Finally - they found the stream. More like a river. They plunged into its depths.

*don't let go*

***I won't***

When they woke, they were laying on a cold stone floor, still side-by-side, hands clasped. Their eyes opened at the same time. The ceiling was far too high in the air - and it was made of glass. Neither spoke nor moved. Willman squeezed first - gently with his hand. Felice answered. Gentle - squeeze. They waited. Finally Willman rose, pulling himself up. *At least I can see again.* Looking around wasn't bad. They were in some kind of conservatory. Turning to Felice, beckoning with his eyes. *Get up!*

**"Where are we?"**

"Don't know"

**"You told me to read it aloud."**

"Yes. Well. Shouldn't always do what you are told should you..."

Before the retort flew off her lips, he turned to grin.

"Come on Felice. Have a sense of humor will you."

**"Sense of humor! Where the hell are we?"**

The answer to the question came loud and clear,

like a gong in a temple.

*"In Grazzely Land! Welcome!"*

The beast that spoke, laughed, the feathers on his head rising - Mohawk style. His face was something else, a sagging waste of excess red tissue, thickened, a burn victim from hell. The warts on his neck swelled when he spoke, looking like they would erupt. This beast was full on volcanic style.

Willman turned quickly, his face focusing on the creature moving toward him, the vision shook him to the core - *Holy Cow!*

"Hello" Willman said mildly holding onto his calm, the holy cow running down the corridor, and he wished, he with it.

*"Well hello back,"* the creature said.

Don't look Felice.

***I won't...*** But she did anyway. ***Bitch! Bitching!***

**"What the hell are you?"** She screamed!

The creature bellowed a laugh, his hurt long since forgotten.

*"Not so pretty to look at am I. Still, I have a pretty heart. You wait and see. Dinner is this way. Don't keep me waiting.*

The creature left, down a long chandelier lit hallway, his footsteps galloping buffalo, herding across the plains.

**"Willman?"**

"Felice!"

Pulling Felice to her feet was an experience.

"For christ sake, Felice. Come on."

***"Don't want to go to dinner!"***

"No choice. We're here. Now come on. Don't want to upset our host do we?"

Felice just could not believe this was happening. She had been so happy to find the long lost book. Now look where she was, and that creature! They were going to eat together - or be eaten! She wanted to cry, tears were starting to well when she looked around, really looked for the first time, noticing things in the conservatory that she had not noticed before. There were plants that were taller than circus stilt men - most looked like giant daisies, at least twenty feet in height. They were in bloom, the white petals outlining the yellow center. But when she looked closer, she noticed that the yellow centers were faces. Human faces. Some looked ill. Her eyes met theirs. They bowed, smiling quietly - knowing something she did not. She elbowed Willman, nodding her chin up in that general direction. He looked up. *Hmmm?* There were pots and pots and pots of these, all lined up, crowding the domed roof, their faces turned, pointing up - taking in the rays of sunshine.

*"Come on, I'm waiting!"*

The creature boomed his voice toward them, tinkling glass carrying his message.

Five minutes later they were all seated around a small round table. Crystal glasses, china plates, and lace napkins, lay before them. The creature waved an arm. Dinner was served.

*"Eat! Drink! My guests."*

Merriment was not the greatest visitor - at least not

for the first two hours, but only because of their own fears – their fears of vision. Although Willman noticed as time passed, that the webbed fingers of the creature touched and moved like a princess in love. And his eyes, they were stormy and yet as quiet as a pool in summer. Willman felt more and more comfortable, for their host had been nothing but courteous, even funny and pleasant. Felice started to glance at her host too, seeing his eyes water as he told some story of a weary soul, his leathery hands rubbing back over his feathered head, his elbow digging into the table top as he leaned into his arm for comfort, the memories eating at his heart. She learned to eat without her stomach turning - in fact, she wondered why it had turned in the first place. Finally, she spoke.

"Grazzely Land?" she asked. "Just what is it you do here?"

*"Come. Follow me."*

Their ugly host rose, moving slowly this time with leaden feet, leading the way down the corridor to the high ceiling conservatory. As they entered, every towering daisy in the room turned toward them - or was it toward the creature - the creature with the ugly face and the beautiful heart – the daisies bowed with whispers of thanks.

Felice nudged Willman.

"Look - that one - with the young face - is that little Jimmy?"

Willman sucked in his breath. It was. He turned, looking at their host full on. "What?" was all he could utter.

This question brought a crooked smile to the face before him - a smile that lit up the folds of disaster - a bright light in a dank alley full of drunks and homeless people.

*"What indeed! My fine young fellow! What indeed?"*

Willman turned back toward the tall plant.

"Jimmy?" He had seen the tiny fellow in Chetsy.

The daisy head just nodded as if in a breeze, before looking back up at the sunlight, through the wide expanse of glass. The creature chimed in.

*"Recuperating! Just recuperating! May survive or they may not. Best I can do. Give 'em a chance at least - a resting place in between life and death. That one there was blown apart by a bomb at Pearl Harbor - still hasn't left or gone back. Can't rush the process - all up to them."*

"But...?" Felice started.

*"Ah, and that group over there. All from the building of that one pyramid, with the falling of so many stones, the engineers made big mistakes on that one... and oh, that singular tall stalk,"*

*- the face looked down at them, a middle aged man with brown eyebrows and a silver beard - "he was beaten by a gang in the subways, his body still lays in a coma at University Hospital. Up to him if he ever wakes up."*

"But...?" Felice tried again.

*"Ha! May be leaving us soon?"* the creature crooned to the three daisies that had turned their smiling faces down to look at him, *"empty pots - room for more!"* His bellowing laughter shifted a stalk or two. He turned to Willman - *"revolution!"* was all he said, *"looks like they are going back."*

They walked amongst the pots, each plant a giant beanstalk. The creature carried a large watering can, pouring a thick oily liquid onto each as he passed.

*"They need this, ten times a day - amongst other things."*

One plant they reached, was black, withering...

*"Oh, my friend, farewell, so many years here, I wish you well on your journey."*

The creature bowed to the dying plant before him, the daisy head wilting to the ground. The yellow face dropped to ground level, close to Willman. Just then, the lips moved, as the blush in her cheeks faded.

*"Too much bleeding... held on until you came... love my husband... tell him, please...*

Then the face wilted into the pot - its petals curling inward.

"Who?" Was all Willman could utter. He would never forget that face. It was not in pain, not suffering, not sad, had a small smile. Just in peace.

*"Jebber's wife,"* the creature said, *"your grandmother."*

Willman watched, startled, as the plant started to melt into the soil - until nothing was left.

*"Fertilizing, ready for the next one - better to pass on what little energy is left."*

T.W. stepped forward, lifting some of the soil, letting it filter through his fingers. *Theadora's mother? My Grandmother?* He looked at the creature then, and saw a tear filter down its face, attempting the difficult course. Willman gulped back his own tears – he saw the grief in his new friend and wondered how he could take it, day after day, night after night.

As he stood mourning, a short thick stalk started to grow out of the pot, an inch at a time, until it reached seventeen feet, with leaves on either side. Finally a bloom emerged, opening wide - its center just stamens. The stamens turned into hair, eyebrows, eyelashes - the center of the bloom becoming pink. Lips taking form, cheeks protruding - until finally, it was a face. Old. Grizzly. Its lips grey. Puckering.

*"Heart attack. This one will probably live to*

*a hundred. Doesn't know it. Won't be here long. Just needs a place to think about things. To realize that life is pretty good. He'll go back soon. No family - just a million friends. Gives more than he takes. Won't be here long as I said."*

Before they had even moved away, the face looked down from the sunlight, smiling:

*T h a n k  y o u.* It mouthed, before the flower melted.

*"Room for another one!"* the creature mirthed, watering can in hand, his tears the source of replenishment, the can never empty.

Hearing a sob, which was not his own, The Keeper looked around - Willman's shoulders were stooped.

*"Come son, we have no control over our forefathers, we just help where we can, accept that and you will be at peace - she knew you would come one day and was so curious to know what you would look like - she got to see you, she left happy."*

Willman thought about this as the creature led them away. He glanced behind once. He saw two daisies starting to droop - the rest of them held their faces up to the glass.

*Who are they?* he thought.

Back in the dining room, they sat, and the creature sighed, a low moan escaping a birthing cow – full of fear and love and pain.

*"Do you understand what Grazzely Land is now?"*

They both nodded. "Thank you sir. Your job is a hard one. Yet you remain cheerful."

*"All souls should be cheerful. Including me!"* At this he laughed, his mirth returning. His laughter was merriment. His laughter was nourishment to the soul. His laughter was needed, a blessing, a thankful sound that fed the waterfalls of spirits and ghouls and ghosts and trolls.

Willman smiled then.

The Keeper of Souls was a fine fellow indeed.

"Thank you, friend."

*"Thank you."*

*Time to go Felice.*

Holding out his hand.

She took it... and they were gone.

When they woke, he was laying in the pink poofy armchair that had previously disappeared. She was in her Thinking Chair. They did not move for a long time, until finally Willman said, "shall we look at the book some more?"

In silence they moved to the table with the wobbly chairs.

"Want to start reading aloud again, Felice?"

"Not really, Willman. Do you?"

"No, not really."

Silence for five minutes, until he could resist no longer.

"So, what does it say now?"

"Don't read aloud anymore."

"Shut up! It doesn't."

"It does really. Look!"

He did look... And it did say that.

"Want a shot of whiskey?" he asked, relieved. She did. Even though she had never had one before. They toasted, clinking glasses. Then they read, well into the night.

## CHAPTER THIRTY-EIGHT

# TOMBHRA AND WILLMAN

Willman rose groggily the next morning, making it to his lunch date just in time. He, Tombhra and Kelly meandered down the lane toward the driftwood-strewn beach. T.W. was deep in his thoughts. Neither he nor Theadora had realized that the spirit from the mannequin was Lillian's daughter - at least not until he had chatted with them that day. *And I'm in love with her - in love with this woman who lives inside an old woman's body. What a mess.* Frowning, he glanced around at the townies passing by. He had come to know many in a short time, but wondered - *what would happen if I stopped here, in the middle of Main Street, and took her into my arms?* His heart raced at the thought, a steam engine going full tilt. It would be Tombhra he was kissing, and he wanted to ever so badly, but he knew it would look like he wanted to take his granny to bed. He didn't care what people thought, but how would Kelly survive. He didn't want to make her life difficult. She could be shunned, treated poorly. Although there would be some, he knew, that would understand true love. His frowns crinkled deeper - *I love Tombhra too much - Kelly too.* He wanted no discomfort for either of them, so he kept his puckering lips to himself. *Maybe I could hold her hand...* His fingers twitched at the thought, but then, with great effort, he jammed his hands in his pockets, knowing right now, that this was for the best.

Tombhra sighed as she eyed T.W. with a sideways glance. She felt sure he had been about to kiss her. When she was with him she forgot she was inside Kelly's old body, rusty and dented as it was. Would that put him off? Would he quit stopping by the shop, asking if she wanted to meet for a walk, or asking to take her for a coffee at Lance's? It had been difficult to get used to at first, being inside Kelly's body. But this was even more strange, because now, as they walked down the lane, the conversation was not a conversation between the two of them, it was between three.

Willman walked on. He felt like Kelly was on one side and Tombhra the other as they meandered along. They were content to be in each other's company. Their walk had progressed along the beach and back - the lapping of the water, the crunch of shells, the call of the gulls, all melded to make a timeless state. Reality, however, raised its head. Lunch break was over. Willman escorted them both back to the chocolate shop. He opened the door, then stepped aside, the tinkle of the bell announcing their return.

"Fancy a night out tonight?" he asked, not being able to help himself - the thought of not being with these two until tomorrow left a burning pain in his chest. "There's a band playing," he added for extra persuasion. "I can invite Thea and Carly as a cover."

"Cool!" Tombhra and Kelly replied together, causing an echoing effect of their voice, "I love to dance!"

This from two of his most favorite voices caused him to break into laughter.

"Pick you up at six-thirty... see you later," his voice gruff with excitement.

"How titillating," murmured Tombhra as she watched her love walk down the red brick alley. She turned to grin at Kelly. At times it seemed they were two separate bodies. Kelly grinned back. Then they both walked as one behind the counter, humming to themselves in anticipation.

## CHAPTER THIRTY-NINE

# DANCING AT THE GREEN COW

Six-thirty came fast and furious. Well, at least for Kelly. The shop was busy, customers came and went, dark chocolaty smells melted the air, freshly baked scones beckoned as Medusa's snakes became roses, and head banging coffee twisted arms into submission – a wrestler in top form. Kelly barely had time to look at the clock, although Tombhra did. Time started to feel a bit like it did when she was locked inside the mannequin. Having to wait to see Willman again, even though she had just seen him, was torture of the racking kind. She sighed more than once, but the anticipation kept her buoyant. Between the two of them, they made it.

Tombhra was dancing on her tippy toes by the time he knocked on the now locked door of the shop. She opened up, planting a kiss on his cheek before she could even think about it. No one moved. But as in the game, stone statues, played in freezing weather, they could not stay still for long.

"Let's go!" T.W. said, breaking the ice. He turned away, a huge grin across his face. *WOW! Tombhra just kissed me.*

The three waltzed over to The Green Cow, fun oozing from their pores, chatter passing back and forth like hors d'oeuvres at a party. The loud music opened the door for them. It blew their hair back, stroked their scalps, littered their ears. It was a humming, drumming, jiving, rhythm of sound. All three felt the thrumming of the walls, the movement of the floor - they started to sway harder than timbers on a stormy day. Old feet may look old, but they never forget the beat. Kelly was back in her younger days - she was swinging. Tombhra was rocking with her and Willman was right behind.

All three waved to Theadora and Carly who had reserved a table with enough seats for everyone. With them was Bunting. She immediately jumped up to join them on the dance floor. The walls of The Green Cow were rumbling like distant thunder. The Willman grabbed a hold of Tombhra's waist, waltzing her around in a small circle, then he did the two-step, the tango - she threw her head back laughing. He released her as Carly stepped up to take the twirling Kelly into his arms. T.W. put his arms out and around Bunting, spinning her around the floor in the same flourish as he had Tombhra.

"See what the rumormongers make of this," he laughed into Buntings ear while casting his yearning eyes toward Tombhra. She caught his look - echoing his sentiment.

Tombhra was ecstatic beyond words. Her world had been deprived for so long, entombed in her iron cast of the mannequin, shaped in the figure of a woman that could not feel nor want. She was so full of emotions that it was a sin to be encased so. And now she had escaped the mannequin to be captured again in a body that was far older than her years. But she didn't care. *She didn't!* She could feel, and talk and walk, laugh and dance. The age of Kelly's mind felt comforting in some ways, and yet, the old and crumbling shell of Kelly's body left them both feeling confused. Tombhra was young. Kelly still felt young inside, yet her body, when she looked in the mirror did not match who she was inside. It was just all so confusing to both of them. How could one be so old and yet feel so young. They talked of this often, both experiencing the same thing, yet from different views. For tonight though, they decided not to care, so they just kept on dancing. Kelly Keen was keenly aware that she would pay for it with more than a few aches and pains in the morning. *I'll probably feel like kneaded dough - bet I won't want to rise though.* This thought made her grin. *Yes, you will granny,* whispered Tombhra. *I'll help you.*

At some point in the evening Harry Tomb stepped over to dance with Kelly. He was grinning from ear to ear not believing that Kelly could dance like that. A grin split his face in half as he gyrated his hips back and forth, his arms jiggling around in the air like seaweed in a storm. Although he had been Kelly's date on Brendan's birthday night, he was not Tombhra's date tonight. Willman interceded, whisking Tombhra off across the dance floor. Kelly stepped back, giving Tombhra full access to her body, but she did manage a glance back to see the bewildered look on Harry's face. *Do the old blighter good,* she thought, *I'm no easy picking.* Tombhra simply sparkled brighter than any star, "thanks Kelly," she whispered.

Brendan was serving behind the bar that night. He looked on in amazement at Kelly dancing like Tina Turner. More than a few comments were launched from his lips, none bad, he really did like Kelly - it was just that he was amazed at how that woman could dance! This was the first time he had pulled himself out of his reverie of despair. The nightmares were still invading his sleep.

It was more than sad when the evening ended. But end it had too. Everyone went home, but at least home with smiling lips. All except Harry - he marched back to his Crayola house and threw himself into his brown leather armchair, not moving until his cat rubbed against his leg. Harry absentmindedly reached down to scratch his furry friend - - he had never felt so perplexed in his life. He could think of nothing but Kelly. That whole night he dreamed of her, she was a belly dancer in some foreign place. And he was the one she danced for. He didn't want to wake up it was SO DAMN GOOD! The same wonderful dream repeated itself, night after night, after which he would eventually wake, early each morning. Then he would belly dance himself into the bathroom full of scrumptious warm memories from the dream. Moving to the mirror one morning, he looked at himself.

"Better shape up old boy! You've got competition." He shaved, took a pair of tiny scissors into his great big hands, snip snipped at the hair that was starting to peek out of his nose, then combed back his silver locks. "That should do it," grinning into the mirror. He didn't feel like breakfast at all. He was in love. He had known Kelly forever, they had always talked - why, oh why, had he not seen it so clearly before. Today, he decided, would be the first day. He was going to woo his baby back from the big guy. So off he set, on a brisk walk into Chetsy to find the woman who had become his heartthrob.

CHAPTER FORTY

# HARRY TOMB NEEDS GLASSES

Harry walked around in town for a while, not having the courage to actually go to Kelly. He'd spotted her with his competition many times since the night of the dance - he wasn't sure what to do. It was later, toward lunchtime that he saw her - headed toward the beach with that big moron! *Should he?* He hesitated, but only for a second. *What the hell, Harry! Go for it*! He called out.

"KELLY! KELLY! Over here..."

The three turned toward him as Harry trotted over.

"Hi, Harry."

Harry nodded briefly at Willman before giving his full attention to Kelly. His eyes sparkled like ice crystals, melting in her warmth. He felt nervous though, squirming at the thought that she might actually turn him down.

"Want to sit with me, Kelly. Enjoy the sunshine. We could chat for a while." Harry's head nodded toward the nearby bench.

Kelly looked at T.W.

"You go ahead, Kelly. I think we can stretch that far, time to try it anyway. Enjoy yourself. We'll just be a short ways away."

Harry looked at Willman in a quizzical way. Just as he thought, he was a big idiot - what was all this 'we' stuff. Still he didn't care. Kelly was choosing to sit with him. His heart skipped like a kid with a rope. He took her hand, she didn't resist - his chest thumped –

who needed a band when your heart could play the drums. Gently he led her to the bench, seating himself once she was comfortable. He only glanced up once to watch the departing Willman. His glance lingered longer than planned. The big oaf was talking as if Kelly was still beside him.

"Jeesus. Hope he doesn't become a total whack job."

"Say again?" said Kelly.

Harry grimaced, deciding not to repeat himself. He didn't want to upset his new girlfriend now did he, so he pulled his attention back to the woman sitting beside him, resisting the urge to turn and watch some more.

"We can go a little ways down the beach my love. It's o.k. I've figured it out. I can carry your spirit a small distance from Kelly's body, then take you back again. We can't go far though. Maybe just to that giant rock. We could sit there, have our privacy."

"Alright. So long as you are sure," replied Tombhra. She wanted to so badly.

Willman reached out to touch the golden shimmering shadow that hazily stood beside him. His hand grazed her. She shivered, moaning slightly.

"Come on!" He took her hand as they walked toward the rock.

Harry sneaked another look. He couldn't help it. *This was bizarre,* he watched the big duffus walking away with one arm held out to the side. He wondered about Kelly a bit then. *Was she a nut job too?* He thought about this for a minute before deciding he didn't care. He liked her just the way she was.

Tombhra and Willman reached the rock. No words were needed, just the touch of their souls. Time alone was precious. Sitting down, they leaned back, resting peacefully, in silence, pondering their thoughts. It was Tombhra that moved first, leaning in for a kiss. Willman did not need to be asked twice. As they melted into one another, their lips touched – tingles, sweet dreams.

Time became nothing. No thoughts. No awareness. No one else. No existence. This earth was their own - or were they in space, floating toward eternity? Tombhra hazed in and out. Willman's heart simply stopped.

After a long while, their lips parted - they leaned back onto the rock, side by side, their hands entwined, content with being together. Some time passed before the rock they were leaning against moved!

"A i v e h a i v a c r a a a m m p..."

Willman stood up quickly then laughed.

"THELMA! How on earth did you get here?"

"M a a y n e k k k... ooooooh..."

The rock moved even more as she stretched her giant neck out.

"Y a z z u u r... t h a t h e e r t... T o o o k y u r t i e m k e e s s i n g d e e d n ' t y o o o...!

Willman just grinned. Tombhra blushed, her golden glow turning crimson at the edges.

Back at the bench, Harry was taking another sneaky

look. His eyesight had been off lately, but... *that rock just moved, I'll be damned if it didn't*, his eyes squinted, until Kelly stood to maneuver herself in front of him.

By now, Willman had become worried - he came down from his Tombhra high.

"Is anything wrong back home Thelma? Why are you here?"

"Eeeel mennn goottt aruunnd thu caive-stowl a miror. Waanted tooo leettt you knoww... toook a reeesk cooming..."

Willman was silent. *Eel Men in the village! Coming to Chetsy. This will not help matters.* But he knew he could do nothing right now except protect the ones he loved - to do what was right.

"Thanks for the warning, Thelma. I'll be on the look out. Can you get home safely?"

"Jooost waait fooor the taide... soonken shieep oot theer weth meero rs."

Then she smiled, the first time Willman had ever seen it. A big toothless smile that made her more beautiful than Cleopatra - she knew she had done what was needed.

"Proud of you taking the chance, Thelma." He patted her then on her long neck, which no longer had the big oozing sores. "We'd better get back, ole Harry there is about to not know which way is up... and this won't help either!" Willman reached his face high to kiss Thelma on her cheek - he had to grow in size to do it. He laughed, knowing that the old blighter was sneaking another look.

*I'll be damned,* Harry thought, peeking around Kelly... his hand in a salute to shade his sight from the sun - *think my eyes are all buggered up!*

## CHAPTER FORTY-ONE

# THE THINKING CHAIR

Theadora was in her kitchen, the fire roaring as a cool wind rattled the windows. The big red door that led to the small kitchen was closed. She stood at the chopping block dicing potatoes, her mind straying. When she was in town a few days ago she had bumped into Tom, an old friend who was raising his two children on his own. What concerned her was Tom's almost weeping report of his son, Jimmy. Jimmy, he said, who was always such a vibrant son, and known as a bit of a prankster to his family, was ill. At first she had thought it was just a normal child illness, the flu or cold. But as Tom had talked on, his emotions becoming more raw as the description of his son echoed in her head, she started to dawn.

In the end, he was talking to her in hitching breaths. He'd told her, that although he had taken Jimmy to the doctors, over and over again, they could find nothing. Blood tests normal, x-rays normal, ultrasound normal. They had even done a C.T. scan. In the end they told him that Jimmy was just tired and depressed. Some had suggested antidepressive drugs. They said there was nothing they could do because everything tested normal. One doctor even told Jimmy to just snap out of it. That or go to a psychiatrist. Another doctor had even indicted that Tom was the problem and that he should get help.

Tom felt let down. Furious. Helpless.

His son was tired, yes, for sure he was. In fact, he

was so tired he had no life left in him. For the first time to anyone, Tom expressed his real fear to Theadora.

"I think he's dying, Thea. He just lays there. No awareness. And no one will help. I don't know what to do, Theadora," he gasped, "I just don't know what to do." He hitched a breath again, "and even though he is so tired all the time, the little tike still plays his hide and seek games. He falls asleep, then in the middle of the night I get up to check on him and he's gone. I wander the house. You know it is huge and rambling Theadora, too many crooks and crannies - Jimmy has hidden in them for more years than I can remember. So I fall asleep on the couch for an hour after searching, then later, I find him back in bed. But... but... he doesn't look right. He doesn't look like Jimmy any more. Some... some... sometimes," Tom gasped, "sometimes, I think that he is not my son anymore. He doesn't look like my little Jimmy." Then he started to cry.

She hugged him, saying nothing, having been hushed into her own silence.

Now she was still in her hushed silence except that her mind was in a roar with thoughts of the evilness of Muckdeannes. It was at this moment that her son returned home. He spent some time each day with Tombhra, while Kelly sat with Harry, although he knew he must stay focused. He stepped in through the door, all fifteen feet of him. Even though it was not difficult for him to maintain his smaller form, he enjoyed letting the magic rest. He liked just being himself sometimes. Usually, when the two were at home together - he would laugh when he watched his mother walk through one of the doorways, the arched top towering above her head, the ceiling of the room even higher. She looked like she was a figure in a cartoon. Theadora smiled too when she heard her son happy. But now he wasn't laughing when he watched her move through the pantry door, nor was she. They took a moment of stillness to lock eyes before Willman moved again. The red door closed behind him as he stepped toward the giant armchair next to the warmth - next to the fire place, that was of course, big enough to roast a pig.

"We have two hours before the crew arrives, Thea. I need to pay a visit. May be the last one."

"I'll be here when you get back." She said nothing more, her silence speaking loudest.

T.W. watched her chop in a four-four rhythm, busy getting a pot of stew going on the old stove. She was as quiet as he, their thoughts mingling in the air. The smell of simmering broth invaded the room as fat dumplings danced on the surface, pigs performing water ballet. The delicious scent of a yeasty sour dough marched behind the broth, climbing out of the earthenware bowl that sat on the tabletop. The clock ticked, until he lifted himself from his comfortable place, needing to leave before their friends came. He pushed through the red door before crossing the smaller kitchen, stepping toward the door to the Room of Secrets - it opened, allowing him entrance. Inside, in the corner, on the wall opposite the mirror, was a Thinking Chair. It was different to Felice's. This one had a high arched back with intricately carved figures - pixies, elves, dragons, fairies and giants. The Powamander breathed fire from the end of one arm.

The Dittermore's tongue hung from the other.

Willman moved slowly toward the chair. *I need help*. That was all he thought.

He sat, laying his forearms so that one hand fell into the fire, the other onto the tongue. He breathed.

In and out.

His breaths became shallow... until they stopped. His chest did not move. Not a wisp of air. He was gone. Time no longer passed.

The first thing he saw made him laugh. It was he. Looking into a shop front, his reflection giving him wings - fairy wings. They were big and airy, spun of golden silk. He beat them a little, watching his feet lift off the ground - his toes pointing down, ballerina style as he rose up.

*Ah, nice, but not where I need to be.*

Nothing again.

Nothingness.

He was in the shipyard now. A figure ran towards him. It was headless, its body charred, yet still the beetles beat - bits of flesh breaking off, hitting the earth like hailstones. The shape ran towards him with the beetle heads running behind, whips lashing louder than a tornado ripping the earth. The body hurled itself toward him. He caught it. Then it crumbled in his hands.

In the room of secrets his chest heaved. Once.

The shipyard went away.

Nothing again.

Nothingness.

He turned his head. He was laughing. The demon daughter caught his lips with hers. They were sour.

His lips became black. Dried up. Putrid. Rotting off his face. She kissed him again, her teeth hitting his, lips no longer there. "My husband..." He shivered, turning away to see what he had been laughing at. It was Tredor. He was dancing. But then he saw he was not. He was jumping to avoid the whips. He pushed the demon daughter then. She fell onto a giant wasp, its sting piercing her chest. Grabbing Tredor, the whips lashing his legs, his lips gone, he ran.

Nothing again.

Nothingness.

The nice eyes crinkled at him. He wanted to stay.

Sophia?

"Not here." she said.

Nothing again.

Nothingness.

The tongue grazed his cheek. It was rough. He pushed it away. *Not here either.* But nothingness did not come.

It grazed him again, pushing his head hard to the side.

"Good fellow. At last, we meet. Wakey wakey. Rise and shine." Dante the Dittermore licked his face again. "Slow to wake, aren't we?"

*Not here!*

"Yes. Yes. Here. Now wakey wakey."

Willman opened his eyes groggily. The creature before him licked again, pushing him onto his behind since he had been crouched to begin with.

"Ready to stand. Bit slow, aren't you?"

Then Dante started to waltz down the tiny path before him, humming a nice tune as he went. He disappeared.

*Knew this wasn't it.*

Seconds passed. Minutes.

*Not it.*

Minutes more. He was still here. *Guess this IS it.*

"WAIT! FOR ME! I'm coming, wait!"

Willman lifted himself and ran down the path into the dense thicket, following the Dittermore. It didn't stay dense for long, just a boundary. Beyond that, it opened up, a mammoth lawn, green and short stretched before him.

The first duck that met him was yellow, talking between mouthfuls of grass.

"Don't step on the grass. Trimming. Now."

Willman followed the path, careful not to step where he shouldn't. The second duck was red.

"Don't step on the grass. Careful. Careful."

The third, fourth, fifth, sixth and seventh ducks were all blue.

"Don't step on the grass," they quacked, pecking at his feet each time. The lawn stretched endlessly before him, ducks everywhere, the path disappearing into the distance.

That was enough! This was the wrong path. He turned around, headed back toward the thicket - *forget Dante!*

The thicket was thick and dense. Willman was happy to enter it after the vastness. Once inside, he slowed. *What now?* Unlike when he passed through the first time, now it didn't end. He walked and walked. Some distance in, although he could continue straight, there was a small moss worn path veering to the east, with a sign and a purple arrow.

Take It! THE SIGN SAID, the arrow pointing to the right.

He did.

It went a long way before it opened into a garden with mustard, cress and mint. Gardenias tall, in full bloom. A large oak tree stood in the middle, one branch, almost as thick as the trunk itself, stretched out to the side. From that hung a swing on which Dante the Dittermore swung - humming to himself.

"Room for one more!" He sung, swinging.

Willman joined him, feeling strange swinging with this creature. Dante the Dittermore had a very long tongue, which he liked to lick out into the distance, picking fruit up off the ground.

"Want one?" The apricot stuck to the tip waiting to be plucked. He flicked it around in front of Willman. "Want it?"

Willman grabbed. It made a squelching sound as he pulled it off the tongue. It was bigger than any apricot he had ever seen, juicy and succulent. He bit into it, feeling better right away.

"Glad you made it at last. Took your time as I said."

"Sorry." Willman said, biting the last bite of the succulent fruit.

Dante jumped forward, shoving the swinging seat way back into the air, Willman with it.

"Off we go then," he said with a dish and a dash, and was gone again.

As the seat swung back to earth, T.W. leaped off, chasing this strange creature yet again. The path this time, was curved, that way and this. Until finally, before him was a house. He saw Dante enter, slamming the door behind him. Willman slowed. He wasn't sure about entering four walls that could enclose around him. He sat down. On the large rock. Thinking. After some time - *still here, better move...*

"Anyone home?" he pushed the front door open.

Before him was the biggest hallway he had ever seen. Not just tall... or wide. It just stretched on forever. He stepped back out the front door again, moving to one side of the house. He glanced the length. *Hmm? The inside doesn't fit.* Then he moved back to the front door. Taking a deep breath, he entered. The hallway still stretched too far - wide, yet narrow at the same time, with doors on either side and bright, like the sun, with no end in sight. Willman walked forward. Either that or leave. He paused at the first door. Hand on the handle.

*N O!*

Second and third.

*N O! N O!*

It went on, until the seventh door on the right. It was brown, deep earth. The knob was round, fitting his hand. He entered. Inside was Dante, smoking a cigar by the fireplace and there were walls lined with books, aisles and aisles of books.

"Take a walk, look around." Dante puffed on the cigar, his tongue wrapped around its base.

Willman nodded his acknowledgement before turning to the left. The rows of books were daunting, the aisles disappearing into the depths. He took the third row and walked. On either side of him the books talked, a million miles a minute.

*Tens of thousands, sizes not important, tadpoles and newts, lightening called*

*Square the root by three, then divide by four, throw in a gem or two*

*Find a camel, take the hump - roast it up with sage and the hand of a Cretznul*

*Take your time think a while*

*Open me, I can tell you where to be*

*Come here, I am the one - bring to me the blue red ring*

*Pull me out, scent of twelve, pain of head, see and sight, no more plight*

The voices went on and on. Willman walked. Not to be distracted. Until he reached the end of the row. Puzzled - shouldn't he have found his answer? Before him was a wall painted pink flamingo. He turned away from it, ready to walk the aisle again. As he took the first step, he heard a swish, a slide. Glancing back he saw the wall no more, it was gone. Beyond was a dining room, with a beautiful round silver table covered with etchings of fables - holding it up, was a hippo with a happy face. All of the seats were filled, except one. He moved toward it. Sitting down, he looked around.

On his left was Hayban, his right Jebber. Directly opposite was Dante. To the right of Dante, was Sophia - to his left was Powamander. On the table in front of him, was Jazz.

*Just your thoughts son, we are just your thoughts - you know what to do - we are here always - look to your right, through the window...*

The light was bright through that window - he had to move closer to see. Outside was a small boy running across the lawn. He fell as he ran, tumbling down the small incline. His tumbling increased in momentum, rolling hard, until he hit the solid trunk of the birch standing tall.

"Ouch! Yowzee! That hurt!" said Willman, looking up at the tall tree before him. He was but just a lad. Reaching his fingers up, he rubbed his shoulder. He felt the damp earth seeping through his trousers, so he stood. Once standing, he still rubbed. He tried to lift his arm, not getting far before he stopped, pain digging in - an ice pick at work - making him wince. On the floor before him was a glass vial that had fallen out of his pocket. He knew that is what he needed for his shoulder. He reached his good arm out, but before his own hand could grab it, another came out of the grass, taking it before he.

"Hey! That's mine!" yelled Willman, his short legs racing after the glow of the vial - his shoulder yelping at him with each leap. He ran for a long time, so long that he had time to grow again. Becoming the giant that he was. His shoulder was still hanging limp, so he continued to chase. He needed that vial! "Bugger it all!" he yelled again.

"Tut. Tut. Swearing is not acceptable."

Willman stopped. *Now who said that?* Then he ran again. The hand in front of him raced along, grasping the silver glass between thumb and forefinger, its three remaining fingers scurrying at great speed. Willman's legs grew longer and longer, until finally he caught up. He leapt, his giant form hurling through the air, his body landing with a *plumph* on top of the running hand. "Got you!" was all he managed to utter before he felt wetness seeping through his shirt. He rolled over, groaning, the vial shattered and useless. He put his one good hand up to his forehead in despair. Now he would never get his arm back. Rolling to his side, he poked at the hand. *Pokey poke.* It didn't move. He rubbed his forehead harder. *What do I know about you? Huh? Hand. Did I kill you?* A shard of glass had pierced the palm. As he lay there, he thought of nothing more to do than rub at his shoulder. Massaging. Back and forth. Until finally, feeling came back. His arm lifted. His fingers moved. Twiddling back and forth. He groaned inwardly. No vial needed. Why had he not slowed down to think. *Pokey poke.* The hand still did not move. *Pokey poke.* After a while, where the silver liquid had stained his shirt, the cloth started to fall apart, becoming fragments of the finery it had once been. His skin scorched beneath, flaking off from the poison. *I was going to drink that - for my shoulder.* He looked at the hand, lifeless, dead. It had saved his life. He sobbed.

He woke in his Thinking Chair.

To nothingness.

The Dittermore's tongue caressed his hand. His other warmed in Powamander's flame. He could not move for a while. Sitting there. His friends carved around him. It was some time before he rose, stepping out through the Door of Secrets. He moved back into the kitchen - Theadora said nothing, she let her son rest in his chair by the fire. An hour passed.

"Maybe you should visit one of the paintings before they arrive." Theadora tuned into her son's state, knowing he needed help. "Go on. Won't take a minute."

Willman stood. He felt heavy. Again the door to the Room of Secrets opened. Many paintings lined the walls. He glanced around. The only one that caught his eye was the one with the Delfars swinging in the trees. So he stepped toward it, melting into the greenery the same as he melted into the mirror.

He woke in the bosom of the Delfars den, laying in the orange glow of one of their swinging homes. Tredor's face hung over him. Chittering. Slapping him lightly. Trevor was close by, stroking his wrist. All he could do was smile. His soul lit up. He sat, raising his body, legs stretched out before him, reaching his arms high up over his head.

"Feels like I've slept forever. Hmm. Lovely."

Rejuvenation.

He was on his feet, ecstatic, hanging out of the round window, pointing at the village in the distance.

"Hey look!" He hadn't visited since going back to Chetsy. This was great. Willman realized that he was the same size as the Delfars. This made him grin. "Let's swing!"

He leapt out of the small round hole while grabbing at the hanging vine that swung him to the next tree, then the next, and the next, vine after vine. Tredor was right behind, chattering the whole way. Trevor followed. Soon, the village was not in sight and different trees appeared. Their vines were different. Willman laughed out loud, swinging high, then... THUMP... he hit the first of the blue oval fruit that hung in clusters from the big leafed tree. Tredor had stopped a short ways back - sitting on a branch of one of the giant orange trees - not wanting to go further. He had never seen the grove with the blue hanging clusters before. When he saw his friend falling to the ground, hitting branch after branch, he lost no time swinging into unknown territory. The last branch that Willman fell from was twenty feet up - he was headed hard toward earth. That is when something pink appeared, swinging beneath, catching Willman, then cradling his body in its palm before lowering him like a baby to the ground. It was The Hand. It rescued Willman before Tredor could. It stroked his face, one long finger gently caressing, the others resting calmly. Tredor landed nearby, Trevor not far behind - they chittered and jittered, hugging each other. Not sure. What to do? Should they dash in, bite fingers, so that they could drag their friend out. Instead, they decided to wait. Still chittering on the ground.

The Hand stayed - stroking.

Eventually, Willman came too.

As he rolled onto his side, he saw The Hand before him. Not being able to help himself - tears started. That is when the words whispered around him... *thinking chair... only thoughts... to learn... you learned... your thoughts gave birth to me. Hand is alive... good man... you.*

Willman calmed, his upset quieting. It was always so real in the Thinking Chair.

*Tredor had been w*atching, he slowly moved closer, creeping gingerly across the ground, his silver hair on end, his pigtail sticking straight out, pink face crinkled in anticipation. He gingerly reached out his arm to touch the fingers. The fingers waited a while before lifting to touch back. Stroking the fur gently. *Tredor likes this.* Trevor, however was not so sure – he stayed back, by one of the giant orange trees. The hand, finally curious, moved toward him like a crab. TREVOR SCREAMED, his mouth a donut 'O', before running as fast as he could to scramble up the nearest trunk. The Hand didn't chase him - just fumbled around on the ground in a wretched way at having scared the little guy. Willman watched. He couldn't help it. He started to laugh and laugh and laugh, rolling in mirth. Tredor joined in. Tizzie caught up then, even though he wasn't in the picture. They all rolled together, until eventually Trevor came out of the tree to enjoy a rickety ride on the back of the very patient Hand.

Next Willman knew, he was back in his armchair in the kitchen. Laughing. Thea handed him his whiskey, glad to see relief line his mouth - then she lifted the trapdoor in the kitchen floor, releasing odors of must, herbs and garlic as she stepped down onto the first cold flag step, and then the next, until her head dropped from view. It was only minutes later that a tap tap tap announced the arrival of guests - the knockers entered as the door creaked open, groaning its greeting as it allowed entry. As usual, Able came first. He jetted across the room, a green and orange blur traveling so fast he left a contrail - he loved Willman. Perching himself on the back of the enormous chair, he neatly folded his wings into place before reaching down to preen the giant's wayward hair. Mandy came next, his amethyst eyes beading their way toward the warmth. On seeing Mandy, Bucklin, Thea's pet grasshopper, crawled higher up the grey stone of the chimney just in case the feline mistook him for a fish head. Once at a safe height he let his bony legs play the violin. Bunting entered, dancing to Bucklin's song (was it a Miles Davis tune?) as she followed Mandy - she took one of the two small armchairs close to the heat, sinking into the cushions with a sigh. Felice, right behind, took the other, shifting her weight to avoid a poking spring. Carly sat at the big rough table, his finger tracing the name carved into its surface - *Hayban.*

"Glad to see you've made yourselves at home," Thea said as she returned from the cellar. "Wine anyone?"

"Funny girl!" Carly said, quickly gathering glasses from an oak sideboard then placing them on the table next to his seat. The cork came out with a gentle plop. Theadora poured - the dark burgundy blossoming as it filled the big round globes. Two of these she left on the table, the others floated over to the ladies that were nestled comfier than robins. Carly swirled the liquid high to the rim - wine art he called it.

"A toast!"

Everyone raised their glasses to aromas of berries, as chocolate and plum filled their palates.

"Hmm. Delicious. Damn good choice, Thea," Felice said.

"What are we eating," asked Bunting, her mind

always on food, "Oh! Yum!" She watched her friend slide a hearty loaf from the stone in the oven onto a wooden paddle. "Can't wait!" She eyed the potent Brie that was starting to melt, ripening to perfection, like a peach in Georgia tasted in the heat of the day. Then she spotted the chunk of English Stilton with its massive veins of blue and green. "Whoa, Theadora! That cheese looks like it has its own legs to walk on! Puurfect! Let's eat!"

"Ttt. Ttt. Slow down, Bunting. Bread needs to cool. Just wait a bit." Thea slapped the air in Buntings direction, making everyone laugh.

After some general chit chat, Theadora broke the bread, placing half of it on a thick wooden board along with chunks of the two stink in heaven cheeses - then she duplicated this on another much used platter. She placed the board on a small round table near to the old stuffed full of stuffing arm chairs, the platter went on the centuries old table where she joined Carly.

"Now you can eat!" she said. This was an order that was not difficult to obey - the smell of baking made even the parrot drool. Everyone dug in, tearing off chunks of the crusty bread, smearing the delightful cheese onto one piece or another. Glasses were raised, more toasts made. Fine aged cheese with a crusty baguette - food of the earth.

Each murmured their appreciation - Willman passed a piece of sourdough to Able, who joyfully grabbed it with his grey Tonka Toy feet before holding it up to his beak to nibble at - some crumbs fell, littering his giant friend's hair - snowflakes not melting in the heat. They talked between one another for a while until the meeting was called to order.

Felice spoke first, telling of her encounter with Setėeva Haar. She informed all about the brand on her head, right in the center of her bald spot.

"I recognized it immediately as a Selon," she told the others, "I see you shaking your heads. I know it is not good news, but at least we know."

"Threats were made," commented T.W., "your heart, Carly's head. "Not good, this you know. We must not take it lightly."

Murmurs of assent resounded through the kitchen.

Carly went next. Everyone in the room knew about Seteeva's encounter with the fish. After all, every one of them had gone into his shop at different times since hearing the story, all armed with some delightful delectable for the infamous fish, who was now living on better food than most of the people in town. She liked everything. Everything that is, except Brussels sprouts, which Carly absolutely loved. He kept trying to convince her otherwise, but so far her normally opening and closing mouth stayed firmly closed when the small green tousled heads were tossed in the air. Carly related everything again, in its full version, right from the moment Seteeva entered through the door.

Bunting followed, telling a story that made everyone sit forward. It concerned a friend who had a daughter. The daughter's name was Lizzie.

"Her parents are worried sick," said Bunting, "they say they hear strange noises coming from Lizzie, chomping and chortling noises. They told me it is giving them the creeps and that Lizzie seems tired to them and a little paler than usual. They even said, in total confidence, that they thought she may be possessed."

Everyone stared at Bunting after this revelation, especially Theadora.

"Let me tell you," started Theadora. She went on to recount her meeting and subsequent conversation with Tom, Jimmy's dad. Everyone sat quietly, listening.

Once Thea was finished, T.W. added.

"I was at Mary Jane's the other day, getting my hair cut. I know. I know what you're all thinking. Hair cut. Again! Still, she never questions the growth and I must tell you that Mary Jane is tight-lipped most of the time, but lately she's been very forthcoming, a sign of stress on her part I believe. I think she knows that something is afoot. She was telling me about her neighbor's child. Apparently, he is displaying similar things, like those that have just been mentioned. Not quite as bad as poor Jimmy, but still bad." T.W. paused. "And, several locals are having unusual nightmares that are affecting their health. Mary Jane told me about Brendan's - it sounds horrible, and we all know that it would take an earthquake to unsettle Brendan, so it must be bad. This raised a few smiles from everyone, especially Theadora. However, the smiles were short lived. The discomfort caused by all of this news aroused too many senses. Each individual in the room had to take some silent time to collect themselves.

After a while, Theadora spoke, "I think we all by now have more than strong suspicions about Better B. Better and Seteeva Haar. Felice identified Better B.'s heritage right away from her scent. We also know that a Muckdeanne is here. Although we don't know where he is."

Willman had his own thoughts on this - he knew that the Muckdeanne in Carly's shop oozed a hatred for someone close - a wife, a child, a brother or a sister. He didn't know which relative it was, but he would bet his bottom dollar the person would be either Better B. or Seteeva. He knew that the Muckdeanne's hatred of a family member made them stronger, because that person would direct the hatred back - this is how they gained some of their strength. Even though Muckdeannes were not strong, they also were not stupid.

Willman chimed in.

"Better B. and Seteeva have threatened several of us - verbally and with magic. Remember the attack on my holding spell - it must have been them. We also know the Muckdeanne is at work - look at the children getting weaker. The pattern is all too obvious. Then of course, there are the nightmares. It takes a strong witch to gain access to a person's subconscious."

Everyone sat in silence – nodding.

Then T.W. voiced a question.

"I would like a vote on whether we should disturb my grandfather, The Jebber, for a group consult. It will deplete him of a lot of energy to show himself in this world, so cast your vote wisely. We could call on him via the black pond."

Of course, everyone said yes – Jebber's help was needed.

At this point, unified as they were, Theadora rose, ladling the simmering stew into large earthenware bowls, passing them amongst her fellow guests.

They ate from their bowls in silence, which was long, but comfortable. Time passed until everyone rose. Felice, Bunting and Theadora pulled shawls around their shoulders. Carly tipped a wool hat over his head as T.W. wrapped a scarf around his neck, his bow tie disappearing under the folds of green wool. This odd looking group of five moved with a purpose to the outdoors. Felice's skirt played happily in the wind. Able hung on to Carly's shoulder, as Mandy, the cat, slinked in amongst their legs. They made their way through the gardens. When they reached the pond, Mandy stretched his neck forward, four feet planted firmly on the ground, his head hovering over the blackness of the water, looking down. The blackness was a real black, blacker than black, and yet when Mandy looked down into the water, his reflection was black and the pond was white. He bounced back, an all four feet in the air bounce. All of the witches saw this - it was a little humor on The Jebber's part. Mandy was disgusted. He was a white cat. Jet white! He didn't bother looking in the pond again. The Willman chortled to himself as he watched the haughty cat plop down, nonchalantly lifting a paw to lick.

The black pond was big. T.W., Theadora, Carly, Bunting and Felice arranged themselves around the dark water. Theadora raised her head, her eyes looking at the stars, the utterance of words to her father fluttering up from her mouth, floating in the air, until they plummeted downward, the letters smashing through the smooth ebony surface, plunging into the depths toward The Jebber.

Jebber knew they would call and was at the bottom of the pond waiting. It was the best way for them to communicate with him without using their mirrors. He knew that leaving Chetsy to visit him for any period right now, would not be good. He was snoozing, when the first word hit him squarely on the head with a dull thud. He was sitting upright in a jiffy. The first word was not that much of a magic chant, it was, "WAKE," then the second word hit him, "UP!" He grinned. His daughter knew him well in his aging years.

"Hi" "Dad" "I miss" "you"

"I" "you" "love"

The 'love' must have airily floated down, thought Jebber, the 'you' overtaking it - warmth for his daughter emanated from his heart. Then the words started to cascade upon him with force, a hailstorm of love and confusion.

"It is time. Better B. Better and Seteeva Haar are indeed strong. It will take our unified strengths to withstand their magic and hopefully incapacitate them. Do you have any advice?"

The Jebber did. He leaned back in his chair taking in a deep, deep, deep breath. A breath far deeper than any mortal could ever take. Held it. Then exhaled. Slowly. He rose up through the depths, like a diver reluctantly returning from a coral field, the surface opening above his head, allowing his giant form to rise. He loomed above, ethereal, floating in the air, the tail of his form still in contact with the ripples.

Hearts became still, the wind stopped speaking. Willman looked up at his grandad, who was at this moment, even bigger than he. A smile cascaded down, showering them with its invigorating droplets.

Jebber opened his mouth to speak - a gentle whisper came forth, a dove calling - he had little time before he would have to return.

"Seteeva Haar is indeed a Selon. Their histories you know. Take her not lightly." He paused then. A long pause, while he looked around. This was followed by a tremendous sigh before he continued. "I have been making enquiries, in dungeons and dark places, with witches that breathe fetid air, that have maggots for pets, and crave stale brew for bathwater. I have found out the worst. Better B. Better is the first female Muckdeanne. This makes her a more potent evil than any other Muckdeanne - even her father. She does not have the weakness that prevails on the male side of this curse. Her strengths will only grow. This one is more dangerous than a river full of crocodiles." He paused as his form quivered, fading a little. A deep breath brought him back to full vibrancy. His arm reached down, toward his beloved grandson. In his hand was Simon. "You will need the little man's help... Simon leapt to earth, happy to be back with his friend. "And this," said The Jebber, leaning forward toward Willman, as he opened his other hand, "is something that you should not open, unless one of your own lives, or someone close, is in serious danger. It can only be used once, so use it wisely. Be gentle with it."

In his hand was a blue velvet bag, pocket watch size. It was fastened at the top with a gold chain. Whatever was in the bag was kicking, or punching, or blowing, or pushing, or something, at the insides of the bag with some ferocity, for the blue plushness would suddenly paunch out at some place or another, a puff of dust blooming from the folds of the material each time it happened. This bag he entrusted to his grandson, dropping it into his now outstretched hand.

"Put it in your shirt pocket - gently, always gently," said his grandad, "If you have no need of it, be sure to bring it back through the mirror. Promise to bring it back. Promise?" he whispered.

"I promise, Jebber," Willman said carefully to his grandad.

"I'll be with you," Jebber purred as his form started to melt back down into the water, his head finally dropping down through the blackness, a kindly sea serpent returning to his home.

The wind that had quieted during all of this, now picked up again, causing Willman's unruly hair to battle amongst itself. The five made their way back to the house, eagerly led by Able, his wings fighting the gusts, feathers in disarray, his squawks filling the night air. Simon followed close behind, running to keep up. Mandy, the cat, followed even closer, totally intrigued by the tiny form as it hopped along like a grasshopper in front of him. T.W. shot a warning look. *NO!* It said. Mandy slowed, frowning, whiskers curled and twisted to match the short curly locks on his back. He dropped back, behind the legs of his friends.

On returning to the kitchen, nothing much was said as they all took their places. Theadora uncorked another bottle of wine as T.W. stoked the fire, then they sat to contemplate before returning to their homes, each lost in their own thoughts. Simon, happy to be back with his friend, curled up on one of the hearthstones, seemingly immune to the intense heat, all of his appendages dangling sideways.

## CHAPTER FORTY-TWO

# WICKEDNESS AT THE USED FURNITURE STORE

Back at the used furniture store, all hell had broken loose. The desk had sold, causing real problems, but now, thankfully, there was an old piano bench that had just about everyone's attention. Every time it sold, the person that bought it tried to remove it from the shop, only to be dragged back across the threshold by several angry people - faces grimaced and twisted worse than gargoyles. Angry people were replaced by furious people, who were replaced by delirious people - the shop shifting and changing its tides, waves of faces coming and going. On top of this bedlam, inside the trunk, Better B. Better's dad was starting to come to, his bondage weakening. To add even more to the situation, Seteeva's eye socket was infected, her black patch no longer hiding the orange tinted purulent goo that oozed out. Orange for a Selon was just not good. Whenever Better B. glanced at Seteeva lifting the pirate patch, dabbing wildly at the ooze, she started to snicker.

"What's so funny?" asked Seteeva.

"Nuthin..."

"Nuthin? What you snickering at? Better not be my fuckin eye!"

"Eye? What eye?" B.B. thought she would die laughing.

Seteeva was just about to explode when Sheila did what she had many days before hoped for - she leapt on Desmond - who had been about to walk off with the piano bench - and clawed his eyes out! Her long manicured nails, painted the brightest red, dug deep into his sockets. Desmond screamed like a woman! He dropped the bench, lashing out with his hands until they caught onto Sheila's long curly hair. For a split second, he held her head, before bringing his forehead down onto the front of her face, feeling and hearing her nose smash under the force. Her blood spurted to mix with his. About this, he felt happy. He still had a hold of her hair, so he did the same thing, again and again, while his eyes hung uselessly in front of his cheeks. Through the screams, his and hers, he yelled.

"Won't get the bench now, will you bitch!" Then he let go.

It was as if his hold on her had kept him standing, for now, he fell to the floor, rolling around, holding his stomach, howling at his own humor. Sheila fell on the floor too - she wasn't laughing though, she was unconscious. No one in the shop seemed to pay much heed because their attention was back on the piano bench, which was once again up for grabs. It was far more important than Sheila or Desmond. The war was reaching atomic bomb level, when, without warning, Better B. yelled, even louder than she normally did when competing with Seteeva.

"ENOUGH! ENOUGH! Tomorrow we will resume our bidding for the bench! We are now closed!"

She cast calm, with the flick of a wrist, a fine brown dust sprinkled through her fingertips, scattering around inside the shop before blowing through the door onto the crowd outside. Everyone quieted, tranquilized, each person looked around, wondering what they had been doing, why they were here. They turned as one, robotically stepping over Sheila, but not noticing her. Bypassing Desmond, who was still rolling in his mirth and anguish.

"Come back tomorrow, ten o'clock, bidding will resume!" echoed Better B. after the departing mob. The Walking Dead. The Zombies. She called a halt, not because she wasn't enjoying herself, but because she could not absorb any more of the angry energy. She didn't want to waste it. It was this energy that strengthened her, but she could only use so much fuel at once, and her tank was on full.

What no one had noticed was that the orange ooze from Seteeva's eye socket had splattered when she swung her head around in Better B.'s direction. The bright orange goo was stuck to the neck of one lady, already a flesh eater. Another woman had it on her cheek - it itched like a flea-infested bed. One other splatter had landed on the head of a dazzling high school blond. Her hair started to fall out in chunks before she reached home, chemotherapy at its best. She ran into the house to the utter amazement of her parents, with half her hair held in her hands, tears streaming down her face, incoherent babbling falling from her lips.

The town of Chetsy was an absolute mess - in more ways than Better B. had ever imagined delightfully possible.

Sheila, Lizzie's mother, never made it home. Her husband called the police.

Desmond lived with his brother, Burt - they were twins. His twin knew something was wrong - he called the police and luckily he called his friend, Mary Jane. He felt a pain behind his eyes as he talked, his heart palpated, knowing it was not tears that stung like that. The police did nothing - several of them had been at the shop anyway, involved in the war. Mary Jane, however, was somehow immune to all the goings on. She called The Willman, just because she had a feeling she should. He was the only person she thought she could talk to, and she felt like this was something that needed to be talked about. Her feeling of oddness was growing.

Lizzie's dad had sat with his head in his hands for hours, only one police officer had responded to him, but even he had acted oddly, saying they couldn't do anything. A certain amount of time needed to pass before they could look into a missing person? *Not in this small town*, thought Lizzie's dad. Those kinds of rules and regulations went by the wayside. The fact that Sheila had not picked Lizzie up from school was abnormal. In fact, now he thought about it, she had been acting different lately, ever since she had started going back to that shop. His wife no longer thought something weird was going on with Lizzie. This was really strange since before this, they had been talking night after night about the problem, voicing their fears to each other. Just last night when he had brought up the subject, she had literally ripped his head off, telling him to stop being so paranoid. He sat for a while, thinking. Then he called his life long friend. She picked up on the second ring.

"Hello," Bunting said.

Lizzie's dad didn't hesitate - the words tumbled out, effortlessly, landing simply in her ear. There was no questioning his worries - he was clear as a bell. Bunting heard every word, and every non-word. When she put the phone down, which was not long after T.W. had put the phone down from Mary Jane's call, she picked it back up to call the giant's house.

CHAPTER FORTY-THREE

# JIMMY AND THE DOCTOR

Jimmy was dead, but the town wasn't mourning. Only his father and brother. No one would take Jimmy to a morgue, or even just bury him, so he just lay in the cold cellar of their old house while Tom moaned through his grief, not knowing what to do. The town had come to a standstill, other than the constant bickering, arguing and backstabbing. Everyone still went out, starting their days normally, headed to work, for coffee, going to the book store, for lunch, for breakfast, getting a haircut, The Green Cow for dinner, but none of it followed the normal pattern. Anger and arguments over coffee, ending up at Better B.'s store, only to bicker again. The schools were empty, children feeling to tired to do anything, at least one parent too busy with their 'shopping' errands to care. The town of Chetsy looked like it was suffering from a hangover. A big one! It had drunk at least a shipload of gin.

Tom sat on one of the old beat up benches in his farmhouse kitchen. He had his head in his hands, yet again. He had done this so often of late, that there were palm indentations in his chin and finger grooves in his forehead. Little Jimmy still lay in the cool cellar, laid out on the cold stone floor. *This is so macabre*, he thought. He almost puked. He couldn't believe that his son was dead, for one. And for two, that he was laying in the cellar, and had been for days, instead of in some funeral home, or as should be, buried already, with a decent farewell. Tom thought about the night Jimmy had died, it was just like any other of late. Jimmy spent a lot of time in bed - he was so tired all the time. They had tried to play scrabble, all three of them sitting on his bed working to keep the board level, but the little boy was just too worn out, so after a while they had kissed him goodnight, turning out his lights to go to bed themselves. But he hadn't gone to bed - he had sent his elder son off, telling him to rest, for he looked wretched too. He himself had sat outside Jimmy's bedroom door, leaning against the wall, waiting. He hadn't dozed off. He knew he hadn't, his mind was just too active, too worried to do such a thing. After a couple of hours he had pushed himself up off the floor, using his back to shimmy up with the intent of checking on his young son. When he opened the door, he just couldn't believe his eyes.

The bed was empty.

EMPTY! EMPTY! EMPTY!

His head screamed at him! No way his kid got past him. Absolutely no way! He had run to the windows in the room. Locked. All of them!

LOCKED!

He screamed inside! All of inside, not just in his head. So again, as of night after night, he searched the house for his son.

NOTHING! As usual. He came up with NOTHING!

This time, instead of sitting on the couch to fall asleep for an hour, knowing his son would turn up, he started to cry. Not only did he cry, he bellowed like an elephant baby, so loud, that his other son woke, coming to him during his storm, holding him as tight as he could. Father and son. They stood like this for what seemed like eons, until finally, the slight creak of the front door stirred them both. It opened just as Jimmy slid to the floor, using the doorframe to guide him to the ground.

"Oh my god! Jimmy!" Tom dashed over.

When the doctor arrived, he looked tired, harassed and pissed off. His wife was giving him fits over some bench or something. When she wanted something, it was bad. This bench thing, well, she wanted it really badly, which was making his life hell. He had been seeing Jimmy since he was a babe - that was the only reason he was here. He had not wanted to leave the house. The pressure of his bitching wife seemed to be overriding everything. He sure didn't feel himself of late, and words kept coming out of his mouth that he hadn't planned on saying. He'd have to talk to her. She was pushing him over the edge. On entering the old farmhouse, Tom hadn't said much, just led him up the familiar narrow staircase, showing him into the room that had been Jimmy's since birth.

The doctor walked over to the bed, standing a while, looking at the still life form. He reluctantly bent forward to take a better look, until finally he placed the bell of his stethoscope to the tiny concave chest. He glanced once at the staring eyes, before snapping the stethoscope out of his ears, standing to leave without further ado.

"Yep," he exclaimed, "he's dead alright."

Tom was aghast.

"What do you mean? Dead! He just fainted. Dead? Dead? Shut up! How can you just say that...

what is wrong with you... you are the one walking around like a corpse, but Jimmy? Dead?" Then his anger dissipated with sorrow behind, his words became whispers. "Dead? You must be mistaken. Not dead. Comatose maybe? Yes? Tell me Doc, just unconscious. Please," he begged.

The doctor looked squarely at Tom, his own face blank - his mind in a distant place.

"Dead as a doornail, old boy, how'd you like that!"

The once good doctor started to laugh, a sinister laugh of the kind you never want to hear - a cruel hag living inside his mouth. He laughed and laughed until Jimmy's dad punched him - straight on the nose. Tom couldn't help it - the old bastard was just so cold hearted. As the doctor held his hand up to his now broken, bloodied nose, his laughter was more muffled, but still there.

"Pwut your dwed swon, swumwhere cwold... no one's cwoming." He marched downstairs, leaving the front door wide open, with a cold north wind blowing, a trickle of blood marking his path.

As the doctor walked smartly to his car, still laughing, the blood gurgling in the back of his throat, a voice in his head, which was his own, (an unusual thing of late), was asking him - *what the hell was he was doing, just what the hell was he doing!* He just shook his head at himself. *Don't know. I don't seem to be in control.* He started to laugh harder as Tom watched from the shadows of the old farmhouse.

Better B. Better had been watching this whole exchange through Jimmy's eyes. Listening through his ears. She was able to do that when she possessed most of their soul. She did it by sitting in a chair inside the crooked house on the corner, taking a trance, until ever so slowly, she passed through space, melding with whichever child she had most recently been sucking on - her ethereal body entering theirs. Tonight she had entered Jimmy. Jimmy, who was laying wide-eyed on his bed. Better B. had entered his body just as the doctor's face loomed over, leaning closer to listen to his heart. Her whole vision was suddenly filled with the doctor's saggy face and fat lips. In fact, the face became so large in front of her that she thought she was there in reality... and that the doctor was going to kiss her.

One of those BIG FAT WET sloppy kisses! Horrors!

She actually yipped out in her tranced state. Seteeva, who was in the same room polishing some of the furniture - her eye no longer dripping since she had poured a steaming hot potion into it - actually jumped at the sound, especially when her stupid friend did that yipping noise again.

"Thought she said she was meditating," mumbled Seteeva to herself.

B.B. stopped yipping as soon as the doctor's ugly face was not looming in front of her, looking like some puckering bottom hole ready to take a dump. She actually sighed with relief as he pulled away. Then she heard him say that Jimmy was dead. That started her laughing inside. *Oh man, was this good.* The energy produced by her evil actions, sizzled inside. She was getting stronger by the day. At this point she decided to leave Jimmy, just in case the good doctor decided to come back to try resuscitation - she didn't think her stomach could handle that. On this thought, she came back to her body, her own vision returning just as Seteeva was pouring more of the boiling liquid into her cavernous eye socket, making it steam and sizzle.

"Do you have to do that in public!" she snapped, momentarily forgetting the glee of Jimmy's state.

Seteeva Haar responded with a glare that would drop a person to their knees. But instead of bitching back, she took the moment to address the most important thing on her mind – Carly Jones!

## CHAPTER FORTY-FOUR

# JIMMY

Jimmy had lain in the cellar for three days now. Tom lay next to him on the icy stone, staring at the ceiling, just like Jimmy. He held his son's lifeless hand as they lay there, side by side, both looking the same, both looking dead, except there were tears on the face of one. The tears of the other were inside. Not to be seen. Jimmy could feel them though. He was in agony. He wanted to scream. He wanted to roll over so he could hug his dad. He wanted to stand up, he wanted to eat, he wanted to pee, he wanted to lie down in his warm bed. He wanted! He wanted! He wanted! Yet he couldn't do anything. He couldn't move. He had tried so hard. He couldn't even lift his little pinkie or squeeze his dad's hand. Better B. Better had done a really good job on sucking out his soul. His hearing was still good, which was a torture of its self - because he could hear his dad now.

"Oh Jimmy. I love you, love you, love you... what am I to do... bury you in the garden... the town... no police... no doctors... its gone crazy... Chetsy has gone crazy. I miss you Jimmy. SO MUCH!"

*NO DAD! DON'T BURY ME! NO DAD! NO DAD! NO DAD!*

The scream in Jimmy's head was louder than the terror of the thought of being buried alive. *He was talking to his dad now, wasn't he?* He was confused. Things kept misting in and out. His mind was foggy.

There were times he knew he talked to a strange creature - feeling like he was nodding at it from up high. At those times, he felt peaceful and strong. He had been in that peaceful place a few moments ago, but now here he was with his Dad and brother again. He could hear them. It made him panicky. *Where had the strange creature gone?*

"He don't smell bad or nothing - isn't all stiff either, you know, like a wedgie," came a familiar voice. It was his big brother - Jimmy couldn't see him because he couldn't move his eyes - he knew that voice though, it was HIS BIG BROTHER.

*DON'T BURY ME!* He yelled in his head louder than ever.

Jimmy's dad came up from his ramblings.

"What did you say, son?"

"I said, he doesn't stink or nothing. Thought dead people started to stink."

"Well, its cold down here, son".

"Doesn't look like he's getting ripe either, you know, like a rotten banana."

Big brother peered closer, daring to touch the prone body with the tip of his finger. He was surprised when a piece of Jimmy did not stick to him as he pulled his finger away. He touched again just to be sure. He thought he felt a tremor when he did it the second time. Made him jump in his skin.

"Are you dead, Jimmy?" he whispered. Jimmy didn't answer. "I won't be mad at you if you're not dead..." he whispered again. "I'll even let you have my old Lego set... if you're not dead that is."

"For christ sake! You're being all weird!" said Tom jumping to his feet. But he too, now peered closer at his child, sniffing as he did so, not so much from the tears either.

"The doctor said he was dead." Tom took another whiff. "And he hasn't moved a wink in days."

"The doctor stinks like a dead dog! Jimmy doesn't," said big brother defensively.

Tom hesitated for only one second before he scooped his youngest son up in his arms.

"Dad! What're you doing?" running behind, as Jimmy was whisked up the cellar stairs, through the kitchen and up the narrow stairway.

"I'm putting Jimmy in his bed, then we'll see. If he starts to smell like a dead dog or we find bits of him in the bed, then we'll move him back to the cellar... what do you think, son?" He grinned then - for the first time in ages.

Big brother grinned back. "I'll go get my Lego... just in case."

Tom took a seat beside his son's bed, pulling up another chair and a small table. Later, with Lego pieces tipped out, they made a rocket ship, an elephant, a James Bond car, then a robot, until both leaned back in their seats exhausted. Four hours had passed and so far Jimmy didn't stink. This was good news because the room, although not hot, was much warmer than the cellar.

With little fuss, father and son agreed not to leave Jimmy's side. Big brother lay on the bed - he decided not to worry that he might be lying with a corpse. At this point, his little brother came before his own fears. He snuggled into the sleeping bag that his dad laid over him. Tom uncurled his long form on the short mattress that he dragged from the other room, his feet flopping over the end.

As Tom fell into an exhausted sleep, Jimmy's big brother reached under the covers to find his little brother's hand. He held it, not letting go all night. "Don't die, Jimmy," he whispered over and over.

Little Jimmy stopped crying at this point. His big brother had said 'don't die', not 'I wish you weren't dead'. He loved his big brother. He did. He really loved him. He went to sleep for the first time in ages, even though his eyes did not close. He dreamed of being a daisy, looking into the light as a strange creature caressed him with language and oil.

CHAPTER FORTY-FIVE

# HARRY TOMB

It was another day - Harry Tomb woke early, hopping sprightly out of bed for a seventy-year-old coot. His now usual morning routine was carried out with glee before his walk into town to see Kelly. Actually, Harry no longer walked - he jogged in a quickstep fashion, along with the rhythm of his heart, leaving his tiny Crayola house behind. The little hamlet of houses sat just outside of town - each house painted in a different, bright, uplifting color like a field of multicolored tulips. Harry loved his home. He loved being near enough to town to walk. He had for many years lived in an old cabin out in the woods, his age eventually making the decision for him to move closer to the population of Chetsy. It had been a good move, keeping him younger than his years as he absorbed the vitality of the town and the goings on instead of letting himself become an old curmudgeon. How he had changed with the move, he thought, doing a little skip. *Seventy, and never been in love before...* he hummed as he trotted along. The hum was a ditty that he had made up himself.

It wasn't long before he reached the outskirts of the town, where his humming seemed to grow louder.

*Funny that,* he thought, *why'd I sound louder?*

He stopped his throaty vibration, thinking that he might be tricky and catch the hum in a trap. It turns out the trap worked - now Harry wasn't sure why he'd set it because he didn't like what he'd caught, for now there WAS another hum and IT did not stop! In fact, it grew louder and louder and louder. It was too early in the morning for such a thing. He had intended on getting to the chocolate shop before Kelly so that he could propose. This was a distraction he didn't need. *What IS that?* He followed the noise, or at least where he thought it was coming from - as he moved, it became more than a noise, it became brain cell splattering! It was giving him a headache for sure and on top of that, it was only half dark out. Or was it only half light? Whichever way you looked at it, something wasn't right. The light itself was not a problem, Harry knew his way around Chetsy by heart, he had lived here all his life, except for the bit in the middle - when he played trumpet with the bands and taught music at the University. But now he was curious, he could not picture what could be making a noise like that. *Some queer things been going on in this town - maybe it's something I should check into.* His ears led him to the shortcut through a clutch of trees, the shortcut led to a narrow street, which led to a corner, and finally to the Used Furniture Shop.

As Harry rounded that last corner, he stopped, dead still, rubbing at his eyes, not because he was tired, but because he did not believe what he saw. His sleep hadn't been the greatest lately, what with dreams of Kelly belly dancing her way to Timbuktu and back, but really, it couldn't be this bad. *I'm a strong man... aren't I?* He rubbed his eyes again. No. What he saw - is what he saw. The gnarly house that was the used furniture store was pulsating, its walls slowly expanding out, then slowly sucking in. It was as if the house was on a respirator... it was breathing. Then a flash of color flickered in one of the windows, filling the entire frame - just plain glass one moment, then more colorful than a cathedral window the next. The nasty noise was coming from inside.

The house was breathing. But Harry wasn't.

At last - he took a big gulp.

"Holy macaroons," he whispered. At these times, everyone knows that you just run. Away! Harry knew he should, yet he couldn't help himself, he had to see. He needed a look. Gingerly, the first tiny step was taken toward the pulsating walls - *just what the dickens are you doing Harry, turn around and run - remember all the horror movies Harry, when she hears something in a room - when she does not run, when she moves toward that room, arm outstretched, hand on the knob, opening the door - remember Harry - you scream out at the screen - Harry - you scream "YOU ARE A STUPID DICKER HEAD! RUN!" And that isn't even real, Harry. This is real. So just what are you doing? Why - just why, the dicker head hell, Harry - aren't you running!*

*I don't know* - finally understanding why everyone else did the same stupid thing in the horror movies.

His feet moved silently forward - once closer, he half bent, a hunchback stance. His heart was beating much faster than when he watched Kelly gyrating on the dance floor. Crawling on all fours for the last fifty feet across the lawn took forever - *still, not bad for an old coot,* he thought. Once he reached the base of the building, he lay flat, while figuring out a plan. The house was still breathing. *Holy shit,* he wheezed, as the cold morning dew penetrated his clothes. He was not sure what to do. Then the breathing house stopped, its walls standing at a tilt. *BeJeezus! Now what? Is it dead?* The strange mind boggling noise continued, as more intense colors reflected out of the window landing next to him, ready to run up his trouser legs and make him scream. It was still half dark. Harry had never known the town to take so long to wake up - *wish it would hurry up.* Never mind that though, he was here. He had to make a decision. Taking a quick breath in, then holding it, he carefully used the wall to inch himself up, until the top of his head and his eyes were framed by the lower part of the window. Anyone looking from inside would have seen him, but they weren't, thank goodness. The only one looking was Harry. Although he wished he wasn't. He wished he'd listened to himself before he had crawled across the lawn. *Why, oh why, didn't I listen to myself...* his mind moaned, sad that he had fallen into his own man-eating trap.

It was the morning after the piano bench war. Desmond had been rolling around on the floor for hours. To begin with it had been in mirth, but only because his mind had become sick with the poisonous spell that had been cast upon him. Later, he rolled around because of the pain in his head... then later still, because the spell had totally worn off, he rolled around because of the talk he could hear between the two demented women in the room. Sheila still lay unconscious. Or more than likely - comatose. At this time, of the two, she was in the better state. Desmond was feeling panicky. His head was on fire. His eyes were still hanging out of their sockets, but he could see in a weird sort of way. It was just that he couldn't see what he looked at, only things beneath whichever way his eyes hung, and even that was all misty. *Brother. Oh brother. Hear me now!* He called silently and desperately to his twin.

Better B. paced across the room one more time, kicking Desmond in the ribs like a cruel rancher with a cattle prod - something she had done at least a hundred times in the past hour. She wanted to splatter one of his eyes.

"Shut up, you idiot, or I'll stomp!" Her foot hovered in the air over the giant marble, ready to squish. She never did - seemed more fun that way. Desmond knew each time he had escaped because the mistiness was still before him.

Seteeva was blowing her bubbles, each one bursting when it hit the wall, destroying the screaming demon within. The man lying on the floor with his eyes hanging out could only imagine what foul things were in the room with him - such things that could make the screams of a slowly burning child. An eruption of color scattered its rays after each tiny explosion, making his mistiness become a searing haze that sent a hammer and chisel pain into his brain. The poor twin groaned, as did Burt in the little house on the outskirts of town, feeling his brother's pain. Outside, Harry's eyes might also have been hanging from their sockets as he continued to stare, his throat cramped tighter than a vice in a school kids woodwork shop. He determined that the nasty noise he could hear was coming from a chest that was by the sofa.

"SHUT UP!" yelled Better B. as she stood over the chest, both hands splayed on the top. "SHUT UP! You moron of a father!"

Better B. had been breathing so hard and with such anger because her father had come to, and was as usual, being a problem, that it had caused everything of hers to breath in the same way. She was connected with all of her belongings - including the house. Things stopped moving when she had taken the time to down yet another glass of wine, but now she was back to pacing and breathing hard, snorting in and out. That is when the house started moving again, nearly knocking poor Harry onto his butt. He held on though - tight to the windowsill.

"What are we going to do with those two?" asked Seteeva nodding in the direction of Desmond and Sheila.

Better B. just snorted.

"Well?" asked Seteeva again. "Won't be long before the crowds are back."

Better B's beady eyes bounced around, her mind scrambling, the din driving her crazy. She focused on the trunk, then Sheila - in seven short steps she crossed the room, grabbed Sheila by the hair, dragging her across the floor with superhuman strength. Sheila's mini skirt rode up around her hips - her urine stained pink panties peeking out. Pointing one long finger at the lock on the chest - it opened - *click click* - the lid rising of its own accord. As it rose, so did her dad, like a ghoul out of its coffin. Harry nearly fainted.

Deftly, without an ounce of remorse, Better B. lifted

Sheila's limp body, throwing her in on top of her father. She saw his tongue flick in and out, serpentine in its manner, strands of putrid intestines still clinging to his wrists.

"HERE, THAT SHOULD KEEP YOU QUIET FOR A WHILE! YOU MORON!"

The lid snapped shut, the lock clicking back into place. Her dad, besides being a Muckdeanne, was known to munch on a bit of human flesh once in a while - especially when he was really desperate. He was really desperate right now and weaker than a fly in a trap. The munching sound was loud - so loud that Harry could hear it right through the pulsating walls of the house. He knew just what it was, without having to hear Seteeva's cry of glee.

"Jiminy Cricket, B.B! Your dad sounds really hungry! Hope he doesn't get too much strength back."

"Naw," responded Better B. feeling a little calmer now that the annoying noise had stopped. "It will keep him barely alive, although I don't know why I bother, it is just that I need more time to think... well, at least we got rid of one of these two cretins." She stepped over Desmond again, kicking him in the ribs as she did. He rolled to his side, his eyes dangling at an angle. Then she bent down, grabbing him by the shoulders. As big as he was, she easily hauled him into the air, pushing him backward into a large armoire that had been displayed with its doors open. He was a rag doll in her hands.

"Make one sound and you're next on the menu," she hissed at him as she banged the doors closed. She may as well have been nailing him in his coffin.

Desmond was stuck in the upright standing position as if he had Velcro on his back, he didn't know how that had happened. His eyes looked at his feet. He could still hear the chomping noise. *Man oh man... brother... wish I was at home with you right now.* He sent out the biggest thought he had ever sent, hoping his brother would have a giant net out to catch it.

Harry had seen enough. Now he ran. But not until after he had carefully lowered himself onto the ground to crawl the fifty feet back across the lawn, like a lucky pig escaping slaughter. Then he ran in the half crouched position putting distance between them. Finally, he stood up straight and ran in the upright position, ignoring his cramped screaming muscles - he was sure someone had tied his legs in a hangman's knot. It was still half dark outside. *How the hell did that happen - dark for so long?*

Harry ran until he reached Chetsy Chocolates. He sat down on the neat bench, panting, his chest wheezing in tune with the wind, waiting for Kelly. He felt more than a little sick. His stomach turned, churning butter. As he sat, it became light, in one quick instant, like a flash of lightening light. First it was half dark, forever - then at the snap of a finger, it was bright light. Harry rubbed his eyes, not for the first time that morning, he felt confused and sorely tired.

*Just what was happening?*

## CHAPTER FORTY-SIX

# HARRY TOMB AND KELLY

Kelly and Tombhra showed up for work half an hour later. Harry Jumping Bean bounced from his seat, ready to meet her as soon as she turned into the red brick alley. He heard his love coming - she was chatting away with no one to hear - *yes, sir... we'll make a good match, I like to talk to myself too... how funny, sounds like she is actually having a conversation. Have to ask her how she does that.* Then he sighed, his distraction short, the memory of what he had witnessed still beating on his forehead, harder than a hammer on a nail.

He couldn't get the horrible vision from earlier out of his mind - it kept replaying like a bad movie. He had recognized Desmond. He wasn't close friends with the guy, but he remembered getting a ride home from him once - from the store - when it had been icy outside. He had been slipping and sliding around, dropping bananas and tins of beans out of his shopping bag when Desmond had come over, putting a hand under his elbow, steadying his old geezer self - even helped pick up his groceries before driving him home. It just wasn't the same at seventy - he didn't walk steady on a tightrope anymore. So, anyway, he liked Desmond, and even if he didn't, he wouldn't just ignore what he had seen. He knew, he thought now, that if he just went home, went to bed, pulled the covers up, he would be safe. But he couldn't. He just couldn't ignore what was going on.

Chetsy was his home. These were his people. And that poor woman! High heels and all! *Oh my god!* thought Harry. Even though he didn't know who she was.

So instead of uttering his declaration of love for Kelly as he had planned bright and early that morning, shedding words that should have been full of beauty and clarity, his muttered words came out black and dangerous - he was in a terrible state.

"There is s...something d d d...dark and d...deadly going on in this tow... town."

Kelly hadn't expected to bump into anyone as she rounded the corner. So besides being a bit shocked at seeing Harry looking like someone had just pulled him out of his grave, she was also shocked at his words.

"Have you gone of your rocker, Harry?" she asked bluntly, with no trace of sympathy in her voice. In that moment of time before he spoke, she had thought he was going to declare his passion for her. He had been hanging around a lot, sharing talk, oozing love thicker than soup on a cold winter's day. Kelly was finding that she really liked him. Now she was miffed that he was here just to let her know he was nuts. She put one hand out to push him aside - not to actually touch him, but as a queen would to wave aside ragamuffins before her.

Harry tried again.

"Kelly, p...please, listen to me. It was almost d...dark this morning..." he began, his voice begging for an audience.

Not one to have much patience, especially when she felt slighted, Kelly responded.

"Tell me something new, Harry. Of course it was dark this morning. Are you dumb or something, Harry!"

Now Harry did beg, he didn't care if he seemed like a sniveling old fool - he just had to tell her.

"No. N...no. I'm s...sorry." He started to sob. "I'm dis...distraught. Let m...me start ag a...again." Then, Harry got it right, everything storming out in one torrential flow, stronger than Niagara Falls, everything from why he had left his house so early, to what he heard, what he saw.

Kelly stood stock-still. Tombhra too. Kelly heard the horrendous story - she also heard the love part of Harry's recountal, the reason why he had left his house so early in the first place. She reached up, giving him one big smack-a-roony of a lip snoggin kiss, then grabbed his hand and pulled him into the shop. Harry was so bewildered, he let himself be tugged along, gliding lightly on water.

"Sit!" She commanded as she moved with great dexterity behind the counter.

He felt like a dog, but he sat anyway, his tall frame folding in. "Good boy," he muttered to himself. A strong shot of coffee was in his hands in no time. As he sipped, his shock receding, he decided maybe it wasn't so bad to obey after all. He tried a playful little growl then, under his breath, wondering if Kelly would like that. G r r r r r g r r z z y g r r r r *Better practice,* he thought.

Now, if Harry had come to Kelly with this story a few weeks ago, she would have pooh-poohed him, put a ping-pong ball into his mouth and given him directions to the nut house. But since she had been hanging out with T.W. and Tombhra, she knew more than most. Not everything, but enough to make her grab for the phone.

The Willman didn't answer, but Theadora did.

They were rolling down a hillside together, in total disarray, words tumbling, hitting the earth with hailstone force. Both of them talked at the same time, Kelly and Tombhra, some words lilted with accent, some not. Theadora listened intently, nodding now and then. Kelly and Tombhra heard each nod, each tap of the fingernail. They even heard the swish of Theadora's scarf as she grabbed if from the back of the chair.

"Don't go near that place!" was the only comment Theadora made. The click of the phone told them she would take care of it.

## CHAPTER FORTY-SEVEN

# THE MEETING IN TOWN

The yellow scarf wrapped itself around Theadora's neck, an affectionate snake curling around its handler, its tasseled ends lifting to sensuously lick her cheek. It was then, that T.W. walked into the kitchen. It took only one look at his mum to know that something was afoot. He watched her gently pull the lively snake down, away from her face.

"Tssk, tssk, lay calm now. I'm alright."

"Mother!" He moved toward her, bending down to take her small hands in his. Quickly, she recited the new information. With this phone call - and the two from Bunting and Mary Jane - they both knew that now was the time to act. Chetsy was going down fast. They as yet, were not quite sure what to do, not wanting to act in haste or anger, with the potential of death to them, leaving Chetsy at the total mercy of the evil doings of Better B. Better and Seteeva Haar. That would certainly end the life of their village. Just magic was not going to win the war with these two. Yes, they were strong, and there were five of them. But Better B. and Seteeva were more than evil. Wisdom is what would overcome, thought T.W. as he decided to take slow steps wisely.

This is why he was now in the Bentley, floating down the driveway, the trees breathing in to let him pass, curtsying with wide skirts of green and moss for shoes. Theadora sat beside him. The only thing different than usual about this drive was that the little man Simon, was sitting in the back. He was not actually sitting in the seat because from there, he could not see out, and not only did he want to see out... he had to. Otherwise he got carsick. So he had scrambled up the leather so that he could sit on the top, his feet dangling over, resting where shoulders would normally lean, his bare bony bum nestled into the softness. His nipples, still as pendulous as ever, flopped onto the upper part of his belly, bouncing in tune with the ruts in the road. His huge penis still drooped uselessly between his thighs, only lifting its head up to smile as the biggest pot holes passed by. Despite all this, he felt good - he was back with his friend. In fact, he felt really good. He started to bob his head to the music that T.W. was playing, even singing along. He wasn't half bad either. Willman looked at him through the rear view mirror, and smiled. Simon grimaced back, a tadpole with teeth. He didn't know how to smile. Or, at least, he had forgotten. Anyway, the trip into town was kind of jovial under the circumstances. At one point, Simon was singing at the top of his lungs to the song.

"When a maaaaan, loves a woman...

Can't keep his miiind, on nothin' else..."

Who knows how he knew it, but he did. He and T.W. were like cicadas in tune. Theadora just hummed along, she knew that singing helped keep her son calm and focused.

When they arrived in their usual parking spot behind the quaint shops and alleyways, Thea and Willman glanced at each other. *Ready?* They each opened their door and stepped out into the sun, their senses scanning better than any satellite for bad magic. They stood, taking the few seconds needed to hone their inner selves, their nostrils fluting wider than a wolf, their ears more sensitive than a bull elephant, their brains throbbing, strong, like it was before mortals ignored them - then, and only then, when they felt no danger, did they nod to each other.

"Safe?"

"Yes. Safe."

T.W. turned, opening the back door - he held his hand out to Simon.

"Come on, buddy. Time to go."

Simon shook his head from side to side. Emphatic! In fact, very emphatic for a naked little guy.

T.W. was gentle, caring.

"It's OK Simon, I'll put an invisible spell on you, no one will see."

Still he shook his head. He folded his arms. Tightly. Crossed his legs, even though it was difficult, and looked the other way.

"Ooooo Kay..." said his giant friend, quietly. "I'll leave the window open. You change your mind, find us, the invisible spell is right here." He flicked his hand, releasing a light from within his palm. The light was green, taking the form as he relaxed his fingers, of a cloak that sparkled emerald. "Wrap this around you if you leave the car, tie it around your neck, that is all you need to not be seen."

The fantastic cloak, a gift from a King's closet, floated unaided in the back of the car. Simon still sat in the place he had climbed to at the beginning of the journey. He looked the other way with a hummph from his lips, then he cocked his chin in the air, with arms still folded as his friend pushed the door of the

Bentley smoothly closed... a touch of velvet.

T.W. and Thea walked off in the direction of Lance's coffee house. Simon turned his head to watch them go. He couldn't believe that they were leaving him. Why hadn't they stayed, spending more time convincing him to go along. Didn't they like him? Why hadn't they tried to coax and cajole him into going with them? Why didn't they offer him treats and bribes? Why? Why hadn't they tried to talk him into leaving, telling him nice things? He'd gotten into the car hadn't he? This was a strange place, this town. He was dubious. It was different on the other side of the mirror. This was a weird place - Chetsy. "Baah!" They'd invited him along, so why weren't they trying to make sure he went all the way along with them.

"Hummmpphhh!" he went.

"Hmmmppphhhh..." but this time it had a little less 'umph' to it.

His eyes followed where his friends had disappeared around the corner. They had fed him, bathed him, talked to him, given him a place to sleep. And above all, they had never laughed at him. In fact, just as in the ride here, they had laughed together, enjoying each other, instead of them enjoying him and his misery. His thoughts went back to the Moat House. He wasn't sure what to think. He felt a bit confused. This was such a strange place. Not like the village. His journey with Jebber through the blackness was frightening, and now they had left him. So, instead of chasing after his friends, he decided to sit there and sulk. Sulking had never gotten him far before, but he decided to do it anyway.

It wasn't long before Simon's better nature got in the way. He had so much enjoyed the ride into town. He started to hum, kicking his heels rhythmically back against the seat - *man oh man, that beat, boogie woogie...* his body starting to bob up and down to the tune in his head, the tune he and Willman had been singing at full hoogie toogie tilt on the ride into Chetsy, until finally, no longer able to contain himself, the words burst forth from his lips, a geyser erupting from the ground.

"WHEN A MA A N LOVES A WOOMAN... CAN'T KEEP HIS MIND ON NOTHIN' ELSE..."

He sang the whole song, loud and gleefully and, in perfect voice. Fantastic it was, until finally, at the end, he slipped off from his high perch, landing in the folds of the well-worn back seat, a parachuter finding the haystack. He lay there giggling, his beautiful face belying the ugliness below.

As this was happening T.W. and Thea were sitting in Lance's waiting for Felice, Bunting and Carly. They had arranged this meeting to finalize their plans, knowing that they needed to make their move now - they needed to organize themselves. Too many lives were at stake and time was running short. Felice was still working - she nodded over to them from behind the counter, meaning she would be there shortly. Bunting walked in soon after they entered, ordered a coffee, then seated herself in one of the armchairs that sat close to the table. Carly was still to arrive.

Also, at the very same time, across town, Better B.

wanted a coffee, but she needed to man the shop due to the insanity of the times, mainly so she could keep an eye on the armoire that housed Desmond, and to make sure her brat of a father kept quiet. Any distraction caused by him could upset the balance she had so carefully developed - she knew that her creepy parent could easily cause enough of a disruption in her life to affect the spells she had on everyone. If someone came into the shop that was immune to the bewitchments, opened the armoire, saw Desmond hanging there, well who knows who or what might get involved then. She was not willing to take any risks. Things were going just far to well. So Seteeva was sent on coffee duty. She was supposed to go to Lance's, but her infatuation for Carly Jones and his pottery shop diverted her, which, she knew, would ultimately lead her to Chetsy Chocolates. *Well,* she thought, *it served coffee, so what if I get the coffees there instead of Lance's.* However, today - even though she had not smoked as much as usual - she didn't make it to her destination of choice. The reason for this was because she thought she heard a little voice singing in her head - it came as she walked down the main street of Chetsy town. *Oh my,* she thought, *I haven't sung that song in ages.* And so she started to sing, slightly out of tune, but not quietly. She was a siren at full blast.

"WHEN A MAAAN... LOVES A WOMAN..." and on she went, singing along with the little voice in her head. Most of the people in Chetsy either were possessed at this time and so didn't care, or were not possessed and just thought it natural for Seteeva to be high. Either way, no one questioned it. And so she had the freedom to sing like a walrus as she walked along.

When the song finished, Seteeva came to a standstill in the middle of the street, she felt deprived, she wanted to sing some more - the last time someone had denied her like this was in baby school - as far as she remembered, that someone was still a slug, perpetually getting its head chopped off - how dare it stop! In her head or not! That's when the little voice came to her again, but now it was not singing, it was giggling. It didn't stop giggling. The twittering sound was not something she wanted to join in with. In fact, it was just an annoyance. That is when she realized that the voice was not in her head - it was coming from something strange in the town. Seteeva put her nose into the air and sniffed - a big ugly witch sniff. Quickly locating the source, she started to move with a determined step. Big strides of a cretin seeking revenge! It did not take her long - she followed that annoying little giggle right up to The Silver Ghost that had its windows wide open. She peered inside, her black pupil dilating, then reached in, grabbing the neck of the giggling twerp like creature and started to shake, like a rat terrier would with vermin. She squeezed its neck, and shook and shook - she had a miser's grip that would not let go. She rattled the strange beast hoping to free him of his brain, all of his appendages flapping from side to side, his large penis banging around. With so much shaking, the penis hit Seteeva's wrist with such force, that a spurt of goo shot forth from its end. The gunk hit her square in the mouth. *Gross Little Monster!*

She yelled inside her head. Seteeva could not believe it. She dropped the flopping beast so that she could wipe the back of her hand across her face in absolute disgust, then she spat onto the ground! Simon grabbed the opportunity as he plopped onto the back seat, his neck no longer in a vice grip, he clutched at the green cloak, wrapped it around himself, leapt invisibly out of the window and raced up the street after his friends.

Seteeva straightened herself, stepping back from the car, a wolf that has lost its prey.

"Where are you, you little jerk!" *Fuck a duck, where'd it go!* "Come here to nice Seteeva!" *Where has that beast gone?* She spat on the pavement again, waiting for a minute, just in case it reappeared. But no, there was to be no Bo Peep, so she headed off to get the coffee, still looking around furtively for the scurvy monster as she moved. She passed Carly's shop, he wasn't there - this made her scurry on. She knew he had another place just outside of town, one that was more isolated. He never seemed to be there lately though, always in town around people. Maybe, just maybe, he was at the other place, which would make it easier for her to get him. *Now is the time,* she thought.

In the meantime, Simon raced up the lane, rounding a couple of corners, smelling the scent of his friends in the air. He knew how to follow them - he was like a bloodhound. He literally flew in through the door of Lance's, cape gasping, belly busting, nipples flapping, spider legs grappling. It caused alarm to his friends as they watched him, the distraught expression on his beautiful face mirrored on their own.

He bounced from the doorway, across the floor and up onto the table, nimbly missing the cups of coffee that his four friends had before them.

"A wicked witch grabbed me by my neck!" blurted Simon. "My Dooh Daah saved me!"

This comment made him look down at the giant penis between his legs. Although most of the time he hated this thing that had been cursed upon him, at this moment he was thankful for the nasty looking appendage. He giggled, remembering the look on Seteeva's face when his Dooh Daah had done its thing.

"Which witch was it?" asked Willman quietly.

As he asked, he took out a small flask from his hip pocket. He unscrewed the top, pouring a small amount of the Irish Single Malt into one of the empty cream containers. This being small enough for Simon to handle, he pushed it toward him.

"Good for shock," he said, winking.

"Oh..." Simon tried to down it in one, but it was still a large shot for a little guy. Two tries did it though, which led him to gasp in a delighted way. He pushed the container back for more. T.W. shrugged his shoulders, pouring the golden liquid once again.

"Which one?" he asked once more.

"Old One Eye," replied Simon simply. Then he finished off the second whiskey.

T.W. turned to the others, all four putting there heads together in quiet discussion.

Before Simon had turned up, Felice had been fiddling with a piece of wool in her pocket, worrying it, she now placed it on the table so she could give her full attention to the discussion. While they talked, Simon lifted his hands to cradle each cheek, his palms coddling his flushing face. He had started to feel a little queer. After a few seconds, he took his hands away from his head, which felt real wobbly, like the Christmas decoration on top of the tree. He started to giggle. He looked down at Dooh Daah, which was hanging limp, but now he was thinking about how Dooh Daah had saved him, so he said, "good bwoy, wanna go fwor walkies?" He reached for the piece of wool that was laying on the tabletop, managing to tie one end around his penis, the other end he held onto with his hand. He pulled the string upwards, making his penis stick straight out in front of him. He pulled again, loosened, then pulled - a puppet on a string. He took a step forward - it was at this point that his actions caught the attention of his friends.

"Simon! Just what are you doing?" asked Bunting.

"Whatsy looky like," he slurred, "twaking doggie flor walkies. Glood dwoggie woggie!" He looked down at his tied up appendage, then strode across the table, jumped onto the floor, and headed for the door.

Theadora, T.W., Felice and Bunting looked at each other in dismay, although Willman had what appeared to be the crease of a grin on his face. The four moved quickly after Simon, following him halfway down the lane, watching his wavy path from behind. It was like watching a squirrel cross the road. Halfway was about as far as Simon got before he crumpled to the ground, snoring loudly. Felice bent down, scooping him up under her arm, giving her giant friend a bit of a glare.

"Not so much next time," she ordered in her clipped accent.

It was getting late by now, so they went in search of Carly. He had not shown for their meeting. They went to his in town shop, which had the "SHUT" sign up. The door was locked with millions of gayly colored fairy lights brightening the inside. Unusual, they all commented, he knew about their meeting. Theadora put her face up to the window, looking in - it was then that she groaned inwardly, followed by a sharp exhale. She had felt something.

"What is it, Thea?" asked her son, concern engulfing his features.

"Quickly. We must go to the cabin. I feel something amiss." She startled them all by setting off at a run back toward the car - Bunting went with her. Felice was the next to follow, but first she shoved the snoring form of Simon toward T.W.

"Here, you carry him."

As T.W. took Simon, the little guy let out a fizzling fart followed by an earth trembling snore. Felice was glad she handed him over when she did - she snickered as she glanced behind to see T.W.'s nose puckering in on itself. She watched him throw the butt hissing Simon over his shoulder, barely holding onto his feet, his face turned the other way. Once she had controlled her snickering snickers, she started to run - so too, did Willman.

## CHAPTER FORTY-EIGHT

# THE BEHEADING SPELL

Meanwhile - which was the reason Thea had sensed something amiss - Seteeva had decided not to get coffee. She had decided instead, to dash back to the shop to get her evil witch friend - because, she had decided, it was time to get Carly Jones good and proper.

As it turned out, B.B. was up for a bit of fun. Seteeva could not believe her luck. The timing was right. They put out the sign - *Gone for Lunch* - locked the door to the shop and quick stepped out. The sporty little red M.G. smirked when it saw them coming, grunting its approval about the mission. B.B. drove, she was erratic at best, speed limits of no concern. The tiny car dashed through the town, grabbing a hold of the road with its gnarly tires, heading toward Carly's olde post and beam building. It scorched up the hill - two leering faces behind the windshield - leaving only dust behind.

Crammed inside, like astronauts in a capsule, they shot up the road - two wicked witches rubbing elbows, one gripping the steering wheel, the other gripping the seat.

"How's your eye?" asked Better B. "Ehhum, I mean, you know, the, umm, hole, you know, where your eye used to be?" She took her hands off the steering wheel, slapping her legs in mirth.

"Heartless bitch," mumbled Seteeva, grabbing her seat tighter, as if gravity would not keep her there.

"What?" asked B.B. - knowing full well what. She turned her face to glare - not watching were she was driving at all - giving Seteeva 'the what for' look. As she pulled her stare back to the road, a tree lurched close. She managed to jerk the wheel just in time - the solid trunk missing them by inches.

"Flippin dickin trickin, B.B. Watch where the fuck you are going!" Seteeva's face was white.

Better B. recovered fast, she just slapped her leg again, leaning forward over the wheel, choking on her own spittle of a laugh.

"LET'S GO GET THE FISH LOVING GAY BASTARD!" she yelled through the windshield.

Seteeva, all too ready for the moment, responded with a smirk, her white knuckles loosening their death grip. Finally, they were in the same place at the same time - their pinpoint black eyes back to the road, two pale faces ghoulishly peering into the approaching darkness. At the turn off to Carly's cabin, the car swerved to the left, before catapulting back to the right down the narrow lane that led to the olde building. They both saw the light in the cabin at the same time - feeling elation in the same instant.

He was home!

Better B. slid to a sliding halt while looking at the distant cabin set back in the trees. It was not dark yet, but it was to be a full moon, the large globe already visible as it clambered over the top of the distant hills. She felt so strong lately, liking the strength the soul sucking gave her - in fact she craved it. Her magic was more powerful than ever. The only thing that bothered her was that she had to keep stepping on the creeping feeling that tried to talk to her, the feeling that her mother would be mad at her, and even worse than that, the feeling that she didn't really like herself. She hated her father for what he was - and now she was doing the same. She was confused - the feeling sneaked around in her head like a pit of vipers. The confusion led to more depression. The depression made her more wicked. Simply put, she was in a state that was beyond evil. In fact, she was feeling so wicked that she just wasn't paying attention when she got out. It was muddy under the car where she parked, and it was muddy under her feet. The brown sludge sucked hard - slurping - a mudslide trying to gobble her up. She slid first a little this way, then a little that, before she slipped arse backwards toward the mucky ground. As she fell, her flowing, red silk jacket - that she absolutely loved - caught on something metal.

It ripped! A great big tearing sound!

She jumped back to her feet, viciously kicking the wheel as she did so.

"AAAAAAAAGH! AAAAAAAGH!" Her pent up frustrations spurted like molten lava. The gradually peeking stars shivered in horror. The growing moon shrunk in terror. The devil himself stopped his beatings.

"MY BEST JACKET! MY BEST! FUCKA FUCKA FUCKA!"

As her scream echoed in the distance, finally disappearing somewhere down in the valley never wanting to come back, Better B. stood up tall, feeling better. Uug*hhh!* She wiped her muddy hands on her pants, straightening her jacket as if it were not in ruins, then abruptly marched off toward the cabin.

Seteeva scuttled behind, wringing her hands in glee. *Get ready, Carly Barely Head, we are a comin.* As they neared the cabin, they crept on tippy toes, ballerinas banned from the ballet. Not that it mattered. Carly was so engrossed in his art, painting away on a dainty teacup - he wouldn't know if an earthquake hit. He'd lost track of time, so infatuated was he with his intricate piece of work that he didn't even realize that he had missed the meeting in town. He was humming to himself pleasantly. Able sat on his perch in the corner, preening under his wing, while Mandy lay in cozy bliss by the small fire.

Silently, Seteeva and Better B. made their way to the square lead pained window, their two white faces - dying moths - as they peered through the lower distorted glass. Seteeva's black eye patch was slightly askew, but thankfully no orange goo oozed out at this time. Their faces changed as they stared - looking like something in a carnival. Pay to view faces. Nasty, contorted, evil and grotesque.

"Looks like we came to the right place," whispered Seteeva.

Carly continued to work, oblivious to the danger lurking so near at hand. As the wicked witches leered through the window, Able saw them - he squawked, he screeched - but Carly payed the crying parrot no heed, his art had cast him into another place where no one else entered.

The two evil witches stepped back, not believing the opportunity that the idiot was casting their way. They turned to face each other - grins set like jester's masks.

"Lets do it, before he hears that stupid parrot."

"Maybe we should have parrot pie later."

Better B. snickered, snorting snot.

The spell they decided on was *The Beheading Spell.* It was a dark spell of very evil origin. They both knew it well, but neither had ever dared use it before.

The black words stormed from their mouths, filling the air like a thunderhead about to clap. Snail shells cracked, worms curled in on themselves, centipedes lost their legs, ladybugs shed their spots, beetles became spiders, and spiders ate the birds. Tree roots gnarled, night owls cackled, stray cats screeched like whores. The earth opened, a chasm filled with crying widows, a cave full of tortured souls, miners with blackened faces, screaming in the night of the dark. The earth opened more, crackling like lightening in a storm. Toads bellowed, their skins falling, frogs fried in the heat, grasshoppers lost their leaping. The earth groaned, creaking and moaning in discomfort. Until finally - it belched forth the creature within. First, only its eyes could be seen. Dark and red and tortured. It blinked. Looking out from the depths of hell. Its tongue flicked, licking up scorched remnants.

"Hasssusssssssssszzzzzzzz..."

It slithered.

Hasssussssssszzzzzzzzzzz..."

Seteeva looked then, glancing over.

"Holy Macaroonies!

"Ssssshhhhh, don't look."

They chanted some more.

"Hasssusssszzzzzzzzz..."

It raised its head, beady eyes blinking - the redness blood. Oozing from its hole over gnarled bodies of skunks and coons and bastard dogs. The head pointed, its tongue sicked, licking the decaying flesh over which it creeped. The body followed – long, slithering, thick and fleshy. Scales peeled back, maggots poked, sores oozed. Yet still it moved forth, smothering the ground with a thick layer of flesh, insects running, vermin scuttling, rat eyes popping, it slithered and slicked its way toward the cabin.

"Hasssusssszzzzzzzzzzzz..."

Seteeva shivered, a cold ripple of death down her spine - *shouldn't have looked, should never have looked, hope it knows its here for dimple head.* She reached up, holding on to her own head just in case.

"Christ sake Seteeva, stay with it, put your goddamn hand down! Want to attract attention?

Her arm dropped like a smart salute. *No pokey chance in hell, nossiry, no attention - need a smokey.* Her hand reached toward her pocket.

"Don't you dare!" hissed Better B. spittle squeezing through her clamped jaw.

"Hasssusssszzzzzzzzzzzzz..."

Gore trickled from its grizzly fangs, its breath skank as a plagued body weeks dead in a flea infested bed.

"Da Da's dead," wept the child her own boils singing their song on her pale skin. "Da Da's dead," as she turned to see the serpentine demon coming toward her - her own head now in the Moat House, saying over and over, "Da Da's dead." After beheading her, as it had been called upon to do so, it had turned to her Da Da, its last meal, rotten flesh with boiling whores, rotten sores and open craws. It was now here, in this time, breathing is foulness outside Carly's cabin. Putrid smells of cadavers long since forgotten, sewer tunnels never explored, massacres in the war fields of demonic justice. A stinking, vile, eruptuous breath - heaving forth its putrid smile. It came. Forth.

"Hasssussssszzzzzzzzzzzzz..."

The warbled glass of the window melted, the frame sparked alight, tree frogs sizzled and beetles crinkled, cracking bodies in the pale moonlight. The devil laughed and demons spat, a chaos of howling skulls, grimacing, grinning, banging back and forth. Skeletal bodies clawed the earth, climbing, clinging, frantic for escape. Scaly arms, creeping behind, dragging their bones, their screaming souls, back to the darkest depths of the blackest battle. Only the serpent was allowed out.

"Hassssusssssszzzzzzzzzz..."

It slithered and raked, gnawed and grimed, spitting forth the spines of porcupines, like darts and daggers, piercing hearts, of robins, nuthatch and spindly mice.

Rabbits hopped, but not for long, its flicking tongue wrapping hard, squeezing life, sucking breath, breathing hard, foul and putrid, green and slime dripping down - drops sizzling, hitting ground.

"Hasssussssszzzzzzzzzzz..."

It slithered.
Up the wall.
Through the molten window frame.

"Hasssusssszzzzzzzzz..."

Its beady eyes spying inside, the bloody tear, now a river, a cry of ecstasy.

"Hasssussssszzzzzzzzzz..."

Lips of rubber trembling dry, cracking warts, tongue a spitting, venom dripping. Pupils wide... mouth, a skeletal grin.

"Hasssussssszzzzzzzz..."

Able flew at Carly, batting him with his wings.
"WHAKE UHHP!"
The rank odor of death filtered through his nostrils, stirring awareness. His hand still, its painting stopped - the brush a finger of the leper. But no bells sang, no voice, nothing ringing crying to beware. Voices only in his head! Only Able flapping at his cheeks! He looked up.
That is when the wind left his body, no words

could he form to combat the vileness before him. He simply stared, his silent scream scraping the chalkboard of hell!

His nostrils melted, his eardrums burst, a brain frazzled. The forked tongue thrust forth, hard, pushing, exploring, up his nostrils first, then out and down his throat - the venom paralyzing in its cruelty. He could not move. Only scream again inside his head. Carly was lost.

*WILLMAN*NNN! NOOOOOO... His mind sobbed as the tongue probed his inner side.

Tongue continued with a driving force, down his lungs, finding nothing there, withdrawing back to explore dark caves, caverns, sinus taverns. The fat and sensuous curling thing, long and lean, finding his eyes, its end split - forked, each prong silently exploring the depths. Slithering around, smooching here and there, behind the glossy globe, finding a nerve, pressing down, pain an explosion in his mind.

*Love you Able, Mandy, Willman, Thea! Bunteeeeeeeeeeeng!* His scream allowing no more.

His head wrapped in the coils, mind still screaming, mouth open, silent in the abyss. Across the meadows they flew, this demon and he. The wind a tornado, the pain a witch's pyre. Its heat creeping down his ears, through his eyes, into his mouth, his skull exploding - a million mind fragments each one a torture of its own. His tongue lolled, drooling out the side - saliva red bright blood. *He wished he were dead.*

His wish led only to the serpentine force hitting earth, apocalypse in its glory, a meteorite finding home. His head swelled, splitting at the seams as the earth closed over. The serpent dug deeper, seeking the blackest screams of hell! Until finally it loosened it coils, leaving the head behind to roll back and forth in a small worn cavern ten feet below the silken forest that crawled bright once more with beetles, worms, voles, and flying bats... shiny frogs, silken toads, plush bunnies and goats with toes.

The small sycamore by the mound of disturbed earth bent gently, reaching one of its limbs forward - stretching out with grace to provide a perch for Able as he swooped close to Carly's grave. The parrot was followed by the snow-white charm of the panting cat that came to a halt above the earthen mound that covered the head of their beloved.

They waited - the parrot clasping hard to the woody arm of his treeing friend, while Mandy preened, sitting atop the mountain of dirt. Her purple haze a lingering trail that disappeared back like a pointing finger through the woods.

Back at the cabin, merriment was at its height.

"Holly shitaroony! Did you see that!" yelled Seteeva as the storm died down. "Good job you ducked B.B. or your head would have gone with him!"

They had jumped to the window to peer as soon as the last word of the last line of the spell had fallen. Carly's head blasting out of the window had nearly smacked Better B. square in the face. Her reflexes had been quick, managing to dodge out of the way, causing her once again to slip and fall. Now, yet again, she raised herself up out of the mud, but in more humor this time. The look of horror on Carly's face as it had shot toward her was almost more than she could take. She snickered snot again.

"Holy cow!" cried Seteeva, her hyaena laugh making her neck bulge in and out.

Better B. Better still snickered snot with a huge smile on her face, until finally, she too started to laugh.

*"Hee hee he. Haw.* Lets go get the parrot!"

They ran around to the small door - pushing it open - *whoa, holy shit!* - Carly's body was still sitting on the stool. It was sobbing.

Seteeva choked as she looked at the pathetic thing before her, bending in mirth and pointing at the same time.

"Jeezus Jumpin Beans! You see that B.B. Unfucking believably hilarious!"

Then she crouched, her eyes becoming slits as she sneaked toward the flailing figure, her soul poiling and boiling, laughing and sassing, amused that a body could grieve that way. The headless *thing* felt her near, its arms flailed wildly, punching thin air.

"Well Jeezus H christ, jab at me, I'll a jabbedy back," mocked Seteeva before flexing her fists to poke like a boxer in a ring, deftly moving away from the beheaded blind man and his movements. She was having a grand time, jabbing wildly as she dodged the crazy whirling arms, when Better. B., who was standing in the corner, hands on hips, said.

"Where'd he go? Ya now, the stupid parrot?"

"Shut up B. B. Can't you see I'm busy," her feet danced - Muhammad Ali in full form.

"Shut up yourself, Seteeva, you're such a moron! The parrot's gone, so no pie-d-pie tonight - just what are you doing anyway, you are such a freak!"

Seteeva had a retort on her lips when she thought better of it, her feet grounding for a second - finding nirvana the best she could - her soul needing rest - *Nah, why bother.*

"Doesn't matter, we'll get the stupid parrot later. Aneeway, that was great, thanks for helping B.B. Let's just go home, back to the shop. We cud celebrate there, yu know, wine and all." Her sweet talk worked - she took one last punch, catching Carly right in his chest, causing him to huff in pain, before she turned toward the door, close on the heels of her friend.

Outside they joined together, jigging in a dancing fashion back to the car, holding hands like long lost spider sisters. Once in the coziness of the sporty vehicle, Seteeva pulled out her pipe. She was in high spirits, but wanted to be higher.

"Hope you don't mind, B.B., I just have to have a suck or too."

"I know the feeling," said Better B. grinning - not thinking of a pipe at all.

With the pedal to the metal, the car lurched forward, careening down the lane. At the last second the swirling wheels swerved into the road, its rear end hitching back and forth before catching traction to take off at lightening speed once again.

The four good witches came in the opposite direction, seeing the sizzling blur of a red vehicle and nothing more. Their focus was on getting to Carly. T.W turned sharply into the lane leading to the cabin. They pulled to a halt in a muddy spot where a piece of red cloth poked its nose out of the brown muck. Simon jumped out first, recovered fully from the whiskey thanks to a little help from Bunting.

Everyone hopped out after the little man – as they looked at the distant cabin, all noses went into the air - there was a nasty mixture of odiferous smells. Most strong was Seteeva's semi rotting eye socket - rank in its intensity. Bunting pinched her nose shut. This was followed by body odor, a bad witch stink that made Felice gag. After that, came some weird, tainted smell that none of them could quite place.

It was this last smell that had them running. Ten legs a leaping. Upon reaching the cabin, before bursting through the door, the horror of the vision of what had transpired came to them all. Their fear for Carly at having been alone to face such terror - was terror to themselves. The melted pieces of window lay glinting in the now clear moonlight. Slowly, they entered the cabin. One by one they stepped through the door. The fire was still giving out heat and all was still except for the motion of the cup that Carly had been working on. It lay on its side, rocking back and forth, a baby in its crib. They looked at these things. The fire. The tabletop. The cup. All eyes looked at these before they dared lift to see the headless body of their friend sitting in his seat behind the table. His body was perched on top of the stool. The one that was uncomfortable - but Carly always said it was the best ever. He didn't look comfortable now though - his body sitting on the high twirling seat, his arms starting to flail wildly in the air, reaching up toward his head that wasn't there.

No one could stand to watch, they stepped back outside, not sure what to do. Felice moved over to the window, finding Seteeva and Better B.'s footprints. Her spit landed square.

"Demons! You two!" She hissed, glaring at the place they had stood to take her friend, until her attention was caught by the small voice.

"Look! Look! Look at the glow leading across the fields."

Everyone looked. There was nothing there.

"What do you see, Simon?" asked Felice.

"Just a slight white blur of a trail, with a purple tinge, leading off that way." He pointed with his disjointed finger.

"It must be Mandy!" cried Willman, "you can see that, Simon?"

Simon did not respond, he just jogged along the trail that only he could see, his long spindly legs moving with ease over the uneven ground. The others followed, floating in a ghoulish way. They covered the two miles quickly, through the fields and bogs, scattering the fog that drifted above the earth. As they came closer to Carly's resting place, a bright star of light beckoned, outlined with a purple glow. Mandy sat still, cool and white. Everyone moved toward him and, toward the voice of Able.

"Whurry uhp. AHCKKK... whury uhp!"

Below the ground, Carly was now conscious of what had happened. He started to cry. Huge, big fat tears, slid down his face. His nose dripped, drool slobbered, smearing from his lips, more tears welled. He went to wipe it all away with his hands, until he realized that he couldn't. He had no hands. No chest, no body, no legs, no nothing. Just his head buried about ten feet under. He thought about this. He shouldn't have. It made him sob harder.

Up above, his friends stood, unsure what to do.

"Willman?" asked Felice, "what? Please, hurry."

Willman stood tall, pondering. He didn't know. He tucked his chin onto his chest... THINK THINK THINK THINK THINK going inside his own head. Disappearing. Turning inside out. In this state, he sent two messages out - one was to Carly.

*Carly hear me Carly Carly Carly CARLY hear me.*

Silence.

*Carly C A R L Y! Listen... hear... it is coming... don't panic.*

Carly stopped his crying as his friend's voice swirled around in his mind - he wondered just WHAT was coming.

The other message Willman sent was to something else - after it was received a scratching started in the earth, deep down, deep below. It came from another place, another time - yet it scratched here in this. It moved fast, moved furious, moved with a deliverance of ease - scratching, scraping, scrabbling and scaling. It pushed up through the earth, easing centipedes, moving worms, brushing beetles, nothing did it hurt. Its fingers dug, mole like, moving upwards all the while.

*Rest Carly... The Hand is here to help... we are coming.*

*The Hand?* Thought Carly. Even though his eyes had dried, his lips still trembled. He was very frightened.

The Hand continued to dig upward, until it finally reached Carly's head - cradling, rocking, gently stroking. Its fingers protecting - encasing his skull like a rib cage holding a gently beating heart.

Calmness enveloped Carly. The Hand gave him peace.

Willman sighed in relief at the vision.

"OK, come on Simon. You know what to do. The Hand will keep a space around his face, it will protect him while we dig." *Besides keeping him calm. Please don't have an asthma attack, Carly, my friend.*

Simon did know, he was already digging, his bare hands and feet kicking, a crab finding heaven in the sand. The hole to be dug needed to be wide, so that it did not cave back in. On the outer parts, Simon gnawed at roots, kicked out rocks, burrowing headfirst.

"Hurry up! We only have a small window of time to save him, spells will not get him out. Hurry, hurry!" Simon yelled to the others standing around the growing hole.

Bunting was the first to jump in, digging furiously. Although no incantation would bring the head out, they did use their magic to help remove the dirt. Huge amounts scooped with each hand movement, much larger than any fist full. Felice and Willman fell into rhythm quickly. It was manual labor, but performed with a hint of special powers. The dirt was easy to move, loose from the Serpents burrowing. Luckily so, for the stench was foul, scales and maggots the road to their friend. They gagged, each one, watering eyes and flaming nostrils stuffed full of wasabi, but still they worked on.

"Move the dirt back, Thea!" yelled Willman to his mother standing high up on the edge. She did, this part done with flicks of the wrist, waves of color and a mix of spit and herbs that she kept in her pocket... the mound of dirt pulled away from the ever-growing hole.

Meanwhile, The Hand crooned, stroked, preened and protected.

Until finally, when they thought their stomachs could hold no more...

"We're there!" yelled Simon. "There! Carly! Oh Carly, Carly," he sobbed.

He scooped the last few handfuls of dirt, his small hands moving with a velvet touch. The Hand still encased the skull.

Willman knelt down. *Let me... take him.*

Hand unfurled its fingers, extending them in a gesture of faith.

Willman reached down, pulling the head upwards.

"Uugh!" groaned Carly, the sudden motion making him queasy.

Willman startled at the sound, almost dropping his friend. *Oh heck,* he thought, *what if the head rolled down the hill into some rabbit hole...* he shifted his thumbs to get a better hold, then took a deep breath. He held Carly's head so that it was face to face with his own. The eyes before him were slow to focus.

"H e l p  m e," Carly uttered through bleached white lips.

"Oh Carly, I am here," muttered T.W.

Then he stood tall, raising to his full height, seeing nothing, his mind empty of the sight before him - he was back in the field with Jazz and Hayban, back in the field until the field became now. Silver sparks appeared in the air, atoms bonding together, encasing both their heads in a cocoon of molten beauty. Whispered words floated, caressing the pain of the tortured.

*Stay with me... my friend - stay with me.*

Willman hugged his friend to him as he melded time and space to take the head that was in his hands back to the body that was waiting. Slowly his outline dimmed, phasing in and out, the silver of their heads shimmering into the void. Until finally - they disappeared.

They reappeared in the cabin where Carly's body was bumping into things, wandering aimlessly around like a mummy escaped from its tomb. They materialized slowly, the head still safely cradled. Once his body was firmly back in this world, Willman stepped forward toward the retched wandering form. He tucked Carly's head under his arm as he reached out with his other hand to comfort. As his fingers touched the clammy forearm, the headless body startled, swinging a fist into the hard abdomen before it, knuckles clenched tight.

"Hey hey, it's me Carly, your buddy."

Carly's arms reached out, feeling with his fingers, a blind man reading the brail of his friend's face. Recognition dawned. *If it had been that bitch, Seteeva again* - he was going to make contact this time. Willman took one of the hands that was tracing his eyebrows and guided it to the head that he held. Carly's hand stroked the contours of his own face - nose, cheeks and lips. The lips smiled at the touch of his own fingers.

"Quickly, Carly. We must move quick - I know that much, or it will be too late."

The body stood still while Willman placed the head on bare shoulders, as he did, paint smeared arms reached up to adjust the now withering thing so that it sat 'just so'. The silver cocoon that encased them sparkled brighter, giving strength to Carly's weakening brain. Inside the vacuum of shimmering tinsel, Willman leaned forward, placing his forehead on his friend's. The glistening vibrated, molding them tighter together. T.W. closed his eyes as words trembled out.

"Satina vel dale, di es minuet."

Knowledge of the spell coming from his readings of the thin red book.

The chant grew stronger, repetitive.

"Satina vel dale, di es minuett.
Te ust delemon, te ust delemon."

Until finally, Carly joined in, chanting once again, uniting their strengths to save the other. For what seemed like forever they stood like this, until the molten mercury slowly evaporated, leaving the two standing together.

Silence followed. Apprehension. *Had it worked?*

Willman finally moved, their foreheads peeling apart, the band aid removed. He looked square into the eyes before him. Carly looked back. He actually looked back! His lips were no longer snow white...and they could speak - and kiss!

"Willman! Thank you, thank you!"

"No. Thank you. Never have I seen one so brave," responded Willman.

Smiles played a happier dance than elephants

released from the circus, until finally, they fell into a hard embrace, laughter and tears warring with each other.

It had worked. The spell had worked! Carly was back.

## Chapter Forty-Nine
# SHOWDOWN IN THE USED FURNITURE STORE

It was now early morning, the day after Carly's rescue - which was also the morning after Harry Tomb had witnessed the things he did not want to witness. That was all yesterday. Now it was today. Really early today. All of the good witches were rested, but the two bad witches had celebrated so mightily about the success of the beheading, that they were sleeping off hangovers. Tomorrow, they had said, they would take Desmond out of the armoire and deal with him. Then, B.B. said, she would deal with her father. She really no longer needed him. But for now, they slept, even though it was tomorrow already.

This early, fog enshrouded morning saw five big silhouettes and one little one, each approaching the small shop on the corner. Simon was told to stay outside - he was left hiding behind a flowerpot as T.W. and the others moved toward the door. Simon wasn't sure if he liked this plan or not - it made him nervous. As he watched his friends walk away, he started to play with his ankles, bending them forward, then all the way back, forward, and back. Being double jointed sure had its positives, but he soon got tired of that game and started to look around for something else to do. He felt fidgety, like an ant on a hot tin roof. Surely he had been sitting here for a long time already. He sighed. *What now?* He looked, nothing of interest anywhere. He glanced down. That is when he saw his big old floppy penis dangling between his legs. His curiosity peaked. *Hmmm?* Wanting only to distract himself from his fear for his friends, without thinking much more about it, he grabbed the thing with one hand, and with a quick flick of his wrist, he thwapped it onto the inside of one of his spindly thighs.

THWAP!

Then he flicked his wrist the other way, so that it thwapped onto the inside of his other thigh.

THWAP!

*Hey,* he thought, *ho,* this was more intriguing than bending his ankles back and forth. Simon was suddenly living in the moment.

So he carried on.

THWAP!

A twist of the wrist.

THWAP!

A turn of the hand.

THWAP!

Back again.

THWAP!

He managed six THWAPS before Felice was on him, the purple billowing skirt looming toward him like some ghostly apparition. Her fingers grabbed his arm.

"For heavens sake, stop that!" she hissed at him. "You'll wake them!"

The horrible thought of the wicked witches waking was enough to stop Simon from thwapping his ding-dong. Felice left him with a frown on his beautiful forehead, chewing on his fingernails, gnarling them with his teeth.

She rejoined the group. Everyone just shook heads in exasperation.

"Did they wake?" Bunting mouthed to T.W.

He shook his head in the negative. His hearing was intense - he could still hear the slight whistle that Seteeva made while sleeping. The whistling sound came through a gap in her teeth from constant use of the pipe. Though barely audible, it was easily heard by him, even outside. That and the light snore of Better B. Better. Both sounds told him, that as yet, they had not stirred. His hearing was so good in fact, that a few moments later he did hear Better B.'s eyelids snap open as her strengthened witch senses kicked in. It was like the click of a pin being pulled on a hand grenade. He motioned instantly to the others to put on invisible spells, which not only made them invisible, but camouflaged their presence, even from other witches - even those as strong as the two wicked ones.

The door to the shop creaked open. It was not Better B. that stood there, but her dark shadow, blacker than coal. Her body still lay on the floor where she had fallen last night after too much wine, their celebrations mighty. She lay now, eyes wide open after sending her shadow to check - she was curious, but just too lazy to get up, so she lay motionless on the floor, although her senses were heightened by something. She just did not know what.

The shadow loomed in the doorway sending out long wispy fingers to probe the foggy air. They found nothing.

The door closed and the form floated back over to Better B., lying back down beside her.

Seteeva still whistled.

Better B. lay awake, on her back, folding her arms across her chest like a corpse in a coffin. Her shadow did the same thing.

Meanwhile. Outside. There was stillness. The five good witches waited.

Simon had peeked out from behind the flower pot when he heard the door open, but when he saw the terrifying, jet black, nasty looking form of Better B., he had ducked back. Since then, he'd been holding his breath, but now he let it out in one long huff, needing a deep suck to replace it. The air was cold and damp and foggy as it filled his lungs. The wetness was irritating. Simon tried not to, but he just couldn't hold it. He coughed! A bullfrog burping in the quiet.

Better B. heard it! Her shadow jumped to its feet and ran to the door, flinging it wide. Once outside, it crouched, a lion stalking its prey before it leaped off the porch, reaching one long jet black arm toward the flower pot, knocking it sideways. The red clay broke, exposing Simon, who now stood, his face stretched in horror, his nakedness shivering. He tried to make a run for it, but only managed a few tiny steps before the black fingers wrapped tightly around his ankle, dragging him screaming into the witches lair. The heavy wood door banged with a thud. Inside, the shadow stood proudly. The upside down form of Simon was swaying to and fro - he may as well have been swinging from a noose.

Outside, dismay played its dismal game on each face - they had forgotten to protect Simon!

Seteeva woke groggily to the little man's gurgled screams, although her grogginess lifted like a curtain for final call at the joy of seeing just who had been captured. It was almost as great as the joy she had experienced only yesterday with Carly's beheading. She shifted herself to sit upright, her short legs barely reaching the floor.

"Oh my," she whispered. "If it isn't the nasty little monster from yesterday."

These words were enough to send one huge shiver up Simon's spine as he dangled in the air. He stopped screaming and started to cry instead. He knew he was going to die, and after he had finally found friends.

T.W. thought he was the only one that could hear what was happening inside, but he wasn't. Carly had also been blessed with extraordinary hearing. He had just witnessed his little friend being airlifted, not to safety, but to hell, then he heard him scream, and now, the crying. This was just all too much, that on top of yesterday. He didn't even think before he moved. He dropped his invisible spell before anyone could stop him - firing himself like a raging bull up the steps to the house, blasting the door into splinters as he entered.

"PUT! HIM! DOWN!" He thundered.

The shadow was so surprised that it dropped Simon, who plonked onto his head before tumbling to his side. The little man grabbed at the chance, knowing that now, he could help - scuttling forward, crab like, he opened his mouth wider than a moray eel, clamping hard into the shadow's leg with no intention of ever letting go. He shook his head this way and that - a rabid dog gone mad! The shadow hopped up and down, trying to kick off the pain that had a hold of it. Better B. was doing the same thing, shadowing her shadow.

Seteeva looked on in shock after having woken up to bedlam. She wasn't even concentrating on Simon any more. All she could see was Carly. AND HE WAS NOT HEADLESS! Her fury was hotter than lava spurting from a volcano - if she could spit darts with jagged poisonous ends, she would, but that was a spell that had always evaded her.

This was the pandemonium that The Willman, Theadora, Bunting and Felice saw as they bolted through the door after their friends.

It took only moments for Seteeva to collect herself. Jumping from the couch - dropping her pipe in the process - her round body took the few steps necessary toward Shadow. Reaching down, she grabbed the nasty little man monster by the legs, and gave one mighty pull.

Simon had huge jaw strength and could have held on forever, but the power of Seteeva's tugging made his teeth feel loose - so he let go. The sudden release caused Seteeva to reel backwards, arms circling like a windmill gone mad. Even though Simon was caught in this tornado, it gave him time to fold up on himself - double jointed as he was - so that his mouth could find another target. It was easy for him to clamp down hard into one of her fingers. His teeth pierced her skin - vampire action - this made Seteeva drop her grip on his leg as she screeched in pain. Sensing his chance for escape, he let go, his teeth sucked back into his mouth. He fell to the floor, landing easily before scurrying for safety under a big wooden chest that was sitting behind the sofa.

Now that Simon no longer had his teeth dipped into the black flesh of the shadow, B.B. managed to stop hopping around like some demented baboon. She glared at the five intruders who stood before her - a fortress with no drawbridge. Turning to her shadow, she pointed, her long, sneaky finger creeping in the air.

"G e t  t h e m!"

Shadow tried, it loomed upwards, a black ghost looking for glory. It opened its mouth - a volcanic cavern filled with gases, the insides white, yet fury hot. It leered upwards before moving forward, its mouth opening wider still, ready to eat them whole.

Willman was the first to move, stepping to meet the blackest ghoul. He stood his frame between them all. The mouth opened further still, emitting spittles of poisonous fumes - the round lipless shape huffing intoxication toward him.

"Today, is not your day, my friend," Willman whispered, reaching forward into the void. His hand groped, trying to find it – yes - the tongue. *G o t  I t!* He pulled. Hard! The poisonous vapors disappeared, the 'O' of a mouth clamped tight, but not before the tongue came out. T.W. stood before his friends, the curling beast in his hand, it lapped up his arm, seeking his neck. "I said! Not today, my friend," as he grabbed a nearby bowie knife, ($10 the sticker said), to stab the squirming thickened flesh, pinning it to the floorboards of the house. The blackness of the ghoul receded, its shadowy arms rising to its paling face - white eyes appeared loud and staring - glaring at the giant before him. Willman glared back. "Step down my friend, and you can have your tongue back." Shadow looked at its maker, her fury at its futility clear on her livid face. It looked down at its darkened outline, realizing that it did not need SHE to be here. Shadow moved away, leaving Better B. to her misery.

"Get back here!" Better B. growled. "Come back! Right now!"

It didn't come back. It wanted its tongue. It slithered away, a black sniper sneaking off - its tongue still writhing, wrapping around the blade that held it captive. Shadow cast a look toward Willman, its eyes asking the question.

"You'll get your tongue, but you need to wait!" said T.W. tossing the words toward the lanky black figure before turning his attention back to the evil witches before him. He felt his friends moving in close behind. They were united.

As Shadow slipped further away, Better B. watched, stewing in her own feverish anger. At the same time, Seteeva sucked on her bitten finger - she wished, oh how she wished that it was her pipe.

"Foul little creature," she muttered to herself, as she sucked harder at the spot where Simon had bitten her. She could see her pipe laying only ten feet away, *if only I could reach it,* she thought - head down, finger in her mouth, eyes slanted, she sneakily surveyed the five standing before her. She noticed that the big guy was still distracted by Shadow and the others were busy glaring at Better B. who had lifted her arm, wiggling her maggot finger at them – *probably getting ready to send a bolt of lightening,* thought Seteeva, *can't she come up with anything better than that!* Seteeva decided to grab her chance. Her tattoo started to pulsate, emitting an eerie green glow from the top of her head, her one eye began to fill up with blood vessels, an intricately drawn map - escaping her eyes, convicts climbing out over her lids, spreading to cover her face that was changing shape. Her nose melted, leaving two deep black holes in the now bloody mass. Her teeth were jagged, no more whistling through a small gap - now a tornado of breath skank its way out, thundering between the yellow razor sharp fangs. She no longer had nails, but talons with the remains of her last enemy still stuck to the ends. Seteeva was gone – in her place was a beast!

Theadora noticed the pulsating light immediately. She knew what was going to happen, but had not expected the change to be so quick. She had only read of the abilities of the Selons – never being unfortunate enough to actually witness their transformation. Her stomach turned as she felt the air around become leaden – she couldn't breath - she pulled at her neck, gasping, knowing that Seteeva must have set her poisonous gaze upon her.

"Willman," gasped Thea, unable to move. She had no time for more before the beast was there, raking at her belly with its poison tipped talons, ripping her apart.

Willman was instantly by her side, a lion in fury. Never in all his life had he felt like this – he roared from his deepest throat. The beast in Seteeva had no time to turn. Willman pulled her arms back, snapping her shoulders like chopsticks made in a cheap factory – the sucking sound the talons made as they pulled out of his mother's belly made him crazy. He threw the writhing beast against the wall, the crumpled body slithering to the ground. The house shook as he stomped his giant feet onto her now withering weapons of death. As he turned towards his mother, he heard Seteeva groan - the beast had left her body.

"Mother..." Willman scooped the wilted form off the ground.

"I love you, my son," she managed to whisper.

Willman felt the blue velvet bag kicking in his pocket – he hesitated for one second. *No. Not the bag for this.* He was not going to take any chances, *what if she did not find her way* - he would take her himself. He remembered the words well from that day in the room with Felice, the words that should be read aloud.

"Heyisam moor teint dies Moorlzt!
Heyisam moor dia sus Zeib!
Heyisam moor parli teint har vient Straulitz!"

He chanted on, the words dropping from his lips like honey.

As Willman and Theadora disappeared, the others were in a full on battle with Better B. She had cast her lightening bolts - that Carly caught and ate - he was sizzling from the inside out, laughing at Better B.'s anger, at her befuddlement that he had managed to benefit from her wickedness. But the lightening was only the opening act. She pulled a blue globe out of her pocket, spitting on it once before looking inside.

"Are you in there, my Pretty One?"

Before the Pretty One could answer, Bunting sent a spark flying. The ceiling above Better B. opened - a scaly head poked out, with red eyes and a mane of thorns. Green saliva dripped from its cavernous mouth, singing the floorboards where it landed. The dragon reared its head back, sucking in the flames around it, turning with a vixen's vengeance toward her enemy below. Flames belched forth as the dragon huffed again and again – the evil witch's head burst into flames, her craggily hair burning better than oak on a cold winters day. Better B. screamed as she turned her wicked stare up. Before the dragon could huff again she cast her maggot finger into the air sending an axe flying. The axe knew what to do, a mind of its own - it twizzled and flexed, cutting of the dragons head which twisted and turned as it fell, missing Felice by inches, landing with a thud, splattering blood onto her pretty skirt.

Better B. was totally pissed. She rubbed the blue ball again.

"My Pretty One – come out to me!"

Before Felice, Bunting or Carly could move, The Pretty one emerged.

"Yes, dear? What is it you want?" It asked of its singed mistress.

"I want Felice's heart – for Seteeva!"

The Pretty One turned toward the three. The squishy white body of the drowned bloated sailor leered toward Felice, slopping across the room. Felice froze. Something about its eyes. It clanked its teeth at her as it reached out, ripping her blouse open, using its little finger and long pink painted nail to draw a circle around her heart. Carly and Bunting were paralyzed, unable to move, even though their minds jangled with frustration.

"I'm going down," mumbled Felice, hoping she wouldn't feel much, she could not utter anything else, no spells, no other thoughts.

Simon was watching in utter horror from under the chest. His eyes darted here and there – *come on Carly, do something,* he willed, wishing, hoping. As he darted his glance back toward Felice, something round and smoky caught his eye. It was slightly to the right of him, partially under the sofa that was in front of the chest. It was one of Seteeva's bubble encased demons, one she had missed. Inside, he could see a creature of some sort – it was banging on the inner wall of the globe. Simon watched, frowning as he read the moving lips, "let me out," they said, "I'll get the bastard!" With nothing to lose, the little man Simon darted forward, a mouse dashing for its hole - he poked his finger into the bubble then bounced back under the chest.

The demon could not believe its luck – freedom at last, after all those miserable tortuous years. *The stupid bitch wants that woman's heart, huh? For Seteeva – my archenemy. I'll be damned!* It launched itself into the air, barreling along, its mouth opened wide, swallowing The Pretty One whole.

The demon burped as it returned to form, standing in front of Simon, giving him the thumbs up.

"Thanks old chap, that's my job done."

Simon returned the thumbs as the demon flew out the door.

Better B. was so annoyed she was ready to vomit, her black gown flapped in a wind that pushed up through the floorboards, creaking its way into the room. The fierce wind howled as Felice's skirt did its final performance, a billowing cloud in a thunderstorm. Bunting was lifted into the air, pinned to the ceiling, a moth caught in a spider's web. Before chaos could ensue, Carly moved quickly, his paralyses gone, catching Better B.'s poison as his mouth opened, his cheeks bigger than the moon. Then he spat the wicked wind back across the room, flinging Better B. into a picture that hung crookedly on the wall. The black clad witch did the slippery slide into hell as she fell, the heavy picture frame following, landing like a hammer on her head before it toppled onto her belly, causing her prone form to wheeze out a huge puff of red tinted air. As the air escaped her soul sucking body, it formed a line that marched right into the picture before it, as if it knew the way.

Bunting, released from the gale, was back on the ground - she pounced over to Better B. ready to do battle if the wicked one rose like some serpent. Felice was crouched on the other side when she felt something grab her ankle. Her immediate thought was to yank away, but something stayed her – a tingle in her spine, that walked its way into her head. *Stay put* – it said.

"Felice, look down," whispered Bunting.

Felice did, her skirt in tatters, she could easily see the small hand that was grabbing onto her ankle. The hand was attached to an arm that was coming out of the painting.

"You've got one too, Bunting. Look..." Felice tilted her chin down, her dimple pointing.

The fingers of the two small hands held on, gripping like grasshoppers on a breezy day.

"Try taking a step backwards," called Carly who was distracted by some plate that he had picked up from a nearby table. It was one of his, *how'd it get in here?* It was one of his favorites with a gayly painted lady who smiled with her eyes. It was the only memory he had of his mother, from when he was a babe. He smiled - remembering the day he had painted her.

Bunting carefully dragged her foot backwards, doing a limping walk, careful not to dislodge the tiny fingers with fingernails made in heaven. Felice followed suit. The arms pulled out of the painting as they moved, until small bodies started to emerge – bodies with chests, legs and heads. The feet were the last to emerge, plopping out of the canvas, frogs headed for shore.

Felice bent down to lift the small form of Jimmy who was growing by the minute, his eyes flickering as his chest heaved. He hugged her around the neck and started to sob. Lizzie cried too, in between running her finger around in her mouth – glad that there was nothing there except the soft pink of her inner cheeks. Other arms started to reach out of the painting – a painting of a room with children, ghouls, monsters, beds and shrews – the arms swaying, bullrushes in a pond of souls. Felice and Bunting pulled each child back into this world, even the one in the yellow mackintosh who struggled to kick the pike from his feet.

Meanwhile, Willman and Theadora had fallen from

this earth and were now with The Keeper of Souls. The Keeper moved fast, wasting no time.

*"Put her here – in this chair next to the pot. Let me see if I can get her to grow..."*

Willman kissed Thea, whispering a song into her ear. He placed her gently in the jade armchair that folded its own arms around her.

*"You must leave, let me do my work. Be gone now, lad. No questions."*

Willman looked at The Keeper and thought for the first time that he was actually quite beautiful. Then he closed his eyes, tumbling, rocks in a landslide, until he felt Carly's hand on his arm.

"She will be OK, T.W. – she will. The Keeper will see to her. He is probably caressing and singing already."

Willman nodded as he looked around at the mess before him. Nothing was in place and there were children everywhere. He motioned for Felice and Bunting to get them outside before turning toward the demon Seteeva. She was struggling to get to her feet, her arms hanging uselessly, like flags flapping in a dull wind. Willman helped her, dragging her unceremoniously over to her hellish partner who was also starting to come to. Pushing them face-to-face he muttered through tense lips.

"Prioasoietta. Tistenuiatto piz tunimo Sssatt!"

A snake appeared in his hands, draping to the floor like a luxurious curtain in a five-story window.

"Ready for a taste of your own medicine, ladies?

He released its scaley form to wrap around the two, its pouncing panther muscles rippling, coiling loosely, but firmly, around them. Its finished at their shoulders, then reared its cobra head as its forked tongue scraped across their brows. It regurgitated then, pushing the mess down Seteeva's throat, its tongue her fork. Better B. Better whimpered like some baby, knowing that she was next.

As Seteeva Haar and Better B. Better stood, ensnared in the coils - venomous stares doing nothing except eat at their own rotten faces - a mirror on a close by wall started to pulsate. It was a tall mirror that started at the floor, its wooden frame intricately carved with spider webs and fearsome beetles. It caught the attention of Willman first.

"What?" He did not know what was happening, but he felt more than wary.

Better B. saw it too. The glass was moving - beating like a live thing.

"Huh?" she shuffled her feet, an unknown dance, moving her friend with her so that Seteeva could be in a position to see. "Any ideas?" B.B. asked.

"Nmm nmm," was all Seteeva could say, shaking her head.

As they watched, the mirror turned from liquid silver to black. It was not a solid black, but a writhing mass of blackness - a blackness that pulsated in and out. It was then that something started to slip out through the mirror. Number one came slowly - the firstborn - but was soon standing semi upright on this side of the mirror.

It was an Eel Man!

Then came another, and another, and another. Whole masses of them started to slide through. Sleek and slithery. The mirror became a black sludge of creamed up coal melting into the room that had started to smell like a dead whale washed ashore.

"HOLY CRAP!" Seteeva said, light dawning. "THEY'VE COME FOR THE HEAD!" Her eyes darted to Carly. They were going to be disappointed. "Hope they don't blame us, B. B. Don't think I can take any goddam more. I feel worse than road kill already."

"Nah. No way."

But each of their eyes belied their words, sticking out from their sockets like marshmallows on a stick.

Willman ignored them, taking stock. He looked around, visiting his options. *Should I rise to my giant height?* The building would go with him. *What about Simon, Desmond and Sheila? The others would be all right. No, no, not a good plan. Don't want their death on my hands. A spell - will it be enough? Will lives still be lost? What if some of them escape – loose in Chetsy.* Move wisely, he heard Hayban say.

The Eel men slithered forward, cascading out of the mirror like winning coins from a slot machine.

T.W. stepped forward to meet them, his foot sure yet hesitant. It was then that another mirror started to vibrate, causing him to glance in yet another direction while keeping one eye on the beasts before him. This mirror was on the opposite wall to the first - its golden frame etched with fine colors of autumn. It's glass shimmering from silver to red - shivering in the morning breeze, tinkling its glass, a bell beckoning those from their bed. Better B. and Seteeva heard it - they shuffled their feet, continuing their dance, so that they could both see.

Seteeva was about at the end of her rope.

"It's probably some snake eating frickin goblin! We don't stand a chance! I just cannot believe this B.B. I'd kill myself except I can't get my witch-ass arms to move!"

Better B. snorted, her fried eyelashes blinking.

They both watched as the ruby glow in the glass became more brilliant - a shape started to emerge, taking form, finally stepping out.

"Theezz shop has maaany meerrors ma flends," said Malamandor as he stepped out of the mirror to face the Eel Men. Many Lizard men followed, flopping forward. The room should have been full, but it seemed to have grown in size to accommodate the masses. The smell of fish was a welcome reprieve.

The Eel Men looked longingly at Willman before shrinking back. They had come for the head, they had heard there was one here. The Giant would have been a bonus. What they had not come for - was breakfast! Many beady black eyes looked with hatred at the Lizard Men before they started to retreat back into the mirror. They slopped backwards across the room, leaving their slime behind. As they retreated, passing near to Seteeva and Better B., their dark pinpoints focused on the two, thinking as a whole. *Hmm, maybe something of a prize to return with!* A tongue shot out from one of their mouths, it slimed up Seteeva's bare leg, inside the coils, up under her skirt.

"OH MY GOD! NO! STOP THAT! STOP! STOP!"

The tongue flicked around, exploring, wrapping, folding and licking, flipping the flaps of her skirt, sliming the hair on her legs, exploring higher.

"STOP! NOOOOOOOO! STOP! DON'T DO THAT!"

The Eel Men realized they may be in luck after all - they did not have to return to the Moat House empty handed. This unusual pair would make good caged specimens for their mistress's parties. It took no effort, very little at all - they grabbed at Better B. and Seteeva, pulling them into their slippery mass. Willman did not try to stop them, he could think of no better punishment than their being held prisoner in the dark rat infested dungeons of the moat house – *lots of food for the snake,* he thought, *should keep them going for a while!* The slime retreated faster now - as The Lizard Men began to move forward - still grasping, slurping, holding onto their prey. The black mass slicked and slipped back into the mirror.

"HELP! HELP! HELP! HELP! HELP! HELP! Nooooooo!" were the last sounds heard as they all slid into the abyss.

There was real silence in the Used Furniture Store. The first time ever.

Willman wiped a drop of sweat from his brow as he turned to Malamandor.

"Thank you, my friend. Your timing was perfect."

"No ploblem. Flappy to olblige. I flope to be plart of the splory plainted on the clave wall, next to you my gleat gliant." He grinned then, a big Malamandor grin. "Bly-the-way," his grin eating his face, "now le are lhere, thlere would not, bly any chance, ble some glood flishing near thlisll town of yours?"

Willman laughed, knowing his friend never missed a chance.

"Actually, there is. But I must warn you, this house will disappear soon, your ability to return may be lost. You need a mirror on both sides."

Malamandor bowed, realizing he must leave now - fishing could wait. He turned to step toward the mirror - he slowed before reaching the towering frame, pausing before reentering the glass he had stepped out from.

"Hmm? Mlirrors on bloth slides you slay. Then slo dlo The Eel Men. Hmm? Tlime spent bletter at The Moat House I thlink, tlo glet ridlle of thleir milrror." His lips parted then, his tongue licking the roof of his mouth. He turned to his clan. "A hlearty meal my flriends? Retrlieve the stolen milrror thley havel, beflore we blockll thleir way around the clave?"

Many heads nodded, tails slapped the floor. Lips licked. Malamandor moved away from the golden frame, headed toward the mirror on the opposite wall. The one The Eel Men had used. He looked at Willman.

"Whill thisll one work? Ghlet usll to the Mloat House?"

"Yes, my good friend. The place, the magic and the time make it so. But, a question before you go?"

"Yesssssll."

"Where did you get your mirror?"

"Haa. Hllaa. Glood qluestion. Itll was Thelma!" Malamandor explained that Dreador, Lillian and Jebber were in on it too. "Yourll glandfather phlet us use his milrror as he no longer clan. You knowll Willman, when I mettle him, I askled him to showll me hisll gleat slize. It was a slight to blehold - blut, well, - don't tell him thisll - blut man, he hasll nothing on you - thatll day, outslide the clave..."

The memory caused Malamandor to bow. Willman returned the honor. Then the lizards with faces of men, stepped into the blackened mirror - visions of a magnificent meal reflected in each eye before they disappeared.

Simon crawled out from under the wooden chest, dusting himself off as he stood.

"That was really frightening," he said, springing into Carly's arms, hugging him like a giant spider. Carly squeezed back, giving a peck on the cheek at the same time. Then Simon turned his head in T.W.'s direction, his face aglow with affection. The Willman winked at him and grinned.

"Good job, Simon!"

He gave his little friend the thumbs up as he stepped toward the thick oak armoire. Its hinges rusted, the doors carved with creeping vines. He pulled the door open, its age protesting the movement, creaking and wincing as both doors swung wide at the same time. Desmond fell forward into his arms - his eyes swinging like bare light bulbs in a dank attic.

"Felice! Quick! Help." He lowered the form gently down, gladly noticing a slight movement in the chest. "He's still alive, hurry." *Dark deadly creatures you two!*

Felice moved fast, along with Bunting, casting a

calming spell before dragging Desmond outside. The house would disappear soon, everyone must get out quickly. It would not be long before things returned to the way they were before Better B. had started this diabolical war.

"All of you leave, now. Before it is too late. I will see to the rest," said Willman.

"No! No!" Simon jumped down, moving across the room to point furiously at the wooden chest.

"The Muckdeanne is in there!" he said with disgust, "I could hear him chewing. You need to do something. And, I am not leaving you!"

"Simon!" growled Willman.

"NO!" He folded his arms just so. Willman knew it was pointless to argue, so he moved quickly over to the chest, worrying about Sheila. He dropped to his knees, placing the palms of his hands flat on the wooden top, exhaling deeply as he did so. It only took moments, flashes of images exploding in his brain.

"Sheila's dead," he said sadly, mourning.

Carly stepped behind - bringing his support, laying a hand on Willman's shoulder.

"T.W., we must keep moving. You know what to do. You are the only one that can."

Willman did know. If the chest disappeared with the house, it might not be good news, no one would know of its whereabouts and the Muckdeanne could eventually escape. He was the only one with the wizard strength to cast this other wizard, even though he was a lowly one, to where he needed to go.

Willman bent low over the wooden chest, eyes closed, ready to chant, when he heard a commotion outside - a voice yelling out

"No, don't go in there!" It was Felice. *What is going on,* thought Willman, turning to see Kelly and Tombhra run in through the door.

"No! Tombhra! Kelly! You cannot be here – leave now!"

"Willman, I was so worried," cried Tombhra, her eyes bright with Willman's reflection. Something moved then, catching Kelly's attention, something wiggling on the floor. She looked down to see Shadow's tongue jiving about. She was so shocked that she missed her footing, falling, hitting her head on the nearby table – the table with Carly's plate on it. The beautiful plate fell, along with Kelly, breaking in half as it hit the cold hard floor. Two beauties - broken.

Carly was instantly on his knees cradling her bleeding head in his arms. He gently placed his lips on the wound, as his fingers grazed her pulsing neck, enticing the beating heart to march on. His healing powers were strong for he knew time was short. Kelly soon opened her eyes, blinking away a tear.

"She's gone, Carly. Tombhra's gone. I felt her spirit bounce out when I hit my head. It's all my fault. I should have fought stronger when she made me run up here - I knew it wasn't a good idea." Her sobs filled the room, sheep bleating at their slaughtered young.

Willman heard her. *Tombhra gone! No! No!* Grief flooded his heart. Not now, surely, not now. His eyes clenched, knowing that he still had work to do, his breathing slowing as he chased his calm. It was then that he felt something graze his skin, something soft and warm. He shivered, opening his eyes. Before him was a golden haze that shimmered – he reached his hand forward and she took it.

"Tombhra!"

He laughed his hearty laugh. Kelly stopped her crying.

"Quickly Willman, the Muckdeanne!" said Carly.

Willman knew - the house was going now that its mistress was no longer here - he needed to work fast. First, he yanked out the bowie knife, tossing the juicy tongue toward Shadow. Shadow moved out through the door, whispering his thanks as he disappeared into the gloom. Then he pirouetted back to the chest - but before the first word of the first line of the spell could fall from his lips, a fine dust sprinkled his head. *Too late...* he thought.

"Outside, now! Everyone!" He grabbed Tombhra's hand, following his friends, just in time as the house started to crumble, the roof caving in, the dust of stones sinking into the ground. They would have gone with it if it had been a few moments earlier, their bodies dissolving along with the house and contents.

They all looked on as the last visible remains of the Evil the town of Chetsy had endured, sank and melted into the earth - like an ice cream dropped, but not forgotten.

Willman wondered where the Muckdeanne was now, his thoughts grave, until his attention was caught by a peeling laugh, one he did not know. His eyes moved to Carly who was smiling brightly – next to him was a beautiful lady - his mother stepped out from the plate.